LOKI

LOKI

A NOVEL

MELVIN BURGESS

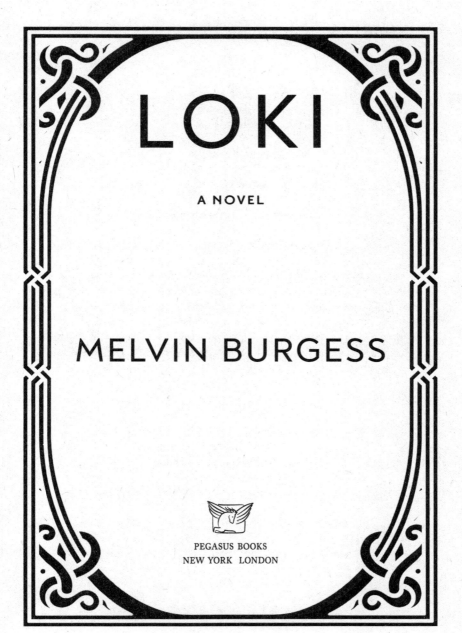

PEGASUS BOOKS
NEW YORK LONDON

LOKI

Pegasus Books, Ltd.
148 West 37th Street, 13th Floor
New York, NY 10018

Copyright © 2023 by Melvin Burgess

First Pegasus Books cloth edition May 2023

ISBN: 978-1-63936-439-8

10 9 8 7 6 5 4 3 2 1

Printed in the United States of America
Distributed by Simon & Schuster
www.pegasusbooks.com

This one's for Heimdallr, and the frost
giants on the rainbow bridge.

BOOK ONE

THE ARRIVAL OF LOKI AND THE DAWN OF THE GOLDEN AGE

Give a dog a bad name they say, and never was there any dog with a name worse than mine. I am a bad person, I expect. You will begin with your suspicions about me and I don't expect to convince you otherwise. How could it be otherwise? In a long life, I have committed many crimes, some of them very serious indeed. But then, look at my peers. Which of them hasn't? And yet here I am, chained to an eternity of torment while they walk free and continue with their crimes.

The truth is a slippery customer. We all have our secrets; it is our right to have secrets, don't you agree? I have no intention of telling you everything but even so, I think you'll find me worth listening to. I can recall your first breath, your first heartbeat. I can affirm, if you're interested, that without me there would be neither. I have saved the gods, the giants, and even humanity more than once. I may be tempted to do it again, if I feel like it – which I might not. Where there is light, there is also darkness; where there is life, there is also death. That's how it is. I am the movement between the two. I am the act of one thing becoming another. It's the same for you, surely.

We all change. I change more than most. Don't thank me. I can't help it.

Yes, we change, you and I – but not the gods. Like books, they are unable to change their stories. They have their natures and their attributes. Their word is fixed. Change is not an ability that sits well, either among their worshippers or among the immortals themselves. The very idea! All-knowing, indivisible, eternal – you know the way it goes. Well, excuse me for pointing out the obvious, but that which never changes, never learns. True knowledge is not about the know-ing itself, but about the ability to learn. Don't you think? If it's true that wisdom is the ability to understand this ever-changing world, then the gods and goddesses are stupid.

Sorry! You wanted wisdom, didn't you? Truth. Certainty. Don't look to divinity for that. They are, as one of them once said, what they are. Nothing can shift them from their natures.

And yet there are exceptions. Exceptions, as you will see, of which I am the first, the main, and the most important. Unlike the others, I adapt. I am not what I was yesterday, and tomorrow I will not be what I am today.

'Oh, ho,' I hear you say. 'This scoundrel, like all the scoundrels who followed him, is going to tell us he has reformed!'

Wrong. I have not reformed. I own it. I own it all – all my deeds and misdeeds, all my mistakes and successes, the lot. Who would I want to convince? Reformation can never lead to rehabilitation in my case. Since my peers cannot change, they can't conceive that I might either. My sentence is long, painful and unjust. There will be no remission for good behaviour, no mercy shown. It is impossible for them to entertain the idea that I might become something other than what I once was. It is beyond them. Those who never change them-selves can never understand that lessons can be learned. Having passed my sentence, they are no more capable of changing my future than I am of changing my past.

All that said, I admit I am not entirely to be trusted. I am a bad dog. But even a bad dog has a story, and I know you want to hear mine.

You will know the stories, some of them anyway. How I made the gods age (true). How I killed the sun – a lie! Go out of your house at midday, look to the sky. What do you see? How I stole golden-haired Sif's beauty. That, as you will see, was a mistake that stemmed from an injustice by her husband, Thor, god of the storm and murder, who then came to me on bended knee, begging me, begging me to make it well again. Which I did, and much more besides.

My aim is not to deny anything. I have my flaws. Unlike the other gods I am aware of them. I embrace them, in fact. They make me what I am. But I have also done a great deal of good in my time – more good than bad, I like to think. I have been your friend from the beginning. I gave you fire, when the gods would keep you in the darkness. They changed my name so that you could not know, but it was me, it was me all the time. I showed you the wheel, the smithy, the plough to name but a few. Believe me when I say that my compatriots have not loved me for any of it.

Listen, that's all I ask. Listen. Then you can judge for yourselves.

Let us start at the beginning – with me. Unlike Odin, or Thor or Frigg or any of the Aesir, or Freya and Frey and Njordr and the Vanir . . . unlike the giants or the elves or men, I am one of those who sprang into being because the world demanded me; it had no choice. They were all bred like cows. I *am*.

MY BIRTH

Picture this: the woods, in the depths of winter. Ice grips the twigs and branches of an ancient forest. In the boughs, the squirrels jump and beneath them the deer lightly browse. Aurochs graze and churn the mud. Under their hooves birds hop and hogs grunt and scratch at the iron-hard earth. In the glades and heaths which the woods encompass, eagles soar, horses whinny, curlews call.

On this night, this wonderful and magical night, the moon, perhaps, is high and full. I like to think so.

So many trees! – but of them all, one stands proud. Highest, widest, most ancient, and yet still in its prime. An ash, of course – it's always an ash. Black buds grace the arching twigs that spring so full of dormant life from its ancient boughs, many of them several dozen metres distant from the great trunk. It is home to millions of other lives – insects, mosses, lichens, birds, mice. A hundred generations have passed since it was a seed. No, two hundred. A thousand! At least a thousand. Maybe more, because in those days of myth, before man, time passed with more grace and lives were longer.

On the distant horizon, a mountain range towers above the sea of frosty trees, and among its remote peaks, a storm is brewing. But what a storm! An earth-splitting storm, an air-smashing, ground-tossing, rock-crushing devastation of a storm. The very daddy of them all. Rock giants toss their spears high in the air. Thunder roars among the peaks and echoes along the canyons and valleys that run down from the heights.

A flash! A crash! – another! The storm is moving down from its birthplace among the snowy peaks into the valleys, following the path of a great river down to the forest. Pow! The river is lit with fire. It flashes sudden gold in the half-light. Bang! Crash! Flash! Again! And again, and again! As the storm moves down to the warmer, wetter air below, it grows in strength. The dissonance grows, the lightning spreads its forked arms and summons charged ions from the earth. Crash! It tears at the sinews of the ground. The beasts turn and run or shiver in their burrows. No human eye or ear is there to witness its terrible splendour; this is before your time. Such a storm . . . *such* a storm! The earth itself bears witness and stories will be told among lesser beings from the memories of the stones themselves.

Behold, now the storm is over the forest. See the dark clouds swell above the trees, rolling and boiling with their charge, swollen with it, overflowing with it. You understand that in those dark and fatal coils, such a charge is brewing that the storm giants themselves recoil from it. The clouds snap and hiss and hum with it. The rain pours down in a sudden torrent that devastates the earth, floods the plains, overruns the rivers. It strikes boulders out of its path and overwhelms the cliffs. It uproots trees like weeds – but still the clouds withhold their charge. It grows . . . it grows . . . until at last not air nor water nor flesh nor bone nor stone nor clod can withhold it. It bursts forth! A bolt tears down from the dark heavens, crashing towards the fearful earth itself. The giants in their rocky strongholds cower and bend, heads between their legs, hands over their ears. The wood trolls yelp and hide. The gods themselves give thanks that they are not there to suffer such power, so much greater than their own, as heaven and earth conspire together to forge a single destiny, one that creates and destroys in a single blow.

CRASH! The charge strikes. The giant ash that has stood for so many thousands of decades splits down its centre as a fiery spear penetrates deep inside. The dense core of the huge tree is hollowed out in a fraction of a second by the force of that tongue of fire. Deep in the ground, rocks melt, and within the great trunk, the sap boils and turns to steam. The tree itself explodes into flames along its entire length and height and breadth. Wet with sap though it is, sodden with the deluge though it may be, nothing can resist that heat, which bursts through the buds themselves like flowers blazing into the darkness of the night. Half the tree sheers off and falls roaring to the ground. Around it the forest is aflame, an inferno of fire. Below it, the earth itself is alight. Above, the storm, exhausted by its mighty expulsion, coils and hisses and at last retreats. A softer wind blows; the clouds disperse. Starlight and a bright moon shine softly on a scene of fiery destruction as far as the eye can see.

Were any witness foolish enough to approach the stricken tree, they would see among the yellows and reds of the forest fire a point of superheated, ionised air, a blue-white womb of preternatural heat, burning deep in the remains of the trunk still standing, despite all, two or three hundred metres above the ground. And . . . what is this? See there – in the very heart of the fire, where the heat is at its greatest! A child. A boy, a baby boy. Unharmed by the awful heat, he even seems to revel in it. See! – he stretches out his tiny hands to play with the flames. And see how the flames twist and turn towards him as if they love him – which indeed they do.

A miracle? Perhaps. An act of creation by fire upon the earth, by lightning thrown down from heaven upon the world. A blessed child, he sits and coos, unfrightened, untroubled by the fire and the heat. In the womb of the tree, he grows and thrives as all around him, the fire rages among the stricken trees . . .

Fast forward a month. The forest is gone. Blackened lands stretch on either side, such was the heat and ferocity of that single stroke. Only the stump of the ancient ash still stands. In its heart, fire burns with the same white heat we saw before. And in the hollow of that trunk, burning but unburnt, teasing with the playful flames that flick around him, the child still lives. Unharmed. Loved by the sky and the earth and all growing things. Sacred. Holy. Born of the purity of the elements themselves.

A baby boy. And his name?

Loki. Yes – it is me. Sired by the heavens upon the earth, a god, the only one untouched by Jotun blood – unlike Odin and the rest, who call their larger cousins dreadful names and pretend to look down on them, even though they are all three quarters giant themselves.

Yes. I, Loki. In this fiery womb I came into being. I have used my words to help you bear witness to my birth.

All that winter long I grew in the womb of the hollow ash, which smouldered on with its miraculous heat. A month, nine months, a year passed. Another year, then another. Not nine months but nine full years was my gestation time. The burning heart of the tree was the womb that kept me warm and fed me. I played with the embers and the sparks. And at the end of that time, the trunk split and I rolled out onto the floor of the springtime woodland, among the bluebells and foxgloves and dog's mercury that had grown up when the forest fell.

And so my childhood began.

Gradually the forest regrew. In addition to the badgers and the bears, the foxes and deer, the aurochs and bison and the birds, I had family. Believe me when I say that my family got on better together than those of the other gods, who spent their time fighting, back-biting, quarrelling, bickering and ultimately, in murder. Famacide is an ugly thing. Where the ash tree fell, the roots still lived and in the spring of the very first year after the fire that sired me, grey shoots opened up into the freshest of green leaves. Within a few years, a sacred grove of young ash trees surrounded the mother tree and from their leaves, in my first natal year, my mother stepped, fully formed, in time to pick me up in her arms, cool as the green leaves themselves, to love and nurse and kiss my forehead. I was unhappy at first at being removed from the heat and wailed for a while until my skin grew used to the cool air of our beautiful northern woodlands. It was the beginning of many happy days.

A little later, my brother Helblindi hatched from beneath the earth, from a womb created where, at the moment of the strike, the first great branch fell blazing to the ground. We heard his wailing, mother and I, and it was I who first parted the leaf mould and found him lying there. Later, in my fourth spring, when the bees first made their nest inside the hollow tree, my youngest brother Byeleist was born. We found him cooing melodiously among the honeycomb, where the bees nursed him and made him strong.

So there you have it. The four of us – I, my mother Laufrey, and my brothers – come into the world in an act of combustion and renewal – in a way, as you plainly see, that the other gods were not. Perhaps they are not as necessary as I. Certainly, they all came about the new-fangled way – dicks and cunts for them, my dears. Whereas I, as you can see, came forth from lightning and leaves.

That is my genesis.

ASGARD

Even then, in my very earliest years, I knew that I belonged with the gods. We knew of them in the Ironwood – who had not? Of how Odin and his brothers Vili and Ve had taken the remains of the slaughtered cosmic giant Ymir and strung his body parts on the gibbet of Yggdrasil, the world ash, to make the Seven created Worlds. How skilled they were in the holy art of creation, and the unholy art of destruction. How they knew how to make worlds from flesh, mountains from bones, the sky from a skull.

Immodestly, perhaps, I believed I had things to teach them myself.

So it was, once I achieved the full spring of my godhead, that I reached for my thickest furs, packed dried meats and fruit into my sack, put on my snow-shoes and kissed my mother Laufrey and my brothers goodbye. I set out on the long and perilous journey to Asgard where the gods lived.

Of that journey, I shall say little here; when you have lived as long as Loki, your life is not a book or a few volumes – it is a library. Let us stick to our tale. Suffice to say that my belief that I had something to offer the divines was not dampened in any way by my journey – on the contrary. The fact was that back then, when the world was new-made, when the blood of Ymir was still warm in the oceans and the sound of his heartbeat still echoed amongst the hills, the transformation of his carcass into mother earth and father sky was . . . well, perhaps not as firmly cast as it ought to have been. Odin and his brothers were mighty gods, no doubt about it. But creation was very young, they were very new to the game and . . .

I'm beating about the bush. Let me be plain: they weren't very good at it.

Yes, the hills rolled off into the distance towards the sea. Yes, the mountains towered above me till I had to crane my neck to see their snowy tops. Yes, the earth was warm beneath my feet and the flowers and grasses nodded in the breeze of that early spring. But . . . not always. Suddenly the fragrant air would be poisoned by a blast of stinking decay. I would turn a corner and instead of a sunny bank, with the hawthorn in bud and the violets and primroses breaking cover under last year's dead leaves, there would be a heap of bloody flesh, writhing with maggots as big as badgers, waving their heads in the stinking air. And yes, the sun shone silver on the rivers as they wound their way down to the sea, but then the moon would flicker, the hot breath of stagnant blood would pollute the air and the waters turned to an evil black-red slime that had me choking and heaving until my stomach was dry.

The world had been made from a corpse, and sometimes, the corpse showed through. It wasn't surprising. We were all young and inexperienced back in the day – but it was an unsettling business, not knowing whether you'd be rejoicing in the young spring air or gasping for breath at the stink of an ancient corpse. I remember thinking even then that it was a good job that I, a shape changer, didn't loose my will in mid-air as the other gods did, when I flew as a bird. Which I did often on that, my first journey, when I got fed up with soiling my shoes on rotten meat.

I found my way, after many adventures, to the bridge where the god Heimdallr guarded the way to Asgard. You've heard of it? Bifrost, the Rainbow Bridge? Not in those days it wasn't. It was a clumsy old wooden thing, just a few tree trunks felled across the void. I was disappointed. Heimdallr stood, armed with a big wooden club with stones sunk in it, unwashed, covered from head to foot in bear grease. But – early days, early days! I held my nose and greeted him warmly. He stood aside to let me in. Despite the bad personal hygiene, Heimdallr had a nose for divinity. He recognised me; some say that, like Odin himself, he had foresight.

You may have heard the descriptions of Asgard in its glory days. The great buildings. Odin's palace, with its doors wide enough to let five hundred men walk abreast . . . Baldr's place, where no dirt, not a single speck of dust, could find a foothold. Well, it wasn't like that back then. The mighty gods were living under heaps of stones, curled up on the clay like oversized rats, smeared with mud, wandering about the place clutching a handful of turnips to their chests and peering over their shoulders all the time, in fear that someone would come and steal them. And the filth! My god. No one had learned even the most simple sanitary arrangements my mother had taught us back in the Ironwood. I thought to myself, well, at least I can teach them to shit at the back of the house rather than right by the front door. Although, as I say, to use the word 'door' for the entrance to those heaps of wood and stones they slept under would be pushing it too far.

Governed by filth and fear were the young gods, in the old days. The truth was, they had plenty to be fearful of. The world was a dangerous place. It was dark, for one thing. We hunched around in the gloom like toads under a stone, creeping out only to make dismal war. Fearful battles were an almost daily event between the Jotun, the Dökkálfar, the dark elves, and the gods. This was in the days before men. Yes, Odin and his brothers had divided the body of Ymir up into the worlds and provided a home for us all, but there was a great deal of disagreement back then about who should live where and why. The Jotun were a powerful race and coveted Asgard; the Dökkálfar were as disagreeable then as they are now, and they had some terrible weapons. Already at this point they had learned how to mine and use metal, whilst we were still scurrying about smiting each other with wooden clubs, clods of earth and chipped stones. And there were monsters – dreadful monsters. In the dark recesses of Ymir's flesh, where the magic had not taken hold, huge worms and maggots bred and feasted on his monumental decay. When they broke to the surface, all hell broke loose. Or they hatched, and came crawling out of the earth like gigantic flies, which is what they were after all, but flies that could belch fire and cough up clots of burning flesh. And there were trolls and elementals and undines and god knows what, other things that no one even had names for.

War back then was a great stony, cloddy affair, with boulders raining endlessly from the sky and clods as big as fields flying to and fro. A good thing to avoid. Much breaking of bones occurred. Yes, friends, the world was in a mess. To make matters worse, the gods themselves were at war with each other in those distant days. The two divine families of gods, the Aesir, gods of patriarchy and blood, and the Vanir, the fertility gods, could not agree about who should own what. It always comes down to that, doesn't it? Ownership. At the time I believed that the war between the Aesir and the Vanir was simply because there wasn't enough *to* own in those long-gone days, when even creation was thin on the ground. Since then, of course, I have seen the numbers of possessions spiral out of control, but nothing has changed. The more there is the more they want, and the more they have, the greater is their greed. What idiots we all are!

So no wonder the gods were stooping about, clutching their paltry possessions to their chests, peering over their shoulders in the red half-light, gulping down their food like dogs for the fear it might disappear off their plates. But what am I talking about? Plates? They had no plates back then. They ate off the ground or out of their hands, like the beasts they were.

Now, I am a man of peace, everyone knows it, whatever they say about me. All I want to do is eat, drink and be merry – to have a laugh and not worry that my neighbour's knife is going to end up between my shoulder blades. I did my best to broker peace between the warring factions – tried to show them that the difference between two rocks was not worth fighting over, that the womenfolk did their own sharing of their favours, whatever the men might say or think of it. That yes, one kind of flint might sharpen better than the next, but there was such a thing as sharing, taking turns and so on. It was no easy task. You would have thought, would you not, that peace is its own best argument, but I have to tell you – perhaps you will not be surprised — that among the gods there were those who actually *favoured* war. Yes, there are those who regard peace and prosperity as some kind of weakness or failure of the will. As if broken bones and young lives cut short and orphans starving in the ruins are the good things in life.

Two names. I give them to you now as they shall figure largely in tales yet untold and in the changing fortunes of Loki. One, the protector of all, from the rich to the poor, from god to man; the other, diplomat and politician, head of the affairs of the gods both at home and abroad. In other words, the gods of thuggery and violence, manipulation and deceit. Respectively, Thor and Tyr.

I met them early on in Asgard, as is the way of things; the bullies always seek out the new boy, isn't that so? So it was in Asgard. But I get before myself, mortal: where are my manners? You will want to be introduced formally to the divinities that sway and prey upon your lives — those who created you, those that guide you, those by whose existence your days are formulated, like it or not. Let me be your roving eye on the earliest days of Asgard, in those distant days of half-light, of clots and clods and boulders, of roughly chipped stone and handfuls of flesh and bone, when the world was young and so were we.

Forgive the half-light, that dull red glow of embers all around us; it is day and the sun has not yet been placed in the bone dome of heaven. Only the dire fires of distant Muspel, the fire world that existed before time began, must light our way — that, and the occasional splash of yellow light from the precious flames we teased from the few damp straws and twigs at our disposal. It will be night soon, and then the surviving eye of Ymir will cast its silvery light above us to show us our way. The other eye was pierced by the spear of Odin as time began and is good for nothing but food for the worms. Be grateful, mortal. If you were being shown the place before my arrival, the gloom would not even have been broken by the firelight, since it was I, Loki, who taught the oafish gods of yesteryear how to strike two flints together to create a spark, which might be teased, using dried fungus, straw and twigs into heat and light. Magic!

So who do we see, crouching in the half-light, with mud up to their shins and their chins in a puddle, as they lap in the ditch like dogs? Why, none other than the mighty Thor and his sidekick Tyr, waiting, the pair of them, like so many in those distant days, for some bright spark (me) to invent the cup.

Pimply youths they were at this early stage in their venomous careers. Thor, eldest son of Odin, already in his adolescence, as big as a bison with enough meat on him to feed nations, should they be tasteless enough to want to try. Already his face is fluffed up by the beginnings of the huge red beard by which he became so well known, as is his arse and his . . . well most of him. His forehead is fairly clear, I'll go that far. Big green eyes that make the women sigh, behind which there is all the intelligence of a hammer. Already he is as tall as three ordinary gods.

And little Tyr, he of the pointed face, acned beyond ugliness, with his limp blonde hair and his thin smile – still two-handed in those days (he had me to thank for his one-handed status before long). Look into his eyes, mortal, and see the intelligence there – the fear, the cunning, the ambition, the cruelty. What a combination! On his journey to what is laughingly called glory, this pimply youth had a long way to go. In time, he became the god of war – most terrible of us all. At this point, however, he was more like the god of throwing stones at girls.

Tyr in those days was a much-bruised boy, largely because every now and then the mighty Thor would get fed up with his continual whisperings and manoeuvrings and lump him one. What were those whisperings? Why, week by week, year by year, he would attempt to lure Thor into his own ambitions and plots, and teach the great red-faced oaf that if you want everything your own way, it's better to be a leader than a follower, to plan rather than crush. It was going to be a centuries-long task, but Tyr was a man with a long patience.

It was Tyr I saw first. I had been invited to a feast of rotting fruit – the nearest we had to booze in those distant days – when this spotty youth came sloping up to me and told me his friend wanted to see me. The company I was in fell quiet, embarrassed, perhaps. Hoenir the handsome, god of shining, if you can imagine such a thing – but much in demand in the days before the sun shone better. Sjöfn, goddess of love, and Heimdallr, good company all – although Hoenir mainly for his beauty I have to admit; the shining god had a brain as dull as his skin was bright.

'Maybe in a bit,' I said – I was having a good time.

'. . . might be better just to see him now . . .' murmured Hoenir, the feckless chicken. So I went along and there he was, the mighty Thor, towering hairily above the young birch trees . . .

'A Jotun?' I asked Tyr.

'Thor – he thinks you're Jotun!' yelled Tyr suddenly. And before I knew it I was hurtling through the air and – splat! Right into a rock. I got to my feet, half stunned, to find my way blocked by the hairy one, who was poking me in the face with his huge, rock-hard belly.

'Think you can call me names, do you? Think so? You can have me, is that what you're saying? – eh, eh? My mate says you think you can beat me up.'

And I'm going . . . 'No, no, I never said that. No . . .' And then splat! I'm face down in the mud with him sitting on my head. And then I'm up, half suffocated, gasping for breath, getting pushed around and then – splat! Face down in the mud again.

What a greeting! This on my first day. But halfway through it I thought – hang on! This is ridiculous. I'm a grown man, a god! And so I turned myself into a horsefly and stung the fat bastard on his eyelid – the skin was too tough elsewhere to get through. But even then, mortal, I underestimated Thor, for his hand flew to swat me so fast I only just got away – my fly snout stuck in that tough skin for a precious moment – and I slid out from under the wind of his fist just in time. For the mighty Thor is not only strong, he is fast – fast as lightning in fact. None of any less divinity than myself could have escaped.

But it ended well. Splat! He got himself right in the eye. He howled like an avalanche and started thrashing around, clutching the injured organ, rolling on the snow, screaming for help.

It was not kind of my friends to fail to warn me what was likely to happen with Thor, but to be fair to them, Tyr had approached as quiet as a cat. He was on us before we knew it, the devious bastard, and none of them dared to speak in front of him. But as it was, I got the last blow in to the mighty Thor and left him with a black eye, which he did not easily forgive. I had to keep my distance from the pair of them pretty much forever after that.

You see! Asgard the beautiful? Ludicrous. A patch of mud and a few fruit trees, lorded over by a fat psychopath and his sidekick. So where were the grown-ups, you might ask? Why was the field left to a bully? A good question, and one that I asked myself.

I needed allies, that much was clear. I needed friends with power. As soon as I'd cleaned myself up I decided it was time to seek out the real gods: Odin; Vili and Ve, his brothers, who helped murder great Ymir and make the world . . . perhaps; but Odin, certainly. His name was the one that everyone spoke of with awe and fear. Such was his sway over the gods at that time, that even Tyr, whose ambition was endless, did not ever conceive of replacing him at the head of the gods – only of becoming his right-hand man and gaining influence over him. The fact is, since it was by the will of Odin that creation itself was maintained, they were terrified that if he ceased to be, creation itself would fail. If that happened, instead of sitting in the mud eating fermented apples, they'd be sitting in a pool of rotting entrails – not nearly so much fun.

Odin, as you may have gathered, did not spend a great deal of his time with his eldest, Thor. He sat at home in his cave a lot of the time, engrossed in the mysteries that he loved so dearly. So dearly in fact, that he mislaid the entire world in the end, as we will see later. When he did come out it was with the women that he preferred to spend his time. There are obvious reasons for this; sex, of course. Food was another. Sif, that rolling boulder of a woman, whose bright hair could shake fruit out of the trees and vegetables from the ground, was popular back then. Fertility goddesses featured a great deal in those early days. Freya was there, she who made the swine farrow and the cows calf, who made love like the empress of sex that she was. Sjöfn too – obviously a popular lady. Eir, who ruled over medicine and curing. In those days there were a lot of infections – what can I say? Of course it was the women who were the most popular deities back then. Thor only got away with it because most of the grown-ups had other things to do. He was deeply unloved back then, by man, god and beast. Only later, when the Jotun wars kicked off, did his popularity increase out of proportion to his actual abilities.

Odin and his goddess, Frigg, lived together with his brothers in a great, wide-mouthed cave – the biggest cave in Asgard, of course, they being the chiefs of the gods – with a huge fire built in the entrance. Vili and Ve were sitting at the back, off their faces on mushrooms, playing knuckle bones, which is about as far as the idea of party had gone in those dark early days.

I was disappointed, to be honest. I had expected more than two hairy oafs and a set of hand bones. Looking back now, I think they were depressed. They were only young – barely out of their godish teens at that time – but already they had killed the source of us all, sacred Ymir, who was neither man nor woman but both, and therefore mother and father of all creation. They had spent the next few centuries dismembering the body and hanging the parts on Yggdrasil, where their brother turned them into the realms of creation. No wonder, then, that their spirits were low. Creation is a wonderful thing, but it was not they who had done that part of the job. They got stuck with the butchering. No wonder they were depressed. And they have been like it ever since.

There were children there, too – young gods, born of Odin and his wife Frigg. Hermod the swift, scribbling in charcoal on the walls – trying to invent writing, I think. I helped him later on. A girl, a little younger, who I had seen gnawing on a knuckle bone earlier whilst Thor had been bouncing me off his fat belly. This was Sigyn. She had since washed some of the mud off herself and was revealed to be somewhat older than I first thought. She made eyes at me.

'Too young,' I told her.

'I can be as old as you like,' she replied. But I didn't take the matter further, not then. I said too young, but I should have said, too severe. She did not look like a girl who loved to laugh. And – those teeth! She had teeth like farmyard implements. It would be like kissing a ploughshare.

And – one more. I should mention her now, since she comes into our tale further on. Angrboda was her name. Aged at that time about ten years, although the years of the gods vary even from god to god and Angrboda's years as a child were very long. But wait! I hear you say. Those of you who have read the Edda, the old tales, will know her name, but not as a goddess. She was Jotun, was she not? Not, mortal!

Do not believe everything you read. She was a goddess, a child god at this stage, not yet Become into her full powers. You must remember that Loki is not the only liar in the Nine Worlds, not by a long way. She ran about in the shadows of the cave, bone-thin, mud-smeared, naked, her hair a crow's nest, her great eyes staring – mad as chaos. She played at her crazy games – staring into the fire, or at the cave wall, or at her own hand, with such intensity it made the skin on your neck creep. Or she would fling sticks on the ground, or scatter rocks, and collect spiders or beetles and throw them into the air, and dance around them, crowing. She had no language, no words, no sense in her that I could see. She scared me, I don't mind saying it, because what kind of goddess would this mad child grow up into? When I asked where she came from, who her parents were, no one knew. For this reason some thought she was not a goddess at all, but one of the seidr, the witches, born out of the void. But many years later, when she changed – when she Became, as we say – into herself, it was apparent then that she was one of us. Only the divine can Become and develop attributes.

I felt sorry for her. Everyone ignored her. I gave her a bone to gnaw out of humanity. Of her, mortal, you shall hear more.

Frigg was there too, of course, weaving blankets out of some sort of hair. I didn't ask what kind. I paid my respects, you can bet. She was an important deity at that time, when all anyone wanted was food, and agriculture hadn't yet been invented. She accepted my gift of a lump of raw flesh and gave a regal nod towards the shadows at the back of the cave.

I didn't see Odin himself at first. He was right at the back, staring at a wall. And – Oh, my lord, I thought to myself – this one is worse than his brothers! A wall starer. His round hairy body, topped with a dense black cap of hair and beard, made him look something like a bear in those days, or some kind of a gigantic furball thrown up by an even more gigantic cat. By his side were his ravens, Memory and Thought, pecking at the bones left over from his last meal. Although back then they'd be better named as ignorance and flatulence; the Allfather was farting like a bear. I made for him – just on the off chance, because I promise you, what I had seen of Asgard so far had left my heart in my boots.

I crouched down beside him, cautiously flapping the birds back a bit. I didn't like the look of those beaks.

'What do you see in the shadows, friend?' I asked him in a friendly tone – trying to break the ice gently, you understand.

I fully expected another grunt but instead he came up with the intriguing idea . . .

'There is a shape behind the shape of things that is the true shape,' he said. 'I'm hoping I may get a glimpse of it here.'

Now that's more like it! I hadn't got a clue what he was talking about and I supposed he was at least half mad, but at least it was a concept. I went along for the ride.

'I know about shapes,' I said. 'I have more than one, you know.'

At that Odin, who had been staring fixedly at the vague shadows on the wall up till then, turned to look me full in the face. He had two eyes in those days, dark green eyes, set so deeply in his head, they seemed to be looking in as much as out.

'Loki,' he said.

For once I was at a loss for words. He knew me already?

'I'm glad,' he said, rising from his place on the floor. 'I've been wanting to meet you. Teach me about shapes.'

'How do you know me?' I asked.

'Shadows,' he said, nodding at the wall. 'I've seen your shape. Under this one,' he added, poking me in the ribs with a fat, grubby finger. 'Under the man, under the falcon, under the snake. Even you, Loki, have a shape of your own, although you can never know what it is.'

Now then! There's your god for you. There's your god.

Odin and I got along at once. He had a taste for mystery; I had a taste for tricks. You would never guess how much those two have in common. If you can change your shape, you are beyond shape; if you exist at the fulcrum where one thing turns to another, you are of both – a mystery yourself. So it was that Loki made friends with the greatest and chief among the gods. Odin and I were as close as kittens in a bag. We talked, drank, laughed and adventured together; all the Seven Worlds he had made were our playground. Of course, that was not the end of the machinations of Tyr, and the rage of Thor, but my friendship with the Lord of All held them at bay. Henceforth they had to make their plans in private, quietly, behind closed doors.

Odin was not just about mysteries; he had the power, he had the knowledge. Already back then his two ravens travelled the worlds over and brought back secrets they had seen, conversations they had overheard. Tyr would have given all he had to own such birds – and he did get to use them in the end, but that is a story to be told later on. Above all, Odin Lord had the gift of life and death. None dared challenge him.

Yes, mortal, it was a clever move on my part, but friendship, as you must know yourselves, can be a fickle thing. Friends love each other for a while, but then they fall out, particularly when the sons of one of them tell spiteful tales and plan the downfall of the other. But let that tale too come in its time of telling. I had further plans for Odin. Many times I suggested to the Lord of Creation that we swear brotherhood together. In that world, at that time, oaths could be made from the roots of meaning itself, oaths that bind beyond love, beyond fashion or taste or blood; they can be tied to creation itself. But Odin was cautious and so, for a long time, all I had to rely on was his liking me. And I knew from experience, friends, that liking and Loki did not always hang together as well as I wished.

My first days in Asgard, then, formed the blueprint for all the others that followed – making enemies and friends within a single breath, enjoying the present with an eye on tomorrow. And helping others to form that most divine of conditions – civilisation.

MY WORK BEGINS

Once I had settled down, I turned my hand towards basics. Where to shit. Hygiene. A clean supply of water. Decent food, medicine. Then, once the gods had grasped the fundamentals, how to wash, and how to tend a simple fire and not to piss in the drinking water, I turned my hand to that most tricky and bedevilled of tasks – politics.

I know! What was Loki, god of clever, tricks and fun, doing messing about with such foolish a thing as politics? Perhaps my very attributes are an answer to that, but I would be the first to admit it should not have been me – it should have been Odin. Of course. The trouble was, Odin wasn't interested. He was always far too absorbed in finding out about the powers behind things to actually deal with things themselves, even if it was the welfare of his own that was at stake.

You sort it out, Loki, I'm too busy . . . Doing what? Oh, foretelling the future, turning base metal into gold, inventing new forms of magic. You name it. If it was impossible, Odin wanted to do it – leaving poor Loki to sort out the problems of the day-to-day running of Asgard. And yet, do the old stories tell of these things? How I led Frigg to sheep for wool and to flax for linen? Have you, mortal, heard the stories about the theft of metallurgy from the dark elves, the Dökkálfar or agriculture from the light elves, the Ljósálfar? Of course not. Did Snorri, who told so many stories of the gods, bother to write mine down? No. Did the Skalds sing of them? No. Loki was always the butt of jokes and, apparently, the cause of strife. Yet nothing could be further from the truth.

That ridiculous war between the two families of gods, the Aesir and the Vanir, that was the first thing. It was the work of Tyr, of course, who had spent the centuries before I arrived on the scene inventing dark stories about the Vanir — some agricultural nonsense or other about which fields grew the best turnips and who owned them, if I remember — which the other Aesir were stupid enough to believe. Result? War. How on earth could something so stupid as turnips get so out of hand?

That war, the first of all wars, was fought by moonlight and the burning embers of Muspel, the distant fire world, home of great Surtr, who existed before existence itself, who will exist forever — long, long ago, before there was a sun in the sky, before love and marriage had been invented . . . before mankind roamed the earth. It was a bitter war, but at last it was settled, with you-know-who (me) appointed by Odin as peacemaker, despite ferocious objections by Tyr and Thor, who of course would have loved nothing more than to go to war forever. Hostages were exchanged, marriages arranged, lands handed out, oaths made. We went so far, as you may have heard, as mixing our spittle, each and every god among us, and making from it a new god, Kvasir, who was then sent out into the world spreading wisdom and knowledge among the Jotun and the elves. Mankind, alas, was too late for wisdom; by the time you came along, Kvasir was long gone. Even so, it was not a popular move amongst the gods, who wanted to keep all the good things in life for themselves — as if wisdom and beauty grew any less the more was used!

And so peace was achieved amongst the gods. Yes, mortal — it was the dawn of the Golden Age. I regard it as one of my finest achievements. And then, with the gods united, it was possible to turn my attention to the Jotun wars . . . and then the Dökkálfar wars. Fast forward several more millennia . . . It took a long time to get there.

Too long, I know. I admit that I did not always focus enough on the task at hand. Even so, after much work, effort and self-sacrifice, peace was at last attained.

Many would have considered that universal peace was enough of an achievement, even for a divinity such as myself, but, reader, I did not pause in my efforts to improve the lives of all – mortal, immortal, whoever. There were great adventures – none of which have been written down. There were achievements – all of which have been forgotten. For instance: Odin, as I have said, had done a marvellous job with creation . . . but there were a few problems here and there. Glitches, you might call them today. You remember when we first met he told me he wanted to learn about shapes? I taught him. I like to think I was generous with my know-how. We set out together, the Lord of the World and I, to explore the worlds he had made beyond Asgard – to Vanaheimr, where the Vanir made their home, to Jǫtunheimr, the giant world, to Svartálfheimr and Álfheimr, homes of the dark and light elves, to Midgard, empty of mankind back then and populated only by the beasts. Down to Hel we went, in those far-gone days where there was no queen to stop us – and further still, up even as far as the other heavens, now lost to creation. But all that is another tale. Know, though, that we set about stabilising the unbalanced world he and his brothers had made. Back then, as I've mentioned, you might be sitting on a green bank with your hands in the water, tickling the pretty little trout that swim there, hoping to catch a nice supper – and then suddenly the water turns to black blood, the green bank to rotting flesh, the trout to a groping maggot, its black teeth going for your eyes.

I, Loki, as the Lord of Change and transmission, the inventor and keeper of knots, all fixings and their loosening – I taught the Lord of Creation how to fix his spells hard and fast in the flesh of Ymir, so that his blood is and was and remains the sea and rivers and lakes, so that his bones stay as mountains, his skull the sky, his teeth the boulders of the earth. It is down to me that you can trust the land you stand on, for although he had a power I do not – to animate, to bring forth life – only I could fix his spells and make change real, rather than mere illusion. You can fool all of the senses some of the time, and some of the senses all of the time, but you can't fool all of the senses all of the time. I, however, can. I made your world real, mortal.

And where is my praise? Where is my sacrifice? Where are the hymns to Loki? There are none left in the Nine Worlds ready to give thanks where thanks is due. Forgive me, then, for my boasts; the truth will out. Perhaps you will admit after reading this, that it is a shame that I am the one who has to say it.

Every time I showed him how to fix the world, Lord Odin would tap his forehead and smile at me.

'It's fixed in here, friend Loki,' he said. 'Fixed hard in here.'

And I was glad about that. I showed him how to do it but it was of course his will and mind that held the body of Ymir, in all its vastness and variety, to be what he wanted it to be. I did not care to spend the rest of my days holding the world in my mind. I am a forgetful creature; my attention span is short. Although I am the keeper of knots, change is my master. I am a god at play. The world is something I want in my toy box, not on my conscience.

So praise Lord Odin! Or . . . so I believed at the time. Since then I've had cause to think otherwise. But that is a story to tell in its place. That place, I promise you, will come before my tale is done.

Meanwhile – the Golden Age! Yes, mortal. Loki had achieved the impossible. War was over, strife contained, terror tamed, weapons beaten into ploughshares and hatred put out to pasture. You'll have heard the rumours, I expect. The rain fell at night, the sun shone during the day. Peace and prosperity for all. The fields ploughed in winter, the seed planted in spring, the harvest in the autumn. Glorious days. Life became settled, life became good. Such a pity you weren't around to enjoy it.

But what am I saying? The sun? What sun? You will remember that at this time we were wandering around in the half-light, the dismal reds of distant Muspel, the dull glow from our own fires. What kind of a Golden Age can it be without the sun?

SURTR'S EYE

This is a story that has not come down to the human beast. To tell it, we must go back, way back – back before the slaughter of the world god Ymir, back to the days of first creation, when only the fire world of Muspel and the cavernous ice world of Niflheimr existed. These were there forever, and shall be. As the mists rising from the ice met with the terrible heat of Muspel, steam was forged that turned into vast blocks of ice, which in turn fell down deep into the space between the worlds – Ginnungagap.

Eons passed. Gradually the huge cavern filled with ice. From the melting of that ice, two vast beings emerged; one, Ymir, the world-god, and the other, a vast cow – no one ever explained to me how they came into being, but then who has ever explained how so much as a single atom came into being in the first place? Atom, cow; cow, atom. Who cares? Take your pick.

You have heard how Odin and his brothers slaughtered Ymir and used his body to create the Seven Odinic Worlds; how they decorated the world tree Yggdrasil with Ymir's body parts, and that the worlds thus created hang like fruits in the void to this day. You know how they populated these new worlds with Jotun and

Dökkálfar, the dark elves, and Ljósálfar, the light elves, and with woods and seas and sticks and stones, and, eventually, much later, with men and women like yourselves. Back then, as they stumbled about in the thick mists of Ginnungagap on their journey of creation, their way was lit not by the sun and the moon, but by the dull, fiery light cast from distant Muspel, the fire world, ruled by mighty Surtr – a world that, like the Ginnungagap itself, existed before all, and where even the gods, as they style themselves, did not and could not ever tread.

When they slaughtered great Ymir like an ox, they took one of his shining eyes up into the heavens, far above us all, which you see today as the moon. That eye only ever opens in the darkness of the night, from fear of his murderous offspring, no doubt. But Ymir's other eye was, as we have seen, pierced by Odin's spear in the primordial act of murder. Thus, the light of that bright eye was lost to us forever.

And so those ancient days were dark. All they had to light their way was starlight and the distant blues and reds of Muspel's fires, far, far away, on the other side of the Gungungengap. There great Surtr slept, back in those distant days, rolling in the eternal fires that burned and burned and never consumed his flesh.

Who is Surtr? Only Surtr knows. All we little things know is, that he was first – even before great Ymir, there was Surtr and the eternal fires of Muspel. It is Surtr himself who burns, some believe, and that he is Muspel and Muspel is Surtr. How huge is Surtr? Of all living things, only Ymir was greater. Like Ymir, the Nine Worlds themselves could sit inside his burning skull.

So the days were badly lit. Everyone waited for the moon.

In this way, centuries passed.

I have to be honest; it was me who first thought of it. It usually is me. Yes, I invented the sun. I think I can make that boast. None of the others had the vision.

It came to me one day when I was walking on the shore of the north sea, bathed as always in dull red light. Dull red clouds, dull red waves, dull red foam breaking on dull red stones and dull red seaweeds. I paused to look to the sky to see if the moon, Ymir's eye, was casting its silver shadow on the horizon, when there was a flash, a burst of sudden light from the east, where Muspel lay. It was so bright it made the gulls jump and even I let out a short, sudden cry, although I knew exactly what it was. Great Surtr lay sleeping, but from time to time, caught perhaps in some dream of love from before time began, one of his eyes half opened and the light that shone from him then outshone everything, and lit up all of creation like – well, like something no one had seen before that time. Let's call it 'day'.

Later, many weeks later as I recall it, I remarked to Odin that if only by some wonderful magic we could get one of Surtr's eyes, what a difference it would make to us! Fierce, terrible Surtr, larger than worlds, who burns but never ends – but from his eye the most beautiful light anyone has ever seen shines, so clear, so bright! Such a light would make life in the Nine Worlds so much more beautiful.

Odin gazed out to the east where Muspel lay and stroked his beard.

'Do you think there's a way?' I asked him.

Odin shook his head. Steal Surtr's eye? Of course not! And so the endless dull red days passed on. But he must have remembered my words, he must have thought and plotted, because centuries later he did find a way. Yes, it's true. The eye of heaven is Surtr's eye; the glory of the world comes from the Fire Lord, big as worlds. How Odin did it, I have no idea. Only this: he went away on a journey, as he often did. He was away a long time, and when he came back among us he had with him a cloth bag; but not what you would think of as a mere bag. This was something that could only have been made by the Dökkálfar. Metal was in it and stone, and cloth too. And magic. Whatever. Inside it there was a great ball, shining, shining, shining so brightly no one could look at it. Burning, burning, burning so hot, no one could touch it. Even in its magic wrap, everything around it smouldered. There was smoke rising from trees a mile away and the stones beneath it cracked with the heat.

Somehow, we wrestled it up into the sky. We couldn't take it out of its bag, or the world would have ignited. It was too bright to look at, so bright and so hot, in fact, that even pinned to Ymir's skull it was too much and we had to place it outside the sky before we could take it out of its wrap. And that eye became the sun, giver of light and life to the world. Even now, many, many eons after, it still shines through a hundred miles of dense bone too bright to stare at with open eyes.

Well, it was some feat. I remember that day – who could ever forget it? It was such hard work, getting that burning, shining globe up so high. But when it was done, the world was beautiful. The light it cast! So perfect, so life-affirming, so lovely. The first sunrise over the mountains, across the seas, the rivers shining like gold in the early light. The first sunset – Surtr's great eye casting its sacred light between the clouds and the golden sea. The dark and silver clouds edged with gold. The young leaves on the beech trees in their brightest, freshest green. The sunbeams cutting the clouds and slanting through the trees, lying dappled among the wildflowers on the grass. Nothing had ever been lovely before the sun came; afterwards, everything was.

We stood there, gods and goddesses, and we watched and loved the world, seen as if for the first time. We stood there for many days before we turned away. We praised Lord Odin then. Who else could have done it? Stolen Surtr's eye for the world, at who knows what peril, what danger, what cost! We begged to know how it had been done, but he shook his head and smiled in his beard and said nothing.

But when at long last we did turn away, another sight greeted us. From Asgard, we have a view over all the worlds. We see everything. Men and women, the Jotun, the Dökkálfar and Ljósálfar. Nothing that can be seen can be hidden from us, even as far as Muspel itself. For millennia we had a view of Surtr asleep, the fires of creation playing around him. And from time to time, that blazing beam of blinding light shooting from his dreaming eyes.

No longer. Now, Surtr was on his feet. He had awoken. So tall is Surtr that even from that great distance we had to look up to see his face. The fires and flame still played about him. His eyes were open. From one shone a blinding light. From the other – darkness.

I turned to Lord Odin.

'You fucking idiot,' I said.

If Odin hoped, as I believe he did, that he could manage the theft without the owner knowing, it was clear that he had failed. Surtr was awake, staring right back at us and at his own eye pinned above the heavens. How had Odin gone to a place too far to go to capture something too hot to touch? How had he taken it from Surtr's living skull? No one knows. To this day he will not say. But Surtr knows. He knew then and he knows now. There he stood before us, blazing with light and fire. And in his hand, his great sword, his sword as long as starlight, ready to cut the worlds to shreds.

They call me a thief. What do you say to the man who stole the eye of god?

And that, my dear friends, was the birth of day, but also of Ragnarok, the end of days. We stood there for an age, waiting for Surtr to step forward out of Muspel and advance on us, to bring about our universal doom. But he did not do it – not then, not yet; but he will. He stands today as he did then, waiting, watching, sword in hand. He will come; nothing is more certain. On that day all bonds will be broken, all doors will open, all locks will fail. On that day, all that can be consumed will be consumed, all that can burn will burn, all that can fail will fail and all that can fall, will fall. He stands and he waits. For what? We do not know. Perhaps he is mourning the death of Ymir. Perhaps to Surtr the Deathless, for whom the lives of gods are just hours ticking by, just a few moments have passed. We do not know, we shall never know. We know only that he will come – courtesy of Odin.

Ever since, from the heights of heaven in Asgard, the gods always try to avoid looking to the east, because when they do, there he stands, great Surtr, a reminder of how puny they really are, how little, how insignificant compared to the true Lord of Creation. How quickly the end shall come to every one of us. Wise Odin, keeper of secrets, shall waft away like smoke in a breeze. Great Thor, whose strength can split mountains, will fall like a grain of sand to the ground. Enjoy your lives, little men and women, and pray that Surtr will not come before your time is over.

And that is how Odin brought the sun, the giver of life, to earth. It was never his to give.

THE GENESIS OF YOU

So our days were won at a cost – but, mortal! Behold the beauty of the day. It was worth it, surely. All us gods were struck with the wonder of what we had made. The days that followed, then, were the days of adventure, of travel, of journeys made for no other reason but to see and be in the wonderful world. To bathe in the sun and the sun-warmed waters and the sun-warmed air; to gaze at loveliness every day. To be a part of it. The eye of Surtr, which is the eye of destruction, became the source of creation. This is the power of Odin. The forests grew, the seas flourished, the fields bloomed. The gods thrived, as did the Jotun and the elves, both dark and light. All of creation, in fact, rejoiced.

Of course, the praise was all to Odin. My part in it was small, so it is perhaps understandable that it was forgotten – even by Odin himself, who as far as I knew never mentioned to man nor mouse that it was I who put the idea into his head in the first place. Such is my fate; it has always been so.

And this is the Golden Age proper. Peace for all under the sun. On this count – I do not see the need for unnecessary modesty – I was the main architect and engineer. And yet! Where are my achievements now? Where is the peace I brokered, where is the happiness I strove to bring about? All around we see war and hunger and greed. But all is not lost! Where there was once a Golden Age, why should it not come again, if only the right people could get their hands on the wheels of power? But listen to me, mortal! Loki, Loki, Loki – that's all I ever talk about. Forgive me, I forget myself in my misery. Let us turn our attention to something of perhaps more interest to you, my mortal readers. A tale of humanity. You've heard my genesis. Now let's have a look at the beginnings of *you*.

You may have heard the story how, after the world had been made, and was at last at peace, and when the gods began to realise that beauty had its purpose after all, they began to conceive the idea – out of pure vanity, as you will see – that it needed *witness*. In other words, they wanted someone around to understand how marvellous they were. Oh, how marvellous, how wonderful, how just, how powerful. How big. How very very *big*. Witness, yes – and worship. Of course, they wanted to be worshipped. You can't blame them. We all like our egos rubbed, and the gods, the vainglorious, ignorant, unlearning gods, have egos that require a good deal more rubbing than most.

So they came across two logs of wood and stood them on their ends and turned them into the first man and the first woman. You've heard that one? Well, it's not true. Mud, that's another story. They shaped the first man and woman out of mud. False. You want the truth? Read on – if you're sure you can take it.

I'm here to tell you that there was no mud or logs involved. I know, I was there, walking on the beach with Odin and his brothers Vili and Ve. The three of them, surrounded by so much beauty, were moved to sing their praises – literally. There was no one else to do it. From death came forth life, from stink, sweetness. As it is written, so it was. The sun, great Surtr's eye, lit up and powered the engine of life. The plants and trees lifted up their arms in vibrant green. The beauty of the world we had made was shown for the first time in its full glory. The old, pre-Loki days of hillsides suddenly turning into slithering mounds of rotting flesh, mountains into teeth and bones, or maggots emerging without warning from the belly of the earth, were gone, thanks to me. Praise be – to us!

Self praise. It was hard work. There were no men and women, no slaves, no nobles to command them. No blood spilled upon the stones, no burnt offerings, no lives winging our way through the upper air. I tell you, we were permanently hungry. So the three brothers were doing the praising for themselves. Oh how wonderful we are! Look at those clouds, aren't they marvellous, how marvellous of us to do that, oh see the lovely hills, the majestic mountains, the rivers, the mighty oceans. Etc. etc. I think it was Vili who sighed a deep long, godly sigh and wished aloud that somehow, somewhere, there might be creatures on this earth who could at least do the praising for us. It would save such a lot of trouble.

But there was no one. The giants had their own lives to lead, they weren't likely to waste time going on about how great we were. The Dökkálfar didn't even care for us, let alone sing about how great we were, and the Ljósálfar weren't interested in anything but themselves.

So we walked on across the sands, the four of us – it was all very pretty, I can tell you, with the new-lit trees and the grasses and flowers and rocks and stones and hillsides – when there hove into sight something that was not in any way pretty. It looked at first glimpse as if a pair of gods were lying on the beach, half covered in seaweed. But no one had ever seen gods like these two. They were hideous beyond belief – deformed, twisted, shape-blighted monstrosities. They were a curse on the very idea of shape. Lying there in the surf, they radiated ugliness. Vili, I remember, who always fancied himself as a sensitive soul, something of an artist, actually let out a cry of horror. It was frankly terrifying that such deformity could exist. For a moment we believed that the earth had spontaneously begat new monsters.

We hurried forward thinking they needed our help – that it was someone we knew who had been cursed by a malignant elf, or torn and twisted out of shape by some terrible force we knew nothing of. But then the wind changed and it hit us. A stink, a dreadful stink as monumental and ugly as the sight itself. Dreadful! Appalling. Disgusting!

And then it became apparent.

It was shit. The drowned gods were no less than a pair of enormous turds. Yes, two vast turds disporting themselves like hideous girls in the newly created surf. Such shits, so vast and ugly, could only have come from the arse of one kind of creature and that was a creature that did not belong there in middle earth, enjoying the sunny pleasure of our creation. The Jotun. Only a giant arse could produce such monsters.

Suddenly we were looking around, because – who else was here? The Jotun were not our enemies at this time, but still – this was not a friendly act. This was Midgard, a pleasant land of beasts, birds and fish, our godly hunting ground. But there was no one there. Whoever or whatever it was had gone now. Poachers, no doubt, and in the middle of their crimes they had pulled down their vast breeks and done a monstrous shit in the clean sea. And by pure chance, the two monsters they left behind had emerged in some kind of vaguely godlike shape.

Once we realised what they were, the fear subsided and there was a good deal of merriment about it. Ve addressed them with a bow and asked if there was anything he could do for them. Vili offered them a chicken leg and pretended to get upset when they refused to answer. Only Odin stood there staring at them in that way he has, his mouth hidden in that big beard, not so grey in those days, so that you never knew what he was thinking. Back then he really was a smart guy, well up to his reputation, very deep, very knowing. There's too much knowing now, of course – but more of that later. Right now, there he is, the Allwise, staring at a gigantic turd and thinking only He knows what.

By this time the other two idiots were mucking about, poking the shits around with sticks.

'Look, I've given it a dick,' yelled Vili, oh so pleased with himself, like it was some kind of achievement, giving a turd a dick. Which made the Allwise laugh himself, and then he got excited and started dancing around.

'Give the other one a cunt – go on, give it a cunt!' he bellowed. Ve was doubled up laughing, while Vili was whacking the smaller one with a stick to give it two legs and then shoving the stick up it.

And then – I don't know what came over me. I just go sometimes. I did what I do right then to those two turds. I leaned forward. Happenstance, I did it just when Odin was bawling . . .

'But who's going to fuck her? Who will it be?'

'Loki, Loki's going to fuck her,' screamed Ve. But that wasn't my aim at all. I did touch them, though. Sometimes I just don't think – I'm my own worst enemy. So I touched them, first the woman one then the man one, and at once they transformed . . . to flesh and blood.

Why? Don't ask! It was an extremely odd thing to do, I admit it. I don't have the gift of life, so the turds didn't do anything except turn pink and stop stinking. Their soft bumpy skin glistened with sea water in the sun, which at this time was getting low in the sky. They were no more alive than when they were made of shit. What a fate, eh? Dead before you even lived! They looked, if I say so myself, utterly obscene.

'What did you do that for?' asked Vili, as if I'd spoiled his fun, which I suppose I had.

I shrugged. I had no idea. Like I say, sometimes I just do stuff. Vili and Ve were on at me then, calling me all sorts of names and being really scornful. But Odin was excited.

'I knew there was a mystery here,' he breathed. The power came over him. His eyes started flashing and he began to order them about.

'Shape them,' he ordered Ve.

'I'm not touching that,' said Ve; but the Old Man insisted and after all, it wasn't shit any more and anyway, once the Old Man gets the flashing eyes thing, you do as you're bid, believe me. So Ve got down on his knees and did his thing – shaping. He rubbed away their ugliness – you can thank him for what looks you have.

'Give them will, give them wit,' the Old Man ordered, and Vili did that too, as is in his gift. Odin stood by and watched, and when it was done – when a man and woman lay there on the beach, moving gently with the push and tug of the waves, then he bent himself and lay his hands on them and gave them . . .

Life. Yes. Only He can do that. I turned them into flesh and blood; Vili gave them form, Ve gave them will and wit; Odin gave them life. It was a four-man jobbie.

The two of them stirred, looked around. Breathed. Their hearts beat. They saw the sky for the first time. They licked their lips and tasted salt for the first time. They coughed up a little sea water. Unsteadily, they got to their feet. Then, seeing us four standing there – we assumed our glory – they sank at once to their knees.

'Lord,' said the man.

'Arise,' said Odin, and he gently put his hands on them and they rose to their feet.

'I name you Embla,' he said to the woman, casting an appreciative eye over her, for Ve had done a damn good job. 'And I name you Ask,' he told the man. 'I have created this earth for you to enjoy. You shall be masters of the beasts and of the plants and of the seas. You shall understand and bear witness to what I have done, here on middle earth. Go forth and multiply.'

Except he didn't say multiply. We were more straightforward back then.

'And never forget to give thanks to me for granting you life and this earth to enjoy,' the old one added.

'And to me, for giving you wit and will,' said Vili.

'And me for giving you beauty,' said Ve – always one to praise his own work.

'And me because . . . of what I have done,' I told them. Which was a big mistake, you know, because people need to be told. I'm my own worst enemy sometimes. But think about it; how would you like to be told you were shit-born right at the start of things? Don't you agree? See? – I was being *nice*.

There was a good deal of celebrating and praising, which went on for ages, before the man and the woman turned to go. But as they did, the woman turned back.

'But where did we come from?' she asked.

And we gods sniggered a bit, because that was truly funny. Odin shook his head.

'That is a mystery you can only know at the end of all things,' he said, hiding his smile in his beard. And lo! They went forth and got on with it.

*   *   *

So now you know the answer to that age-old question – where did you come from. Out of a gigantic arsehole. Congratulations! Which has given rise to the names we sometimes call you. Shit-born. The Brown Road. Sea-floater. Kiss-me-Quick (the quicker the better), Beach-stinker, Rimmer, Bog-trotter, Midden-flown, Arse-born, Shite-in-Flight, and so on. Don't feel bad about it. Most of the rest of us came from a cow. It could be worse, I'm sure, although I'm not sure how.

BOOK TWO

ALL THE GOOD THINGS I'VE DONE

So there you have it, Arse-born: the Golden Age. The Seven Worlds were open and at ease. Travel was simply a case of going and coming home. The sun was in the sky. There were no troubles, no frontiers, no jealousy or conflict, no theft. In that world, the world Loki made, Loki himself was happy – and would have remained so, had he been allowed.

Reader, I married. You remember that girl, the one I met hanging around in Odin's cave way back when I first came to Asgard? The one with the teeth – Sigyn? It was her. She had – what shall we say? – she had grown up. Blossomed, in some ways. Actually, there was a lot of blossoming going on during the first Golden Age of Asgard. The gods call it the Becoming – when young godlets acquire their aspects and powers. Think of it, if you will, as a kind of divine adolescence. Ran, goddess of the sea, began to smell of fish and learned how to breathe underwater. The goddess Eir learned how to heal . . . Gna, the messenger, grew swift of foot. And Sigyn – I could not say she was the most beautiful of the goddesses – far from it – but her attributes more than made up for that. Winning, that was her thing. Who could not love that? It was a kind of premonition. Games, competitions, she was always there standing next to the winner before they won. It made betting superfluous – she had to be locked up if anyone wanted to place a bet. She was one of the first of the Valkyries, those swift flyers who pluck the spirits of the slain from the battlefield and escort them to Odin or to Freya for their taste of eternity. I suppose the idea was that to die in battle, that was a form of winning too, although, excuse me if I might prefer to lose.

Yes, mortal, I married the goddess of victory. At the time I thought myself enormously clever. Who could ever defeat the husband of victory? As you will see, with that move, as with so many others, things did not turn out as I had planned. I would like to tell you that I loved her. I believed that I did at the time. Certainly, for a while she was my world. Since then I have known other kinds of love and looking back I'm not so sure. I was flattered, I think, that she favoured and adored me – who would not be pleased to have Victory in their bed, even with all those teeth?

We had children, two fine sons, Narfi and Vali. Strong boys. I taught them tricks – magic, sleight of hand. I hoped, as the gods must always hope, that my children would acquire aspects of their own as they grew older, and become true gods, like their father and mother. That, like so much, was not to be.

Those teeth. I would like to say something sensible about them, but I cannot. I never understood. So strong, so white, so perfect. So *big*. She could nip off the head of a leg bone with the tip of her incisors. Sometimes I would sit at home eyeing them up and wondering . . . Why? But I never found out. Odin only knows why the goddess of victory should have teeth four sizes too big. And yet . . . Somehow, it seems right.

I wish I could say that these times of peace and prosperity lasted longer than they did – that they coincided with the rise and spread of your own race, but I cannot. In the apple there was a worm. Under the warm sun, grim Tyr was growing cold and bitter for the want of spilt blood; Thor was impatient for the want of heads to smash and brains to smear across the pasture. What is a Golden Age for some is not a Golden Age for others. In some ways I sympathise. Peace has its own pleasures of course – but they are not glorious in the way victory is. It can become, dare I say, a mite boring for those who love uncertainty and conflict.

So it was, that even during the Golden Age, there was discontent below the surface. Rumours were spread in Asgard about the Jotun and their stupidity and greed, about the elves and their perfidy. And, of course, about the progenitor of the wealth and peace that abounded in those days – about Loki. How he plotted against the gods, how he was really more Jotun than god. How he was secretly planning for himself all the time he pretended to be doing good for others . . .

You will know by now the source of those belittling jokes. Who was it had an interest in smearing my reputation and bringing me low? It was all done behind the scenes of course, whispered into ears that didn't understand whose mouth spoke, and why. Stories were spread in the night, notes tucked under doors, forgeries strategically placed to be discovered perhaps centuries later. Over the millennia the steady drip, drip, drip of rumour, professionally spread, did its work.

There were disasters, I'll be the first to admit it. Volund's forge blew up behind him while the smith god worked on the anvil, as I was teaching him how the metal worked. By sheer chance I was unharmed. I investigated the matter myself and found explosives in among the coals. I tried to show the evidence, but no one else understood how such things worked, and I was blamed for blowing his balls to Ragnarok.

It's true that he was having an affair with my wife at the time, but he was one of many. Anyone whose star was about to rise was in her bed by nightfall. I was innocent, reader, innocent! Of course such accidents were cleverly timed, what would you expect? Ask yourself who had an interest in such an accident? In smearing my name with falsehoods?

Once, late at night, coming home past the newly built dwelling places that I had taught them how to build, down a narrow passage behind a drinking house, I passed my enemy Tyr in the dark. It was so narrow we had to lean against the walls to squeeze past one another. It was, for me at least, an uncomfortable and vulnerable moment. But he passed, and the moment with him. I watched him slide along the shadows, and on a whim – I had drunk a quantity of ale that night – I called out . . .

'Tyr!' And he paused. 'We can be friends, why not? Let's make peace. We could accomplish so much more as allies than as enemies.'

He turned his pock-marked face towards me.

'What do I want with peace?' he sneered.

He turned and the shadows closed around him. There you have it, Arse-born. Exactly said, friend Tyr. What does the god of war want with peace, of all things?

I did not give up. I tried and I tried, but what Tyr wanted was the one thing I could not, would not offer: war. I turned to Thor, tried to butter him up. I built him a palace, one of the first and finest palaces of the gods, when I first invented architecture. Thor was pleased. But the palace wasn't as well built as I'd hoped. Bits broke. Things fell down, often on top of the sleeping thunder god. A very fine sculpture of a pussy cat once fell and broke his balls as he lay sleeping. It was funny – I admit I laughed. But to this day, I insist it was not me who filed through that leading leg and caused it to fall in the night.

I should have known that the Golden Age – the Age of Loki it should be called, since it was I who wrought it – was coming to an end. There were omens, forebodings. The first and foremost of which was my own dear wife, beloved Sigyn. I awoke one morning to find my wife was not in the bed with me. Not an unusual thing – as I say, anyone from an athlete winning a race to a king winning a throne attracted her favours. But that wasn't it this time. She was at the mirror, a sheet of polished bronze in those days, twisting and turning herself from side to side to admire her new fashion – a winged helmet on her head, a robe, a trident in her hand.

'What on earth are you doing?' I asked her. Up till then she favoured the simple slit robes and low gowns I admired myself.

She turned to look at me thoughtfully.

'Loki,' she said. 'I'm afraid our marriage appears to be in trouble.'

At the time, I thought she was referring to some indiscretion or other I had committed – I would never deny them, mortal, they were as real as the floor she stood on. I jumped up to reassure her that it was her, her I loved, now and forever.

Sigyn smiled and looked away. She never said, but I see now I had missed the point. Victory, my mortal friends, as I now know to my cost, is a fickle mistress and a fickle wife, too. Sigyn was moving on.

THE END OF THE GOLDEN AGE

Once there was a bridge, a neat and well-built bridge of dressed stone, strong, broad, easy to walk. Many do walk over it — Jotun, elves and men as well as gods, even though it leads to Asgard. In those days, the Golden Age, The Age of Loki, we had open house. There was no need for vigilance. The bridge had of course changed a good deal since I arrived. Back then, it was little more than a tangled heap of raw wood, hewed out of ancient tree trunks with simple stone tools by captive giants and trolls. Now it was neat stone, strong, attractive to the eye. Fit for purpose and good to look at.

Can this be Bifrost, the Rainbow Bridge? You will look in vain for the rainbow, since the Golden Age did not need glamour and plush. There was no status, no wealth gap — only full stomachs and open doors.

Beneath the bridge, the worlds. Very different worlds from the time before Loki, when you would have looked down and seen . . . darkness! — the nameless darkness, deep and lush and velvet, hiding all manner of revolting, flesh-devouring monsters, breathers of fire and venom, drinkers of blood and souls.

All gone. Now, only health and wealth can be seen to the traveller who casts his eye down. Above, the bright eye of Surtr casts its unwavering gaze upon all us insects that toil in the worlds Odin made. Surtr, at this time in his ageless life, was light giver, hope giver, bringer of warmth and growth.

Behold – a figure on the bridge, both large and ugly. Is it Jotun or troll? We see, as Heimdallr lifts his lamp to peer into the traveller's face, that this is a young god. A big god – huge, in fact. As big as a troll already. Bigger. His young body is wracked with muscles like a sack of boulders. Over his shoulder he carries a huge club of granite that he has torn from the rock with his bare fingers and given to the Dökkálfar to encrust with crystals, pieces of unsmelted iron, obsidian and other bone-crushing minerals.

This was back in the days before copper and tin, let alone iron, when we used stone for our shields and flint for our arrowheads. The young god got through those clubs at the rate of one a week or more, so he was forever going back to the dwarves and begging them to fashion him another. He had a million curses for Ymir's bones, which were as weak as water, as thin as buttermilk, as small as a weasel's thigh etc. etc.

Yes, Arse-born. This is the young Thor, off on the murder trail. Look into the traveller's eye. What do you see? A curious intelligence? A questioning nature? A desire to benefit from the views and opinions of the other, that is so rich in the world around us, in this peaceful time, this Golden Age? I think not. Come, let us be generous. How about a desire to protect his loved ones from the manifold dangers of the world around us?

Not even that.

What you see behind the beetling brow of the thunder god is perfectly simple. Indeed, simplicity would sum it up very well. But along with his native stupidity you will find prejudice, bigotry, xenophobia, misogyny, homophobia and any other phobia you can think of. And above all – rage. The thunder god is angry. For some reason he fears that he is permanently belittled and laughed at behind his back. He may be right. Add to this the burning desire to take vengeance for it on the entire world and there you have him – Thor, protector of peasants, Lord of the Storm, smasher of skulls.

What a bastard.

And what is he up to, the young Thor, with his great club and his blazing eyes? To negotiate with the Jotun for his wife, who, apparently, has been kidnapped by them. Why the Jotun, who have plenty of women of their own, should pick the most troublesome one of ours they could catch, no one seems keen to question. Heimdallr, who at this time was of us all best able to peer into the future, nods and says Pass Friend. Well, that is Heimdallr. There is a certain class of person who feels safe with a psychopath by his side. At least he's *your* psychopath, which, as everyone knows, is always better than someone else's psychopath. For a while, at least.

That word – negotiate. And Thor. Thor, negotiate. Negotiate – Thor. You see the problem? There is a dispute between Jotun and god, that much is true. Thor's wife Sif has disappeared; that is also true. A note, purporting to be from the Jotun lord Skrýmir, offering to return said wife for a deal on a certain commodity much in demand before and since, had been delivered, read and now, apparently, acted upon.

No doubt the desire for said commodity and the disappearance of said wife were linked, although personally, I don't actually think Skrýmir had anything to do with the disappearance of Sif. He certainly was adamant in his denials. My own belief is that were you to investigate further, you'd find that someone else, someone whose name comes just a tad later in the alphabet, would more likely be behind it all . . . But enough speculation. Let us stick for now with what we know.

But what, I hear you ask, Shite-in-Flight, with your keen human senses attuned to rhythms of logic and analytical thought – what was the commodity that the Jotun so badly wanted? Why, can't you guess? Isn't it obvious?

Apples, Arse-born. They wanted apples.

IDUNN OF THE APPLES

Let us cast ourselves back a few millennia. Picture this: a shield polished to such brightness that the blazing eye of Surtr himself might blink in surprise. Over the bright metal, a pool of clear water and the whole set in rock, a bone of Ymir's rooted so deep that should all of Jotun jump, not a flicker or a whisper of movement would stir its pellucid waters.

Into this bright mirror, the vain and the mighty come to inspect their beauty. Freya of course, most beautiful and desirable of all women. Her brother Frey, Hoenir the bright god, both considerable beauties even amongst the beautiful. Frigg, vain in her own way; she liked to practise her stern look, her kindly look, her forgiving look, and to see which profile suited them best. Even Odin came, to look into his own eyes and see if there were mysteries there he had not realised. And each day, each of them see only beauty and mystery and youth gaze back at them.

But what is this? It is Hoenir, the bright god, Lord of Vanity, come to luxuriate in his own loveliness. Bright – a bit of a misnomer in his case, because although he was bright in one sense, in another he was positively dull – but let's leave his personality out of this. Let us instead watch him as he bends over the mirror pool to check his beauty, his glowing complexion, his white-blonde hair with its carefully razored motifs . . . but what's this? A frown clouds his lovely face. What's the problem? You may well ask, since his beauty surpasses anything you, Rimmer, can ever hope to see. But his eye is sharp for this sort of thing. The fact is, that the golden light that shines from his skin, from his eyes, from his teeth, from his hair, today has a slightly different hue. Where before it was of the purest gold, today, a touch of silver has crept in. Just a touch, the slightest touch, shining around his mouth where that neatly coiffured beard frames his full and pretty lips – so kissable, as I can attest.

Silver, Arse-born. Very attractive, as it happens – just another form of beauty, you might say. Then why does the Bright One let out a cry of horror and stumble backwards, as if he has been dealt a vicious blow?

Yes, Arse-born; grey hairs. Old age seeping into our lives. The gods live long, but they do not live forever. The quest for eternal life had taken up much of our time – Odin's time, I should say. To the quests of Odin we shall come shortly. How he paid with an eye . . . how he paid even with his life, but was still unable to crack open the secrets of eternity.

Yes, Arse-born; the final enemy was not Jotun or elf, but grim death herself. Read then, and learn, how the gods came to live forever. The story will make a pleasant holiday from the main matter of this book, my downfall. It is not a good one for the gods, I'm afraid, nor for me. So buckle down and man up, those of you who like your divinities spotless. It's not a pretty sight, but a true one for all that.

It was apples that did it, just as the stories say. The wonderful apples of youth, which were bred by the Ljósálfar, the light elves, in Álfheimr. Just as the Dökkálfar, the dark elves, make *things*, laces, hammers, boats that fold up into your pocket, arm rings that drip arm rings and the like, so the Ljósálfar, the elves of light, practise husbandry. It was they who invented the peach, for instance – so different from the bitter little thing we had before. And the plum, and the pear and the quince . . . so of course it was they who grew the golden apples that give the eater not eternal life, but that which is even better – eternal *youth*. The Apples of Rejuvenation, we should call them, but if you get one every thirty or forty years or so, the effect is the same. You just need to secure your supply.

The Ljósálfar were never a very politic race. They were too full of sunbeams to care much about the mucky doings the rest of us got up to; but even they knew enough to keep quiet about the apples. That tree was and is and always shall be the greatest treasure of the world. Kings and gods, giants, monsters, men and elves, all things living, every one of them would die to live forever. The Ljósálfar did their best to keep the secret, but they were not before then a particularly long-lived race and after a while people began to wonder where their wrinkles were. It was Hoenir first; he was one who noticed these things the most. He cornered Illarvis, Lord of the Elves, and demanded where he was keeping his crow's feet these days.

Illarvis looked modestly down and told him it was all down to exercise, diet and a strict regime of moisturisation. Hoenir returned and complained to Odin that a valuable beauty aid was being withheld. Enquiries were made. The elves were asked, politely at first, by Jotun, Dökkálfar, Aesir and Vanir; then not so politely. Eternal youth doesn't mean you can't get broken or hurt, or killed. The tree was located soon enough and Illarvis 'agreed' to share the fruit.

So began the visits to Asgard every ten years of lovely Idunn, the spirit of the miraculous tree. Only in her hands did the apples have their miraculous qualities. We gods would line up to get one each – that's all you ever need. At another time she would visit the giants; at another the elves, etc. It worked well enough for a while, but to be honest it never sat well. Gods as a rule don't like to queue. Nor do giants. This was the Golden Age, of course, so we all did our best to be gracious. The problem was that the tree could only bear so many apples. There were numerous attempts to propagate it. We all became horticulturalists for a while and there was a period when it became somewhat depleted due to the number of twigs that were stolen for cuttings. None of them took; it could not be bred. It stood alone, barren, eternal, unique, like immortality itself.

Discontent grew. The numbers of gods, giants and elves continued to grow; the supply of apples remained the same. There were complaints about how many apples each race was being assigned.

The gods were getting too many, the giants were cheating. You know the kind of thing. Fights broke out. It became clear that the elves weren't up to the job of keeping it safe and so, obviously, the gods had to step in and take possession of the tree to make sure it wasn't stolen. That was the opinion of the gods, at least. Both the elves and the giants took a rather different position. After yet more lengthy negotiations a compromise was finally reached. The tree stayed with the elves in Álfheimr for a period of one hundred years. Then the gods took over for a hundred more. Then it was the giants. From one to the next, from one to the next. And so on, forever.

And amazingly, it worked! A miracle! Or so it seemed. Then one day, when the tree was happily growing away in the woodland garden of Illarvis, the guards turned round – and the grove was empty. Gone. Tree, apples and Idunn – all gone. They had simply disappeared overnight.

There was fury on all sides, particularly from the gods. The elves had been in charge of security. They had warriors and magic of their own at their disposal. It seemed obvious that they were the guilty ones. It was just common sense. But the elves denied any involvement at all. It had to be the gods! Or the Jotun . . . or what about the Dökkálfar, the dark elves, who hadn't been having any apples at all and had been dying like flies lately, from some disgusting underground bug.

An extensive search for underground tunnels was carried out. Dark elven lords were captured and roasted over a slow fire, but no information was gained. Accusations flew. Searches and raids were carried out, wars duly fought, all to no avail. The apples had gone.

Who could that thief have been? The tree was well guarded by spells and by arms. Who had such cunning, such cleverness, such effrontery and bravery to take the whole caboodle, tree, apples and Idunn, from under their noses? It would take a master of disguise, of course, someone with planning who could yet think on their feet and of course talk their way out of anything.

You'll have guessed, I expect. It was me. Under orders, I hasten to add. I'd never have done it for myself. For anyone else it would have been impossible. Even for me, it wasn't easy.

*   *   *

My first attempt to steal the apples of youth was as a wren, a holy bird to the elves. They would never stop a wren from flying into even their most holy groves. There's a lot more magic in that little bird than you might think. I flew into the sanctuary, the sacred grove where the tree grew and tried to turn it into grain of wheat, which I could have carried away triumphantly in my beak; but it didn't work. I tried then to turn it into a stone, a seed, a nut, an apple pip. None of them worked. Some force, some great and powerful force, was stopping me.

I should have guessed. The tree was barren, as I say. It bore no seed and took no grafts or cuttings – who needs children if you live forever? It was itself, then, now and forever. Fire cannot burn it, time cannot touch it. And if time cannot change it, what chance had I?

So much for the tree. It was undying, indivisible, unstealable. I had to think of another way in. And the one I came up with was . . . Idunn.

You should know that every tree, then as now, has a spirit, or sprite, or nymph – an elf as we knew them. Sometimes, if the spirit is strong enough, it can emerge from the tree and walk the earth. These then are the light elves, the Ljósálfar. Idunn, lovely Idunn, was as immortal as her tree. Only for her did the apples fall from the branch, only in her hand did they keep their magic. If you took them away from her, they lost their bite and savour within the hour. Idunn was every bit as important as the tree itself. In fact, they were one and the same.

Mostly the elven folk like to stay among their trees and soak up the sunlight high in the canopy, where the branches are thin and few can visit them. In the sunlight, their bodies become lighter and lighter and in the end, when death comes, they go in a soft flash – a sunbeam shining upon a leaf – and return to the sky that gave them birth. Few gods ever bothered to visit them. Most of them simply lack the curiosity. But I did, when I was free and they were still about. I could turn myself into a bird and fly up and perch on a twig if I wanted to, or as a lizard and run up the trunk. Thor might pass through their woods on one of his psychopathic missions of destruction and shake the trunk and demand feeding. Odin passed by, once in a century perhaps. They didn't care either way. The elves kept themselves to themselves.

And Bragi passed by.

You must have heard of Bragi? Bragi the wise, Bragi the singer, the poet, first of the Skalds, the musician poets of our northern lands. Odin sent him out, long, long ago, to journey the world and to sing of the glory of the gods, their wisdom and ferociousness, their benevolence and cruelty, their charity and prowess in arms. You might be better calling him the god of propaganda, but let's not talk politics just now. Instead, know that he was beautiful, that his voice and playing were beautiful, and that he sang of the heroes and gods, stopping off wherever the fancy took him to sing, to entertain, and to educate.

And although they were not even actually interesting, it came to my notice that of all the peoples he visited, he visited the elves more than anyone.

I wonder why?

I knew Bragi. I liked him. He was good with language, like me. Eloquent. Witty, even, when he wasn't too busy gilding arses with his sweet tongue.

'I sing to them of sunbeams and leaves all bright with the new sap in the spring, the sun shining through them, and they are very happy,' he said, when I asked him what lured the Ljósálfar down from the trees.

That's what he said, but it soon became apparent that although he spoke about visiting the Ljósálfar, when it came to which Ljósálfar exactly, it was always one in particular. One Ljósálfar apparently more beautiful, more clever and interesting than all the others. In short, Bragi had fallen in love. And his love was returned, by none other than . . . Idunn. Immortal Idunn, lovely Idunn, keeper of the apples of youth that everyone so much desired.

It has a certain symmetry to it, don't you think? – that the keeper of wisdom and the keeper of youth should fall in love. Obviously, they had to be together. And now that I knew their secret it was easy to arrange. Idunn of the apples was more than happy to leave the treetops for her lover. I turned the pretty wooden casket in which she kept the fruit into a nutshell and I turned her into the kernel. In the shape of that little wren I flew with them out of the forest, away over the sea and far away, across the bridge, all the way to Asgard, where a warm welcome awaited her. Odin himself presided at the marriage ceremony. Everyone was *so* delighted to see her. Because where Idunn is, the tree is. No need to turn it into anything. The next day, there it was, magically growing in the courtyard of her new home, for her and her hubby to look out on each morning.

The Jotun and the Ljósálfar weren't so happy of course. That day I left behind me such a howling and raging, such a flurry of leaves and a crashing of trees. Legions of soldier elves were executed in the aftermath, I hear, for bringing death among them by their carelessness. Had they only known, it didn't matter a jot who'd been guarding it, for I am the Prince of Thieves. Once I put my mind to it, I can slip in anywhere and take anything. You won't even know it's gone. Bingo! Say goodbye to youth, my elven friends, and say hello to grim death.

Yes, I was the one who brought death to the Jotun and the elven race, for which they have never forgiven me. The light elves are a beautiful folk and there are few, so very few of them left these days. I tell myself that is not because I stole their tree, but because their love of sunbeams is so great that they congregate on the topmost branches of the highest trees, where, in time, they turn to sunlight themselves – gaining a kind of immortality that way instead. Remember that, next time a sunbeam warms your back or your face, or lights up a glade, or passes across a meadow. It's the light elves, making a pass across their old home.

But it is true that there was a great deal of death when I took the tree. Scores were slaughtered among the Jotun and the light elves in the apple wars that followed. The Jotun were a tough bunch, who worshipped war in their own way, and were used to death, courtesy of mighty Thor. But death made the light elves depressed as a race and they began to reproduce less often. I have my moments of guilt, but I don't feel bad about it very often; death was common in those days, just as it is now.

But to get back to the tree. Despite all the lies and deception it soon became apparent who actually had the tree, because while the Jotun and the elves aged and died, we stayed young. More rage, more wars. To be fair, Odin was actually very generous with its fruit. True, some sour souls took the view, that given that they were not his apples, Odin had no right to be generous with them. Even so, he handed them out to giants, light elves, dark elves as well as among the gods. Not to you, of course – not mankind. I know – it's not fair. I did my best for you. I have a weakness for the human race, perhaps because I had such a big part in bringing you about. My condition for stealing the tree was that it be shared fairly. Odin kept his word in every respect except for you.

'They're just fucking machines,' he said. 'At it the whole time, churning out babies like biscuits out of the oven. No, Loki, I'm sorry. The Jotun yes – but not them.'

Well, he had a point. You people breed far too often ever to be sustained as a race by one tree. It would take a world of trees to keep you alive. Even with death at your shoulder, you swarm across the continents like grass across the field.

The most important folk were at the head of the queue – the gods first – all of them. Then the Jotun lords, and so on and so forth. The light elves had their share too. He even included the dark elf lords this time. But the tree remained one tree, and the giants and the elves became many. First off Odin decided that the dark elves could do without – they lived long enough anyway. Then the light elves, who were kicking up such a fuss. Finally, he decreed that the giants had to embrace grim death as well.

So ends the Golden Age, my friends. Once there was enough for all, but when the apples came, then there simply could never be enough. Even among the Aesir and the Vanir there has been strife over the apples. The tree bears a few hundred fruits each year. Any children we have these days are destined for herohood, not godhead. So it has been for time out of mind. So it shall be till mind out of time.

And yet war did not come at once, Arse-born. Both gods and Jotun were reluctant to bring the catastrophe down upon us. There was a great deal of talk. Odin did not intend to keep all of them from the life eternal forever and as I say, there were some apples destined for the great Jotun lords and their immediate families. Skrýmir being one of them. How strange, then, that Skrýmir should chose a sensitive point in those negotiations to kidnap the Thunderer's fat wife.

Now then, you see – we have returned to mighty Thor as he set on his journey to rescue his kidnapped wife. How do you suppose that ended?

See there? Those huts burned to the ground. See those pretty shapes scattered carelessly across the grass, higgledy-piggledy? Yes; the bodies of slaughtered children, scattered about like chickens after a visit by the fox. See that blackened heap to one side of the village pond? The burned bodies of their parents. That grey and gory mess outside the meeting house? The brains of the elders. See the weeping woman, bending back and forth over a body of fallen Jotun? Her dress is torn, his face swollen from violence to her person. The raped wife of the man slain at her knees, and the sad bundle she holds in her arms? – the body of their new baby. The other children, of whom there were four or five, cannot be told one from the other in a tableau of mangled limbs, crushed by stone and wood, that lies at the entrance of their dwelling hut.

And a similar scene at the next hut, and the next; and the next village and the one after that . . .

So has Thor avenged the kidnap of his wife. A crime which, on investigation, turned out to be somewhat less than he imagined. Yes, he did find Sif, hidden in an underground grain silo, some-what dazed but otherwise unharmed. She had not been there long, apparently. Up till then she had been locked away in a cave . . . whereabouts? Ah, poor love, she has no idea. And her food and drink were lowered down to her on a rope from above, so she never saw her captors. And she was blindfolded and taken off to the silo in Utgard only a few hours before she was found. And . . . how odd! She never even heard the sounds of mighty Thor destroying and crushing Utgard and all who lived there, which is very odd since . . .

. . . could it be that she was only put there *after* the massacre? That would be very strange because, why would the Jotun go to the trouble of bringing her there for us to find even while they were being murdered in their beds?

Strange. You would almost imagine that Sif had actually been kidnapped by other agencies, who then wished the Jotun to be blamed . . .

There were rumours of course. Who would play such a trick? Who is cunning enough, malevolent enough . . . nasty enough to want to foment war in such a low way?

Why, me of course! Who else could it possibly be, other than that well-known mischief maker, Loki? Obvious, when you think about it.

Reader, there is another who loves lies. One who has an interest in discrediting poor Loki and causing strife for his own ends. Let me introduce you to him. Not a broad fellow, with a strong arm and a noble brow. More a beetling kind of fellow, a lipless man, whose smile is rarely seen, whose laughter is weak and withheld, not open. One who walks with a limp and deals in whispers. One who prefers the shadows to the daylight, the unseen rather than the seen. A narrow-minded, vicious kind of fellow. Yes, friends, you have already met him once or twice; Tyr. Are you surprised at his narrow demeanour and his thin arms? Don't be; it was ever thus. That broad-chested, hail-fellow-well-met kind you like to think of when you think of warriors? He's just the fighter. Behind that likeable young man is an older one, one with a mind powerful but narrow, penetrating but bitter, who spurs the warrior on with lies and bigotries . . . one who invents insults from imagined enemies.

And the result of this chaos, this mayhem? The Jotun of course demanded wergeld, blood for blood, to settle the massacre. But Odin was unwilling to give up his eldest child to anyone. And so . . .

War. Welcome back, old friend.

It was round about this time that my wife began to spend more of her time with Tyr than at home with me. Victory, my friends, is ever the bitch. Don't be deceived by her flattery, it won't last.

THE WALL

Yes, Arse-born; war returns, with its attendants, greed, hunger, cultural impoverishment, barbarism, injury and death. I could go on. Forgive me if I omit glory. You know the way of it. When your enemy hurls a gigantic boulder at your head, and it misses and crashes into your house, splattering your baby, your wife and two or three visiting toddlers, he is a monster; when your boulder narrowly misses him and crushes next door's family instead, it's collateral damage. When you chose to bite off their chief's toes one by one, slowly, with your yellow, troll-like and very blunt front teeth, it's an unfortunate but necessary piece of information-gathering to safeguard the innocent; when one of them tugs out the fingernails of your mother-in-law, it's an act of unfathomable barbarism.

It was ever thus.

Lovers of peace, such as myself, who were blamed for starting the conflict in the first place, were branded first cowards for our reluctance to fight, then traitors for talking to the enemy to find peace. My stock, already low due to the lies spread about me about the kidnapping of Thor's wife Sif, sank even lower. But I stuck to my principles, Arse-born! There were those still living then, who knew. Democracy had yet to be invented but peace always has its fans. Where are they now, those Jotun, men and elves who once loved me and planned with me for peace, who came to my table to ask for my help in finding a way through the terror? All dead, all gone and buried, slandered for their efforts. There are no markers on their graves. And the gods and goddesses who begged me to help? Quiet now, if they still live. Peace is dead, and terror has no rivals.

And yet . . . and yet. The fact is, I was a god on the side of the gods. I sued for peace, I talked, I manoeuvred. I was tireless in my efforts, yes; but I did not slack when it came down to us against them. There were times when we in Asgard were on the very brink of destruction, and at those times you can be sure that Loki was there for his kith and kin, for his friends and family. Even though it was the foolish gods who brought an end to the Golden Age, I would not have us defeated – could not, would not allow it. Many times, as the following pages will recount, it was Loki who saved the day. If not for me, the gods and all their glories would be shadows in the stones, their deeds forgotten – the very acts of creation which brought about those stones would be unrecorded and gone forever. It was I who made us safe, I who provided us with our most potent weapons. Read, Arse-born, and learn to whom the gods owe their greatest debts.

You rejoin my story at a dark hour for the gods, Shit-face. The wars were bitter, protracted and terrible. Everyone wants to live forever. Human beings were far too puny to do anything about it, although they liked a fight well enough. The light elves were simply not warlike and the dark elves were too vulnerable to sunlight to do much – fighting in the dark just doesn't present the opportunities for sustained violence to those of us who live under the sun. But the giants – the giants were another matter. They knew how to fight. For a long time it was touch and go.

You join us at a time when the Jotun were at our door – frost giants, rock giants, trolls, goblins, the lot. Wave after wave of them coming at us. No sooner had we repelled one army than another began to mass on the other side of Bifrost, our bridge to the other worlds. The great void beneath it was filling up with the corpses of the slain, and the fear was growing among us that sooner or later, it would be full to the brim and the forces of darkness would just stroll across and take us out face to face, fist to fist. We were exhausted. We had fought and fought and fought for a hundred years, but the armies of the Jotun showed no sign of slowing down or of wanting peace. Thor was slaughtering at a ferocious rate, but still they came. Tyr was planning and plotting, conniving and lying, but none of it to any avail. The Jotun had generals as good as ours and their forces outnumbered us a thousand to one. We were doomed, mortal – doomed to die. Unless . . .

There was only one possible way out at that time – one plan, one plot. We could not really hope to win, but if only we could somehow miraculously hold them off for just a few more years, give ourselves a short break in which we could catch our breath and re-align our plans . . . devise more and better weapons . . . uncover further mysteries . . . grow and raise a few more gods . . . maybe then we would stand a chance.

We needed defences. Specifically, we needed a wall. A big wall. A big beautiful wall, too tall to climb, too deep to burrow under, too thick to knock down. It had to be big. It had to be beautiful. Fire must not touch it, nor the backs of giants topple it. We wanted that wall and we wanted it now. We wanted it yesterday. We didn't have it. What's more, we hadn't got the slightest hope of building it ourselves because already, we had decided that we gods were too important to labour.

That's right. Behold your creators, mortal! All that stood between us and the armies of frost giants, rock giants, trolls and other monsters from deep in the earth was Heimdallr and his little stone bridge. And yet we were too proud to roll up our rags and build ourselves a wall. Ridiculous.

One day, one fine day towards the end of the year, when the fires were lit and we gods were looking anxiously across Bifrost at the angry hoards on the other side, we had a visitor. A Jotun. One of the biggest we'd ever seen. As bigger than one of your normal Jotun as a normal Jotun was bigger than a man. And fat. A big fat bastard, but not that kind of wobbly fat bastard that comes from glands and cakes. He was that other kind of fat bastard – the strong kind. He had the kind of fat that carries layers of muscle underneath it, the kind of fat that makes a man stronger, not weaker – the kind of fat needed to back up all the beef he carried. A mason, he said he was, a master at his trade. Heimdallr had let him cross the bridge, so that meant something. Heimdallr let no one cross unless we had a use for them.

So this Jotun offered to build us the wall, the wall that we all dreamed of, so tall that no Jotun could climb over it with ladders, so deep in the ground that no number of dark-delving elves could dig beneath it, too thick to push down. A wall made of stones as big as houses, fitted together so tight, even a fly could not crawl through.

We knew of this fellow; his reputation preceded him. He had built the great castles and cities of the Jotun . . . beautiful Utgard, for instance . . . huge and perfect citadels that we had never even attempted to storm, such was the thickness of their walls and the height of their battlements. There was no doubt that he could build us our wall, and no doubt that we wanted him to build us our wall. So of course, when he came to make a deal, we went to listen to what it was.

He had a horse with him, a stallion, a Jotun horse of course, bigger than he was. I tell you, that beast stood on the wintery plain in front of us and as we watched, his hooves sank into the frozen ground by the sheer weight of him. Strong, so strong – but not bulky the way a big horse often is. You knew he would be fleet as he stood there. A wonderful horse. I never saw his like before or since. The muscles on his back and legs – his gleaming coat, his neck, his fine head. Yes, that horse had all the graces a horse can have. Unlike his master, who was strong but stolid, tall but bulky, dressed in his mason's apron, as if visiting the gods to tender for a job was something he did every day of the week, and he could hardly be bothered to comb his hair or wash his face for it.

'Why?' asked Odin, his eyes shining brightly.

'Why what?'

'Why does a Jotun want to build us a wall to keep the Jotun out?'

'It's my job,' he said. 'I do it for pay.'

We were all staring at the mason, trying to work it out. A trick? Well, maybe. The Jotun are better at throwing tantrums than thinking up tricks, but there are exceptions, some of them great exceptions.

'So,' said Odin. 'What is your pay?'

The mason lifted his big chin off his barrel chest and pulled in his fat belly. 'I want the sun and the moon to light my house,' he said. 'And I want Freya for my wife.'

The sun. What a fool. If anyone had any doubt that this was just a Jotun – a big Jotun but as stupid as all the others – this put an end to it. If he had just a pint of the sun in a bottle, it would burn down his house and all the houses around it, and all the houses around that, and half of Jǫtunheimr too.

And – marry Freya? A Jotun marry a goddess? There was a lot of yelling and shouting at that, which was all nonsense of course, since there was plenty of Jotun blood standing on the godly side of this interview, although none of them ever cared to admit it. You can bet, too that the ones shouting the loudest were those with the most Jotun blood. What? A Jotun, take Freya as a wife? Beautiful Freya, lovely Freya, Freya who was desired by any and all who set eyes on her, god and goddess, man, woman, giant, dwarf, human or beast. Freya, goddess of love, queen of sluts and whores? Tied to one mere Jotun? You must be joking . . .

Excuse me. I speak only the truth. Humankind loves to romanticise their divinities, but do you really think that the goddess of fertility opens her legs just for her hubby? No, no, no. Freya slept with anyone she felt like. Big, small, man, woman – it made no difference to her. I've had her myself countless times. If you doubt me, I can tell you a story or two that will put your mind at rest on that score.

So they said no. Which was the right decision. And so it would and should have stayed if it wasn't for Hoenir. Stupid Hoenir, worshipped only by the mirror in his bedroom, who never had two thoughts to put together, who got confused if you asked him the time of day.

I know. You will have heard differently. You will have heard that it was me who suggested trying to get one over on that giant. Not true! Since my imprisonment they have tried to tie me up in all the knots they tied themselves, smeared me in all the shit they shat, blamed me for all their sins. Everything is laid at Loki's door. It's convenient. I'm not around to defend myself. As I think I may have said before, it's the winners who get to write the books, and I am most certainly not a winner.

But the truth remains. Odin knows. Surtr, whose eye is above us all, sees. It wasn't me; it was Hoenir, that's the truth and there's an end to it. But it wasn't his fault – I could see that at once. Hoenir was a shiny and beautiful creature, like some kind of exotic antelope, right up until he opened his mouth, when he revealed himself for what he was – a bleating, tongue-stumbling fellow, his leaking face-flaps spilling onto his chin, his tongue twisting around his tonsils and tangling itself in knots.

'Even so,' he said, 'it would be a shame to let such a chance go by without taking some advantage of it. Why not put some conditions on it? Make it hard. In fact – make it impossible. Negotiate. He's a giant,' he said. 'They're stupid and greedy. He will agree to anything we want if he thinks he's going to get his paws on our Freya.'

Now, Hoenir never spoke like that. He was neither clever enough nor loquacious enough. He had been coached, I saw that at once. And I knew who by.

'Why do you say that, Tyr?' I said. 'Or should I say – why *don't* you say it yourself, Tyr?'

But my words went unheard. I hadn't got to the end of my sentence when Freya let out a terrible shriek and went for Hoenir with her claws. She'd have cut him open with her nails if she'd got to him, but the others stood in her way, Hoenir yelling, 'Would you strike a fellow god? Hold her back, dear friends!' in that obsequious way he has.

It was obvious to me what was going on, but alas, divinity doesn't always include more than half a brain and he set a number of them thinking. Thor for one. And of course as soon as Thor began stroking his beard and nodding his head, the others began it as well.

This was one of those times when you would expect Odin to put his foot down. But no. You might well wonder what the wisest of all is doing allowing decisions to be made by the meanest among us. But that's Odin. Some say he sees far and wide; we lesser beings often do not know what consequences he sees. I say otherwise – as I shall attest shortly. But for now, know that, yes, the gods did indeed do a deal with the mason and the deal was, that he would have his prizes *so long as he built the wall in one year.*

Clearly impossible. I wasn't so concerned at that point. But the mason pressed back, showing that stupid though the Jotun sometimes are, not all of them are all the time. He argued OK, yes. So long as he could use his horse, Svadilfari, to pull stone.

And the gods agreed.

I argued against it. I did my best. I flattered, I cajoled, I promised, I lied. I even told the truth. I had Odin by the beard, yelling in his face to stop them. None of it made any difference. They all wanted the wall too much.

'Oh come on,' someone said – Hoenir again, I think. 'What difference will a horse make?'

But not any horse – *that* horse! You never saw such a horse. He was beautiful and he was strong. When he stamped his foot, the earth trembled. When he tossed his head, the wind sighed. It wasn't until the Jotun came back within the day with the first load of stone that the others began to have their doubts. What a load! There was a mountain on that sleigh. The runners sank into the earth under the weight of it. Svadilfari was pulling hard, but not by any means at the full extent of his strength. Not only that, but the stone was already dressed. They hadn't reckoned on that of course. I'd warned them to make sure of what they were bargaining for, but as usual, their desires made mincemeat of their common sense. The giant had prepared the stone before he even came to us. Not so stupid after all.

Freya was incandescent. They'd made serious oaths to that Jotun, there was no going back on those oaths – he'd made sure of that, in his riotous stupidity. The last thing Freya wanted was to get exiled into a life of being rogered once a week by a scruffy rock giant in the frozen wastes of Jǫtunheimr. There wouldn't be much else on the menu either, because one thing you could bet – no way was he going to let her get up to her old tricks, that's for sure. She went up to watch him at work. I tell you that Jotun was tossing those stones into place – 1, 2, 3, 4, one after the other. They fell exactly where he wanted them, neat as a honeycomb. No problem. He paused to wink at her.

'Don't worry, pretty Freya, I will make you happy when you are
my queen,' he bellowed, wiping his dusty paws on his piss-stained
robes.

Freya let out a howl like the banshee and went straight for Hoenir
again. She'd have scratched his eyes out if he hadn't curled up in a ball
on the ground to protect his lovely face. As it was, she had to be content
with stamping on his feet and kicking him from behind in the balls till
he howled like a calving cow. Because it was clear right then, right
from the first load of stone, as we watched the Jotun start to pile them
up, that he was going to earn his wages. No doubt about it.

So the year went on. Freya was getting more and more upset about it.
There was a plan afoot by Thor and a few others about carrying the
sun to the Jotun as the first part of his payment and frying him like
a vast fat sausage but Odin wasn't keen and no one else had a clue
how it might be done. Thor might have cracked the mason's skull,
but you should know that the gods at that time had this thing about
honour. You can crack a man's head open for shaking the wrong hand
or for murdering your mother and raping your sister – but if he was
related to someone who had done you a favour in the past, you
couldn't touch him, so you had to pulp his brother-in-law instead.
You can kill his brother-in-law so long as you have enough money to
compensate him, sleep with his wife so long as you're prepared to get
your son to marry his daughter, unless it was the first Tuesday in the
month . . . you know the sort of thing; I forget the details. I never
understood it myself, but oaths had been made, and there was no
going back on them.

The only recourse was trickery. Dirty work. Something below the
belt. Of course, the high-born gods could in no way get their pristine
hands soiled with such work. So they did what they always did; they
looked to me.

I knew it. Right from the start when Hoenir first opened his lying
mouth, I knew in my bones exactly how it was going to turn out.
They were going to regret it and they were going to want me to sort
it out. The whole time they were arguing about how to save Freya, I
could see them eyeing me up. In the end I got fed up with the whole
thing.

'Just ask me if you're going to,' I snapped. And everyone drew a big sigh of relief.

The horse was the secret, of course. Without that horse the Jotun would be like a man with only one leg. I remember when it all came to a head. We were all standing outside Odin's palace watching the Jotun at work, tossing those huge stones into place like they were loaves of bread. Big, heavy stones, big as cottages, one after the other, bump, bump, bump. You could feel the earth move under your feet. They landed and they stuck. And the horse, he didn't need leading. He didn't have to be tethered or told what to do. The Jotun had already loaded up the sledges at the quarry, so all the horse had to do was slip into the harness and set off, one load after the next, regular as the moon itself rising from out of the sea.

Without the horse, he was done. No more loads of stone arriving at his feet. Him having to fetch it all himself. Without the horse, the bet would be lost.

We'd tried all sorts. Food. Hay, the sweetest hay. Carrots. Cake soaked in honey. None of it worked. He was loyal, that horse. We tried sex – mares, dozens of them, one after the other, each one more delightful, prettier, stronger, sexier than the last. None of them worked.

So there we were. I was gazing out there, looking at Swadilfari, his fine flanks, his ears, his neck forward as he trotted lightly with his heavy load, a load that would have had a team of ten ordinary horses heaving and slipping in the icy mud like pigs on skates.

'What can we do, Loki? Please. You're the Prince of Trickery. There must be something you can do?' Freya begged.

'It has to be a mare,' I said, watching the horse drop the load of stone, slip out of harness and trot off to fetch the next sledge. 'But no ordinary mare. It has to be something special – a princess among mares, a queen. A sexy mare. A mare so overflowing with love and desire that even this stern, strong stallion will turn his head to her. A wonderful mare. A beautiful mare, whose neigh and whinny will fill his belly with a fire he cannot withstand . . .'

I had begun daydreaming about it, I admit it. But then I felt a presence by me, I looked sideways, and there was Odin, staring at me with a frown on his face – a fascinated look, half wonder, half horror, half admiration, half disgust. His eyes widened. I shrugged.

'You're going to fuck the horse, aren't you?' he said.

I was feeling very quiet then – the feeling that you get when you are about to embark on a great adventure. I shrugged again and went for a little walk alone to clear my head and settle my nerves, and when I came back, the others were all clustered around Odin. I could hear the words he was saying even from a distance – so sharp are my ears.

'Horse,' he was saying. And – 'Fuck,' he was saying. And, 'Loki . . .'

I was incandescent. I mean – really? He was supposed to be my friend! I would have done it, you understand – to save Asgard. Of course I would! But quietly and in secret. This was dark business. I didn't blag his secrets, not that he ever told me any. But Odin, the great All-gob, Odin the gossiper, like an old woman in a queue at the grocers – he just had to spill the beans, didn't he? As I came up they were all looking at me in utter disgust.

'Well, I'll tell you what, big mouth,' I said to the Allfather. 'I'm not going to do it now. If anyone's going to fuck the horse – you do it.'

Odin started spluttering away – him, the Lord of Gods – how dare I? – monstrous etc. etc.

'Fine,' I said. 'Let the world discover that the gods lie when they make their promises. Give the Jotun his wages instead. Give him the moon and the sun and Freya and let him have your gold, your arm rings, your favourite weapons. Let him fuck your daughters and use your sons as serving boys, since that's how it is. But don't look to me, that's all. Because, you know what? I have honour of my own and I'm not going to fuck the horse either.'

Uproar! The noble gods didn't want anyone anywhere near them to be a horse fucker. On the other hand, neither did they want to lose Freya to a Jotun, or have the shame of having lied known to all, or give up the sun. Shame, shame, shame!

In the end, if there was to be shame, they'd far rather have me carry it than themselves. So they were in a mess.

I made the most of it, of course.

'OK,' I said. 'OK. I'll do it, I'll fuck the horse – on one condition. That every one of you, every single one, gets down and begs me – seriously begs me, on bended knee, to fuck the horse.'

And they did, I tell you. Freya was first among them. It wasn't the first time she'd been on her knees before me – just the previous night actually, although it wasn't begging she was doing then. Great Odin on bended knee. Frigg touching the fur on my tunic reverently. Frey, trying to make it all noble by making out it was this great sacrifice. Tyr, who was actually furious that he had to get me to clear up what was his mess. He wanted that wall more than anyone, and if it cost Freya or even the sun to get it, he was happy to pay. Him, Sif, Njordr, father of Frey and Freya, Lord of the Vanir, the lot of them, one after the other. All the way to Thor. When it got to his turn, he stood before me trembling like a child.

'God of thunder and the sky, protector of peasants, eater of goats, splitter of skulls, plougher of furrows, mighty Thor, terror of the Jotun, protector of the gods!' I cried. 'Your turn. On your knees and beg me to fuck that horse.' I admit I was enjoying it. Odin should never have spilt the beans.

Great Thor ambled up to me, his tawny beard all tousled and roughed up because he was so upset, his face red with shame, his huge stone club trailing in the dirt behind him. He stood before me shivering and shaking. He twisted, he turned, he coughed, he farted. He almost shat himself with shame, then at last he turned to Odin and bellowed . . .

'I can't do it! I can't beg him to fuck a horse! I can't bend my knee to a horse fucker. Father, forgive me!'

And he began blubbering. Everyone gathered round him, begging him to beg me, comforting him, urging him on. All to no avail; it was simply beyond the poor guy. And me? – well, I pointed my nose to heaven and said that, in that case, he could go fuck the horse himself.

So that was that. Except, I did go and fuck the horse. Why, I hear you ask? The reputation of the gods? – people say I don't care about these things, but I do, of course I do. Freya? I liked her. And then there was eternity. We had enemies at the gate, we needed that wall.

All this was true, but there was another reason that flipped the scale. Most of all – I can admit this to you, can't I? – most of all, there was Svadilfari.

I wandered off to let them fret. Quietly and secretly, I became a mare that very afternoon. I trotted out of the woods at night, when only the mother moon was watching, and perhaps Odin, whose face I saw across the frosty fields. Beautiful Svadilfari was under the trees waiting for me. I whinnied, he whinnied back and came galloping across the frozen ground towards me.

Svadilfari, Svadilfari! There never was such a horse like him. His flanks rippled with strength and ran streaming with lustful sweat as we raced along the river banks, his hooves like obsidian clashing against the rocks. His neck when he reached across to bite my ears was a sculpture in flesh and his teeth were ivory. We ran right out of Asgard and across Bifrost; Heimdallr ordered us to stop, but neither of us cared. Down to middle earth we galloped. Across the ice lands we ran, out of Europe and into Asia, up through the endless tundra. We galloped across the frozen rivers of the north, over the sea ice up to the farthest northern point and back. When he entered me, his rod was like a second spine inside me and when he released his seed, it was like a fountain; I overflowed. Beautiful Svadilfari! I loved you in your day as much as I loved any god, any human or Jotun woman. Now he's long gone; there were no apples for his kind. But I would give a century of my life to have him back. To feel his weight against my rear as he mounted me, to hear the clatter of his hooves as he charged across the mountains and the plains – to feel his rod probing so hot and deep inside me.

As we ran, other horses came and tried to take me off him, but he kicked them aside like dogs; and if he didn't, I did. I wanted to know no other, and no other horse has tempted me since. He had then and has since no equal to walk this wonderful earth. No lover has ever loved me so hard, so fierce, so deep. You on middle earth may know love, but you will never have such a love as Svadilfari was to Loki. Beg it in your prayers, offer it to the sky, sing our praises! No one saw us, no songs were sung. But for those few days, we were the greatest of love stories ever told.

Then at last, he was spent. Even he – so spent he was on his knees. Only then did I break my spell and let him go. I walked away and left him on the ice to make his way back to his master, who had lost just one week to love – but it was enough. He cursed great Svadilfari, cursed him and beat him like a mule. I would have gone to his rescue but I was exhausted too. Only when I came round days later and saw him treated like that, his sides and back covered in deep wounds from the whip, only then did I try to go to him. It broke my heart, and I wanted to take revenge on that Jotun, but the gods were frightened that the builder would see me and guess who I was, that the trick would be discovered. So they stabled me securely and left me there. I wept, while my love dragged stone after stone across the forest floor until at last, the day before the year ended, Svadilfari's great heart broke and he died and lay, cooling on the forest floor while his owner cursed and spat at his corpse.

The sun went down on the last day of the year, and the wall was unfinished. The Jotun cursed the gods, called them liars and cheats; so they were forced to deal with him for failing to keep to his side of the bargain properly and insulting them. Thor split his head open. His brains tumbled out and he was buried that day in the woods like a common thing, greatest of masons, together with the greatest of horses, deep in the woods. I visit the grave sometimes and sometimes, I shed a tear.

As for me, I stayed in my shape as a mare for two years. Perhaps you will have guessed the reason. Yes; I was with foal. No living creature could love Svadilfari and not take his seed. And of course I could not change my shape then, with the foal inside me who would not change, so I was forced to stay and bear my child. Besides, I wanted to honour his father. I did my time and in due course, my time came and I dropped a foal, a foal as strong as his father and beautiful as his mother. A wonderful foal. Freya, bless her, who stayed with me through the birth, thought he was deformed because he had too many legs. She wanted to smash his head in there and then, but I stood between her and my young one. I bared my teeth at her and drove her off. Then my baby came to me to suckle, and we settled down to sleep in the sweet-smelling straw.

The gods came later and many of them were of Freya's opinion that the foal should be killed, with his eight legs. But Odin was wise then and he saw that all those legs worked, each one as well as the other, so he said the foal should live. Years later, when I presented my son to him, he accepted gratefully. Ever since, Sleipnir has been his steed. There is no horse faster, and none more beautiful. He can fly through the air and over the water as well as he can over the land. I would say no horse was ever his equal but there once were two who were. His father, who sired him with such passion all those years ago. And – dare I say it? – perhaps his mother, too, had the edge on him when it came to beauty.

As for horse fucking, what can I say? Don't try it at home. Unless you're a mare of course. And even then, you could look all the days of your life and even mine, but you'd never find yourself anyone to compare with my Svadilfari.

THAT WRETCHED HAMMER

Such was my first great deed of service to the gods. And were there cheers for Loki? Were banquets held, speeches made, praises sung? Was his name on every lip? Were the children taught to look up to him as an example? Was he feted, held in high esteem? Were there even thanks, by any chance?

No, there were not. War stalked the worlds, turmoil and strife were everywhere, and yet the gods were safe behind their great wall. If it wasn't for me, they'd all be face down in the dirt with the frost giants up their arses and all they could say was – 'Horse fucker.'

I know the stories they tell, the old Asgard propaganda. That it was me who got them to tempt the Jotun to build the wall . . . and then look at the shameful way Loki got the gods out of the trouble that *he'd* caused! In some ways, I'm my own worst enemy. I was furious with Thor for killing that poor giant – who after all had only tried to make a deal and then stick to it. They got what they wanted. If they were going to kill him, just do it in the first place rather than make poor Loki go all around the horses trying to find a way out of it for them.

I had a go at Thor about that – and Odin, who at least had the decency to look shamefaced. But for Thor, killing folk was just like drawing breath. Whenever I tried to take him to task about it, he just stared at me as a horse might stare at the moon, huffed and turned his head away to find something more interesting – like food or ale or a woman or a nice, fat murder.

Murderers gotta murder. So long as they kill the right people, who cares? But horse fuckers? It seems there's no such thing as the right horse. I got a lot of grief about Svadilfari from the Aesir.

'Oh Loki, tell me, is your pussy still sore after the hard fucking that horse gave you? Did you like having that big dick up you? . . .' etc. etc.

The Aesir were always a stuck-up bunch. Honour, right and wrong, how things should be done. You know the sort of thing. After Svadilfari, things were never the same between me and Aesir. Never mind that they had their wall. Never mind that Odin had the fastest horse that ever lived, or would live or could live. Never mind that the sun and the moon still shone brightly in the sky. Overnight, I was turned from amusing, clever, quick, useful Loki into something else. Horse fucking, apparently, was *so* much worse than murder, killing babies and all the other delightful activities mighty Thor got up to when he was out and about. He was a hero. And me? I, apparently, was little better than some kind of pervert.

It rankled. Thor in particular rankled. So keen to call me a pervert, but I was willing to bet that he had his own kinks. The violent usually do, don't you agree? – one reason why they love these things not to be talked about.

I resolved to find out – and to get my own back in the process. Like all my tricks, it ended in me being excoriated, but leaving the gods better off than when I began. As you will see, it was a trick that gave the gods the final edge over the Jotun. Once I had done, never again did they need fear being overwhelmed by any enemy. And yet once again, Loki, who gave so much, came out of it with his ranking lower than before.

Did you know – probably not, this is not well known, needless to say – that mighty Thor, with elbows like boulders and biceps like bears, actually has ridiculous skinny legs? Yes, it's true. And his cock – how can I put this gently? It's not a big one. Rather small in fact. The giants used to tease him about it back in the days before he developed into a full-blown, over-weaponised psychopath. Thor Spindlelegs, they called him. Thor Smallcock. So did I, once or twice, but I got fed up of ending up flat on my back in a bed with my ribs cracked and Idunn tending me and telling me crossly she was sick of handing out apples for me to heal and that I had better start being nicer to Thor.

So I had to get my own back another way.

You'll have heard of Thor's wife, Sif? She of the long golden flowing locks of hair. Something of a harvest deity, with that golden, ripe hair. I've seen images of her, slim, beautiful and bounteous, but the reality was very different. Sex goddesses might be slim and willowy – they might not – but a harvest deity is going to be *fat*, all tits and arse and belly. Sif in particular is shaped like an anvil. She had to be, wedded to Thor – Thor the head breaker, Thor the mountain splitter – but also Thor the pelvis crusher. Believe me when I tell you, no ordinary woman would willingly put up with that. Yes, I know! – how come you never heard about it? Use your head. Why do you think? There has always been propaganda, it's nothing new. I should know. I invented it. But that's a story for another time.

Sif, I would say, is at least three quarters troll. Nothing else could account for a woman with a shape like that. While Thor was off on his long journeys, breaking giants' heads, murdering dwarves and crushing the pelvises of mortal women, Sif was left at home feeling hard done by and lonesome. Back then when the world was young and the spirit of life was rising up into our nostrils, most of us were falling in and out of love, or at the very least, in and out of lust from week to week. But not Sif. It was nothing to do with her appearance, you understand. That era, like most eras, enjoyed the fleshy layers and curves of a fertile woman. Why not? Who wouldn't want to luxuriate in the health and wealth of the well fed? It's only your own etiolated age, with your lakes of milk and cheap fats, that imagines beauty lying in the bones and not the fat of fine women.

No. Sif was as lusted after as any of us – but she was married to Thor. And Thor, although he enjoyed spreading it about himself, was an early advocate of do-as-I-say-not-as-I-do. In short, he expected his

lady wife to remain chaste at home while he shagged his way around
the world. Leaving Sif – a fertility goddess, remember, who had the
sex drive of a herd of bison in must – prowling around Asgard in a
state of sexual anguish, until she was able to grab some hapless king
or farmer and crush him like a ripe plum in her passion. So when a
handsome stranger came calling at her doors, a young man as tall as
she was broad, strong, handsome – and not only that but willing to
actually get down to it with her, there was no stopping her. Sif had
to take her chances when she could. There were not many willing to
help her out, given Thor's reputation for losing his temper at even
the slightest insult.

So Sif and the tall, well-built stranger spent a night rolling about
between the linen sheets in mighty Thor's mighty palace. And in
between bouts of exercise they talked, as lovers will, and the thing
the handsome stranger liked best to talk about was Thor. Those of
you who are not strangers to infidelity will know how curious lovers
sometimes are about the foibles of those they are cuckolding.

Ah, yes, pillow talk! So many secrets leak out in the happy aftermath of intimacy. It seemed that Thor, with his spindly legs, Thor
Narrowshanks, Thor Twiggydick, Thor Tattsack, when he was in the
bedroom with his beloved spouse, liked nothing better than to cast
aside that ridiculous floor-length goatskin coat he always wore to
hide his diddy leggies, and to stride around the bedroom while Sif
told him how mighty his sinews were, how his legs were like bison's
thighs, how his manhood was more like a battering ram than a mere
penis.

'Careful, go slowly, or you'll split me in half!' she had to yell out,
when the mighty thunder-willy came into action. And – 'It's too
big!' etc. etc.

So . . . once I had all the information I needed, I sent her to sleep
with a song, tied her to a rock for good measure – she was almost as
dreadful as he was in a fight. And then I stole her hair.

The hair theft was unfortunate, but necessary. Sif's hair was
extraordinary, so long, so luscious, so golden. And inimitable. I tried
to imitate it, believe me. I tried and tried. Every spell and incanta-
tion, every rune, every twist and trick I knew; but although I could
make things look like her hair, nothing could ever imitate it. It

happens, with gods: we have our attributes. They are not things that can be reproduced. Thor's strength, Freya's sex drive, Tyr's lust for warcraft, my gift to change my shape and desire to help mankind . . . Sif's hair. It made the crops ripen. When she shook it out near a corn-field, you could see the heads ripen from green to golden in a few minutes.

So you see I had no choice. It wasn't painful, relatively speaking. She was asleep anyway. I was always going to give it back. It was temporary, that's all. Just a loan.

I changed again, this time to look like Sif herself. That was hard – that hurt. Then I fitted her hair onto my head; and I went off to seek out the great one himself – mighty Thor!

Thor in those days was always out and about, looking for victims, or enemy aliens as he liked to call them. Not for him the safety of sitting behind the wall. He'd given up using lumps of granite to pound his enemy's heads to juice; the dwarves, those dark delvers, had refused to make new ones for him ever since he stupidly began crushing them with their own weapons. Instead, he used oak trunks, studded with flints and bits of other stones he picked up on his travels. Of course those clubs only lasted a day or so – they just weren't up to the kind of use he put them through – and to spend any time with Thor was to listen to endless whining and moaning about how inadequate the world was, how badly Odin and his brothers had done the job, since there was nothing fit to make even a simple club with.

I found him at a long hall in Midgard. The lord there was enter-taining him. I don't think he'd said who he was, and so they were having to pretend they had no idea – as if the country was full of four-metre-tall gods with huge red beards, arms like walruses, legs you could weave a basket out of, who could knock back ale and mead a barrel at a time. Such is the way of things. He was sitting in the hall bawling filthy songs and feeling up the lord's daughter, a girl of less than sixteen summers who looked terrified, as well she might be. If she was thinking his member would be a body tearer, she was to be surprised; but she wouldn't be walking for a month, if ever, I can promise you that.

I approached the longhouse up the valley, and as I passed, the cornfields turned golden. It was a wonderful sight, I can tell you. The peasants bent over the soil, dropped their hoes and gazed in awe. It was only May, and the corn was tall and ripe already. Some of them ran on to tell the lord that an enormous, fat giantess was coming, with magnificent golden hair that could ripen the corn; so Thor knew at once that his wife was on the way.

On my entrance, everyone bowed their knees, except for Thor, who was frankly put out that his wife had come out to join him on his travels. It wasn't something she usually did and let's face it, it was spoiling his fun.

I made up for it. I ran forward, putting out my arms.

'My lord! I could wait for you no longer. The thought of missing you for another day – your strong arms – your staff of love so deep and strong – the sinews of your thighs . . .'

He brightened up immediately. It was fine. You can be as corny as you like with the god of thunder. He likes it.

So of course they killed some more oxen and broached some more hogsheads. We all sat and ate and drank, coughing in the smoke of the hall because, my friends, this was in the days before mankind invented the chimney. Thor drank several hogsheads more of ale and ruefully tore his glance away from the lord's daughter, who was more than grateful to me and spent much of the next twenty years sacrificing to Sif. If only she knew . . .

Then at last, time for bed. And let the swiving begin!

I admit I had miscalculated. I thought as a god I could bear it, but reader, believe me when I say I could hardly sit for a week. I swear my backside is flatter ever since then. Subtlety is not a quality of the Thunderer. Fortunately it was not a long process. I pulled his favourite tricks. Be careful, my lord, or you'll split me in two! Oh, my god, look at those huge mighty shins and knees! Help me, help me, it's in my throat!' And so on. He was done in five minutes – five minutes, I should tell you, of pure thunder and lightning, I'll give him that. No one fucks like the god of thunder. He has only one trick up his goatskin, but my god it is some trick.

I suggested to him a trick or two, involving a little backdoor love – it was necessary. He obliged; and then it was over in a moment.

Mighty Thor knelt panting behind me, getting his mighty breath back. I waited a moment or two . . . timing is all in these matters. And just when he was patting my arse affectionately and preparing to pull out . . . I turned. And lo! Suddenly the god of thunder, that great womaniser, that spreader of babies across the land, power of the storm in his loins and blossoming right fruitily with homophobia, found himself stuck up the back of . . .

Me.

'You!' he roared, scuttling backwards out of me like a startled sow.

'Darling,' I murmured.

Great Thor began thrashing around looking for the missing wife.

'No good – she's not here. It was me all the time,' I announced, and produced the golden hair, Sif's great glory, from behind my back.

Thor went crazy – absolutely crazy. You never saw the like of it. He tore that longhouse down, broke the beams, broke the rock it was built on – killed a hundred men, women and children as they lay there as well. I was gone – turned into a fly and was off, dashing between the flying splinters and shards of rock and the bodies hurtling about like slops flying out of the bucket. He couldn't get me; he didn't stand a chance. And although you're probably thinking he would sooner or later – well, there may have been a broken bone or two on the horizon. No more than that though, since Odin was my best mate, and had absolutely outlawed deicide as part of the Aesir/Vanir peace treaty. And although mighty Thor had a mighty temper on him, he was also mightily docile when it came to obeying his father. Because . . . well, there are worse things than being beaten up, put it like that.

As for the broken bones, I had hopes of avoiding that as well. I waited until he paused for breath, then pointed out to him that if he didn't pack it in, I was going to tell that he'd had me up the arse.

'No one will believe you,' he said.

Which was true. When you lie as often and as well as I do, people soon learn that the truth, if it is ever found in your mouth, is only ever there by accident. But . . .

'As soon as they watch you deny it, yes they will,' I pointed out in return.

And that was true, too, you see. Because great Thor, for all his might and main, is also the world's worst liar. As soon as he opens his mouth to mislead, the eyes swivel, the nose begins to twitch, the mouth starts smirking. He sneezes, he stutters, he smirks . . .

And everyone would know it was true. Yes, great Thor the Thunderer, womaniser, man-love hater, had just been stuck up a man who was a known man-arse lover and horse fucker; both terms he had used for me in the not-too-distant past.

Welcome to the club.

There was a lot of roaring and wailing, but I had him then and he knew it. I tormented him a little. Told him I could tell by how hard he'd got how much he liked it; that now that he knew the pleasures of man, he would never be able to give it up and go back to mere women. And so on. And Thor raged and roared and he roared and raged.

It was all going so well. I put on the hair and began prancing up and down the hall, waggling my arse at him, while he fell to his knees, roaring and threatening and weeping. I had him. I had him right there in the palm of my hand – and then it all went wrong.

'The hair! The hair! The hair!' he began to howl, staring at me like a madman.

'What about the hair?' I said. But even as I spoke I could feel it turning cold on my head. I rushed to a polished shield to see, but I didn't need to. I knew. I could see it on my hands, around my knees. The hair was dying. It turned from golden to grey to white. From shining to dull, from full to thin. In the space of a breath, it turned from the handsome hair of a goddess in her prime, to the dull strands of an old woman, ready to die.

Sif's hair was her glory and it was gone. Away from its mistress it had died and there was nothing I could do about it.

And that, my dears, was another kettle of fish altogether. You can do pretty well what you like as a god, but to take their life or their attributes away – that is not good, not good at all. If the hair stayed dead, I had in effect de-deified Sif. There was no worse fate for a god than to lose their attributes – unless it was whatever Odin would do to me when he found out. And find out he certainly would.

So great Thor looked at me and I looked at him, and I don't know which of us was the paler. Because how on earth was anyone going to fix that?

Well, we both rushed off back to Asgard to Thor's palace, to see if the hair would regain its powers and beauty once it was back where it belonged, on Sif's head. Of course, the mighty one refused to actually go in, for reasons I've never truly understood, but which I assume are down to the fact that he is scared of his own wife – a fate that some-times overwhelms the toughest of man and god. He hid outside in the bushes while I went in to get Sif to try on the dead thing that was once her glory. And I think he must have known from her howls of rage and dismay that it didn't work, because when I ran outside to get him in to help me calm her down, the great one, cracker of skulls, smiter of Jotun, terror of the Seven Worlds, was nowhere to be seen. Only a damp patch amongst the bushes where he hid testified that he had ever been there at all.

I don't know why he was so scared, I was the one who did it. We all knew well enough that Sif, muscle-bound troll that she was, often had endure beatings from the defender of the poor. Maybe it was because he felt he should have protected her; maybe it was shame from having given his old friend Loki such a damn good seeing to. Either way, I was left alone to calm Sif down, which was a matter of the most enormous importance, because if I failed, death would be the least thing I had to worry about. Odin and the others have plenty worse things than that up their sleeves, as I have learned to my cost since.

So I promised and I promised and I promised, and I lied and I lied and I lied. Even for someone like me, who has carried these two arts to such a high degree of sophistication, I had to excel myself. It was hard work, but in the end, I did it – I convinced her that I was able to replace the hair and its gift of fertility, in such a way that no one would ever know that the goddess had been bald in the first place. In fact, I think I must have convinced myself, because when, the follow-ing day, I presented myself at the workshop of the great Dökkálfar maker Ivaldi and told him that I wanted him to make a cap of hair, made of gold spun as thin as real hair, that would shine as beautifully in the light of day as Sif's once had, and that would make the corn ripen as she passed by, I felt a distinct twinge of surprise when he told me that no such thing was possible.

'You know that as well as I do, Loki,' he said. 'I can make a cap of hair spun from gold that will grow on Sif's head as soon as she puts it on, yes. But no maker and no amount of magic will ever hold the attributes of god or goddess, even if it's to return a gift they once had. That, as you know, never can and never will be done.'

Yes, my friends, I felt a distinct twinge of surprise, and disappointment and yes, I admit it, of fear. No, scrub that twinge of fear; it was a stab of terror. Because if I wasn't able to give Sif back her godly attribute, how on earth was I going to avoid the dreadful fate Odin had in store for those who commit that dreadful sin, the worst sin of all; deicide? Believe me, the fact that Sif still drew breath was going to be no barrier to that fate at all.

A difficult thing. Quite likely no one alive could have escaped that fate – perhaps, no one who has ever lived except me could have done it. I understand the whims and wishes of the divinities better than anyone else on earth, and yes, brothers and sisters, I did it, as my presence here testifies. How? Well, the law as it had been drawn up left precious little wriggle room, I can tell you, precious little – but it did leave some. Think about it . . . Suppose, for example, Odin wanted to kill some god or deprive him or her of their attributes? – what then? Would he have to suffer the fate he had himself decreed? Not likely. Suppose some monster god arose who declared war on us all? Suppose someone went mad? Suppose . . . but I leave it to you to suppose. I suppose you can suppose along with the rest of us. Suffice to say that the law as written had this one, single, solitary loophole; that the perpetrator of deicide could be let off if enough of the other gods wished it.

All I had to do was make myself indispensable. Which was a pretty unlikely thing. So I resorted to a better, far more faithful old friend instead of indispensability: bribery. Which, let's face it, amounts to more or less the same thing.

It was difficult, even for me. Lord, it was difficult! I had to get a gift for every single one of the gods – the lot! You may think you have trouble with your Christmas list, but trust me, that is as nothing compared to what I had to do. Gods and goddesses, by their nature, have pretty well everything they want. The let-out clause of course is that they only actually end up with the things they *know* they want. My job, therefore, was to get them the things that they hadn't even thought of yet. Thankfully, most of the gods are creatures of very little imagination so the task was more easy than you might imagine.

Even so . . . it was tough. But worth it, for my life, my sanity and my health. And also, incidentally, for the welfare and happiness of the gods themselves.

Let me give you just a taste of the gifts that I got for the big names. A spear for Odin, Gungnir – a spear that always hit its mark, and upon which any oath taken could never be broken. Handy, for a man who liked to keep his mysteries to himself. An arm ring, again for Odin, Draupnir, the Dripper, that dripped eight arm rings made of gold just like it, every ninth night. The Old Man always liked his gold, and he wasn't the only one. That one made people sit up, I can tell you. For Frey, there was a ship, the biggest that had ever been seen, but which folded up into a wallet you could slip into your bag when you wanted to. Plus, it always had a good wind in its sails. Also for Frey, a great golden boar that could run across the sky and sea as well as the land, fast as the wind, whose golden bristles always lit the way, even in the darkest night. Wonderful. For Tyr, a map of all the worlds that showed the geo-politics in awesome detail and which changed as they changed. Fantastic. For Freya, a necklace called Brisingamen, that made her even more radiantly sexy than before.

I could go on. There were a lot of gifts, I can't even remember them all. I shall mention just one more, for him whose word was going to be the most important of all in this – great Thor himself. For him, I got two gifts – a hammer, a mighty hammer, Mijolnir. It could never break, which would be a new thing for the Thunderer, who, as you know, was always smashing his weapons to pieces. It would always come back to his hand when thrown and finally, it could shrink and grow so that it could be hidden in his pocket, and then taken out and used to strike down the biggest Jotun. Also, a belt. As soon as it was strapped around his waist, his strength increased three-fold. Unnecessary, you may think, since he was already ten times stronger even than the strongest of us. To which I answer – belt and braces, Arse-born, belt and braces. My life was at stake!

How about that? It always comes down to the weapons. Bravery and skill are only so much use, as your own wars have shown over and over again.

And that is how I came to provide the gods with all their greatest treasures. Sif wasn't happy – I admit that the cap of golden hair I had made for her, although it fitted like a glove and although it grew to Sif's scalp like her own true hair once had, and which was, many would say, even more beautiful than the original, did not and never could make the corn ripen as she passed. Her vote I did not get – but she was the only one. She spent a lot of time after that shedding bitter tears at having lost her godhead . . . and it's true that Thor did take a lover from the Jotun shortly after, with whom he spent more time than with Sif herself. But then, there are winners and losers in any game, don't you think? All the winners voted to let me off. Losers' votes don't count. Those who had two gifts voted twice. And here I am!

As a footnote I should add that there's been a lot of speculation about how I got the dwarves to make for the gods such wonderful gifts when they had steadfastly refused to make anything unless they got good payment for it. This despite the fact that there is no secret to it, as I've told the story many, many times. I simply set them up in a bet against each other. Not that bright, dwarves, very competitive, and when they heard that another maker was boasting how much better they were than they, they were all quick enough to start pulling out the stops to undo each other. The other stories that have been put about by my enemies and detractors are just that – stories, made-up lies by jumped-up little liars. It was cunning that got the gifts for the gods – sheer cunning and cleverness, perpetrated by the god of clever: me.

It was a good game and I escaped with my life. But there was a cost, a very great cost, to the world in general and to the Jotun in particular. That world map I gave Tyr – the very first map, Arse-born, invented by none other than myself – meant that he was now able to use his strategic godhead to greater effect in the Seven Worlds. Odin forbade him from fomenting war in Asgard, but everywhere else, he had them at one another's throats like weasels on rats. There was a terrible slaughter almost everywhere.

And even more regrettable – Thor. After he got his hands on that hammer and the belt, the Thunderer became impossible. It was the weapon of weapons – the nuclear warhead of the age of gods. Once he realised he was unbeatable he became increasingly psychotic and arrogant – forgetting utterly of course that his impregnable condition was bestowed on him by none other than myself. For that, I apologise to the universe. I wasn't thinking straight at the time. What can I say? Sorry.

The war that had been begun by Tyr came quickly to an end – thanks to me. The Jotun became somewhat more peace-loving, and who can blame them? The hammer never misses its mark, always returns to his hand. That hammer and the belt that trebles his strength whenever he puts it on, together they turned the tables. These and other remarkable treasures made the gods more or less invulnerable.

And everyone lived happily ever after. Well, the gods did anyway. Everyone else died.

Maybe it would have been better for us all if I had allowed myself to suffer the fate Odin had decreed rather than loose the horror of an invincible Thor upon the world. Perhaps. Better for you, Arse-born. But far, far worse for poor little me.

BOOK THREE

ODIN AND I

Your Christ turned water into wine; I turned shit into flesh. Who is the greater god? You must see, even the dullest among you, that Loki has been a force for good in the Nine Worlds. Who was it who saved the honour of the gods, at the expense of his own? Loki. Who was it who ensured the completion of the great wall, behind which the gods of Asgard could at last grow and flourish in safety, and where their great palaces could be built? Loki. Who was it who gave flesh to the human race and provided the gods with a people to worship them? Who secured life eternal? Loki. Loki, Loki, Loki. None of this is boasting; it is simple fact. It would spare my blushes if, like the other gods, I had priests and worshippers to give thanks to me, but that good old Asgard propaganda has done away with any of that, and I am forced to blow my own trumpet.

Perhaps it's not surprising that I have been reviled. To achieve my miracles I had to fuck a horse and get my hands dirty. Instead of praise, I have been called names. Father of lies, horse fucker, taker of the big dick, man-lover, falsifier, shit shaper. But the fact is I am owed a great debt of gratitude by both gods and man. That debt is yet to be paid. I do not ask for much; I am the cheapest of all the gods. Some want lives, some want wine and meat, others, gold or beautiful objects. All I want is a glass of wine and a pat on the back. And my freedom. That would be more than enough for me.

Sometimes it seems to me that the more good I do, the more I get reviled. Perhaps that is my fate. People do not want clever gods. They want mysterious gods, who nevertheless agree with them at every turn. I am none of those things.

Early on, Arse-born, such was the plotting against me, that I feared for my life. Long before the Jotun wars, even before the dawn of the Golden Age, I found that in every dark alley or quiet woods I walked, the crack of a twig or the scuff of a shoe made me turn my head anxiously, for fear that my enemies might be planning on ending my story before its time. For this reason, as I have already related, way back on my very first day in Asgard, I set about gaining myself an ally. Friends and allies, Arse-born! We all need them, and in the hothouse of corruption, lies, propaganda and the scrabble for status that was Asgard, you need them more than ever. And trust Loki to get the best of all on his side.

Odin. Let's talk about him.

OTR'S RANSOM

Yes, Shite-in-Flight, the Lord of Gods and I were friends, good friends, back in the day when the world was young and innocent, before he learned how to betray those who loved him most. I helped him nail creation; I gave him shapes to wear and introduced him to the deepest secrets of my godly attributes. And yet, although he was happy to be my friend, he was unwilling to take matters beyond that.

Brotherhood, Arse-born. That's what I wanted from Odin. An oath sworn on the roots of creation; commitment, you can call it, if you like. Friendship is subject to fashion, to time and tide; oaths are another matter. If made correctly they cannot be broken on the whims of like and dislike. For a long time I sought such an oath of brotherhood with the Lord of Creation, but the Lord of Creation held out. No matter what I gave, no matter how willingly I gave it, he offered no more than simple friendship. For which reason, whenever we went on our travels together, I always had half an eye open for some new service I could perform for him. Some new prayer or mystery, that would bend him to fulfil my hopes, and leave me safeguarded forever from the plots and wiles of the gods of murder and war.

I had many such chances, and I performed many such services –
all to no avail. I have told you one story of how he, his brothers Vili
and Ve and myself went travelling in the newly illuminated lands of
Midgard, as soon as the sun, Surtr's eye, rose in the sky for the first
time, to enjoy its beauty, its pleasant glades and wooded streams, its
moors, its seascapes, its mountain tops and winding rivers. That was
only one of many journeys we made together in those early days. Vili
and Ve did not always join us. Sometimes it was just Odin and I.
Once or twice I even went travelling with Thor, mainly in the hope
of holding him back from his worst excesses.

Most often it was Odin and myself, sometimes with another god
for company, who went forth to adventure in the world. We two, we
happy duo, friends, companions and adventurers as we were in those
golden days of our youth, when the impossible was a daily occur-
rence. Those days! The times we had . . . I could sit and talk about
them forever . . .

On the particular day I have in mind, Odin and I had been joined by
Hoenir, god of bright lights and stupidity. We were on a riverside
walk – a pretty river, running here between meadows, here between
rocky gorges, there alongside forests and heath. A pleasant way to
spend a few months, walking its banks, hunting the game that came
to drink from its waters. Such a lovely place was Midgard, the most
lovely of all the worlds, before you, Arse-born, came along and ruined
it. Lovely enough, in fact, that many others who did not live there
came to holiday. The Jotun of course – we've already mentioned them
and their legacy, haven't we? But also the Dökkálfar, the dark elves,
and the Ljósálfar, the elves of light, and all manner of various other
folk from other branches of Yggdrasil, the world ash. Later, like the
beasts, they came into conflict with the humans who multiplied so
chaotically out of hand; but back then, there was room for all.

So we followed the river along its course until we came, as the sun
was getting low in the sky, to a waterfall. We were in a woodland of
young oaks and we heard the water before we saw it, so we sped our
steps. Everyone loves a waterfall, I think. We turned among the trees
and there it was – a fine cascade falling four or five metres over several
steps into a large pool. And we were not alone. Sitting on a rock

under the spray from the final fall was a very large and very beautiful otter. He had caught a huge salmon, over five feet long, and was eating it just to one side of the water as it tumbled and crashed down around him. He was intent on his meal, and no doubt the water churning around him hid the sounds of our arrival. We saw him, but he did not see us, and instinctively, we backed off slightly into the trees to keep ourselves hidden.

The otter was an exceptional beast, with a fine pelt – reddish brown with hints of gold, unusual in its kind. Also unusual, looking back, is the way it ate its meal, barely lifting its head to look around as they normally do, without a care in the world. He was a young, strong animal, with that enormous fish all to himself, and seemed utterly at its ease and unafraid.

It made us laugh to watch him, snuggled down beside his fish, taking big red bite after big red bite, looking for all the world like a little man who had forgotten his table manners, and was enjoying his dinner at home on the kitchen floor.

Well, friends, I wanted that otter. If I'm honest, I was offended by his careless approach to eating. We were gods – three mighty gods – the wisest, the cleverest and the brightest. And yet this beast didn't even bother raising his head. And – that pelt. It shone in the sun like polished bronze. So long, so slick, so beautiful. He would make a fine pair of gloves, or a hat. Otter pelt lasts the longest, you know. Otter-skin gloves are warm to the coldest day. They are waterproof and will last so long, you can leave them to your son after a lifetime's use.

'Look at him,' I said. 'Not a care in the world.' And stooping, I picked up a nice round stone that lay at my feet. It fitted snuggly into my palm and I threw it straight at his head.

I am a god; in those days the world itself blessed the things that I did, but even so it was surprising just how good that shot was. The stone sailed through the air and landed neatly on his temple – you could hear the crack from where we stood, despite the water. The otter died at once. His head jerked back and there he lay, his jaws still deep in the red flesh of his salmon. Just the end of his tail flickered a little as the nerves died. Dead. Just like that. A lucky shot, you may say. Or an unlucky one, perhaps. Such a chance! Maybe fate played a hand. I expect she did.

I dove into the river and fetched the otter and his fish back to shore. What a fish! It was almost as long as I was. The others had to jump in and help me. Two with one shot! A fine meal, enough for us and more, and the best otter skin any of us had ever seen. We were all impressed – even Hoenir, who was a hunter himself. Even me; and I was used to myself.

The light was beginning to fail. As we carried on our way down river we kept an eye out for a decent camp site, but in the event it was not necessary. Within a mile or so we came across a habitation. Not a house as such, not a cave, although part of it was dug out of the cliff face. In front of the rock was a wooden structure, covered with turfs; it was the first time we had seen turfs used for a roof. There was a pool in front of it, with a path running around it. Curious. Smoke was easing its way through a hole in the turf, which gave it a homely look. We could smell food cooking. Cooking and fire, warmth and food, these things can never fail to make a place seem inviting.

There are rules of hospitality in the wilderness, then as now. So we checked ourselves over to make sure our godliness was kept within – no point in scaring the natives, is there? – and made our way forward to ask for shelter for the night. A night under cover would be welcome. Also – we were curious. Who lived there? You humans were still hacking at flints and chasing aurochs into pits. No Jotun would fit through that door. Dwarves didn't build out of wood and the light elves couldn't bear to be under cover of any kind if they could help it. So . . . who?

A woman and her two sons emerged. The mother, Hreidmar, was tall, taller than her sons, with deep-set eyes and black hair, with ginger streaks – a thing I have never seen before or since. Very beautiful, very fierce. Her head was wide at the top and narrow at the jaw, she had an arched nose and no lips, which gave her an odd appearance, somewhat fishy I'd say, but in no way did it detract from her beauty. The boys were similar – not so tall, not so handsome, not so unusual. Maybe the father was a mortal man or some such. They were all striking – but Hreidmar was really worth looking at.

'Volur,' said Odin under his breath. Volur; a witch. A seeress. She had a magic of her own. The sons, Fafnir and Regin, were not so much to be respected or feared because if they practised her arts, it would make them weak; this was a gift for women.

The Volur. What to make of them? They came into being right at the beginning of things, like the Jotun, the gods and the elves. They had no home of their own, no world, no language, no kith and kin. They must have come from deep down, near to the roots of Yggdrasil. Some sort of spillage, I would imagine. They, like the gods, can bend the way things work. Their magic, seidr, opened up the veins of the future and could sometimes change the path of time. Odin was fascinated, as he was fascinated with all mysteries; and he was greedy for it, as he was greedy for all magic. Hoenir elbowed us — let's go, let's go, he hissed under his breath. They were dangerous, the Volur, even to us gods. But Odin was curious. He could never let a chance for a mystery go by. And me? I was always up for adventure.

I didn't get the feeling that she was keen to see us — maybe she knew what we meant, who knows? The Volur dine with the Norns, the ladies of fate, from time to time. But she knew the rules of hospitality and invited us in.

And fate walked in with us, I do believe. Fate is fascinated with the gods. She works for us or against us, but always with us. There was that tingle you get when fate steps out among you. You feel the hem of her cloak brush against you. This was such an occasion.

Well, we made ourselves at home. Shared our fish; Hreidmar roasted it on the fire. There were mushrooms and fresh leaves and orchid roots as well. Ale and mead — a proper feast. We told tales and sang songs, but each of us, they as well as us, kept our identities close to our chests; hospitality does not mean secrets must be shared. When the time came to sleep, we lay down on the mats she put down for us. Odin rose shortly and went to see her, but he came back soon enough — rejected no doubt.

It took us a while to settle down and sleep. Yes, friends, the air was full of destiny that day. But, sleep we did, at last. Perhaps the mead, perhaps the ale. Perhaps she helped us. Who knows? Perhaps all three.

We woke up sooner than expected — in bonds.

Yes, Shite-in-Flight — gods in bondage. In the night our feckless host seized us and tied us up. We were helpless, bound hand and foot.

And that was a big surprise for no one went against the rules of hospitality, at risk of being flung out into the outer darkness by enemies and friends alike – unless some truly monstrous breach had been committed by the guests. We were furious, of course; we made our moves to escape, which would normally have been an easy thing. Hoenir began to shine – he could burn his way out if need be; it's what he does. I began to change shape, Odin began to flex and flash his eyes, but as soon as we began to manifest our godly gifts, they died around us. The Volur wasn't stupid. Those were no ordinary bonds that held us. They were iron for one thing. Iron at that time was unknown to god or man; only the dwarves knew how to deal with it. But the Volur knew. And there was seidr in them – seidr strong enough to cancel our gifts, even Odin's. None of us had come across such a power before. That was a surprise, I can tell you . . . and there we were, as helpless as sausages, unable to help ourselves in any way at all.

'What is this?' demanded Odin, spluttering away like an outraged auk. 'We are your guests . . . what sort of action is this?'

Hreidmar looked down at us coldly. 'You have forfeited the rules of hospitality,' she said. 'You have forfeited all rules, by murdering my son.'

So saying, she held up the otter skin, which of course we had shown her when we were telling her about our day's adventuring and how we caught that fine salmon.

'Otr,' she said.

'A bloody shape changer,' I groaned.

'My murdered son,' said the Volur. 'And death will be paid for by death. No one will criticise us for that, even for your deaths, Odin, Loki and Hoenir.'

We flinched, all of us. Gods have many names and titles, but it is not nice manners to name us so directly. Behind Hreidmar, her two sons, Fafnir and Regin, appeared, red-faced, angry, swords drawn. It truly seemed that for us three, time had run out.

Who can blame them? Otr had been beautiful and quick; now he was in line to be a pair of gloves. We had only one line that we could argue, and argue we did – that it was unfair and wrong to take our lives, when we had no way of knowing that the otter was a boy. How could we tell? As a shape changer myself, I could testify to that. How many times had I risked swatting, shooting, stamping and flicking on my own person? Beyond number. I argued our case myself, and in the end I won their agreement. Under the circumstances, they would forgo our lives. Instead, they would accept wergeld. A ransom. Gold. Rather a lot of it.

'This is the price,' said Hreidmar. 'My son's skin filled with yellow gold; and then the whole covered with red gold so that not a hair, not one single hair, can be seen.'

'That's a lot of gold,' said Odin, licking his lips.

'It's ridiculous,' said Hoenir. And so it was. The world was young; mining was a rarity. You humans were still banging stones together. The dwarves, the dark folk, had some but they guarded it closely and even they hadn't been at it long enough to amass all that much. A mound of gold so big would be no easy matter to raise.

'You're gods. My son was a shape changer. Of course the price is high,' said Hreidmar. 'We will release one of you,' she went on. 'And so we may be sure they will come back, it will be the least of you.'

Well, I turned my eyes to Hoenir, the bright god. He, as I say, knew how to shine but not much more. No way, I thought. If it was left up to Hoenir we were dead. Hoenir the ditherer, Hoenir the indecisive. Couldn't make his mind up what to put on every morning of his life.

Unbelievably but fortunately, it wasn't him they meant – it was me.

Reader, I was mortified. Of course, Odin was the greatest among us – no one would ever argue with that. But to put Hoenir above me? Ludicrous. I was insulted . . . but also relieved. Let's face it, if any of us had a half-decent chance of finding so much gold, it was me.

Odin and Hoenir didn't seem too happy about it. Perhaps they had been listening to rumours about me spread by Tyr and Thor back at home in Asgard. But it made no difference. Hreidmar had made up her mind; me it was who was to go free. She and her boys undid my bonds with tools and spells and I rose to my feet and rubbed my sore wrists. 'My thanks for your trust,' I said.

Hreidmar shrugged. Let's face it – she didn't need to trust me.

'I'm assuming,' I said, 'that since you ask for so much gold, you may have some idea where I might be able to get it . . .?'

Hreidmar shook her head irritably.

'Try Svartálfheimr,' growled Regin.

Which made sense. Svartálfheimr, world of the dark elves, who spend all their time mining. Where else?

'Andvari might help you,' said Fafnir suddenly, and Hreidmar shot him a dirty look, but didn't stop him. 'He has more than enough,' added Fafnir.

'The pike dwarf,' I said. Regin nodded. So the stories were true. Andvari was another one, like me, who could change his shape. It's hard to explain to people such as yourselves who are stuck in only one body, but put it like this; he had a spare shape. That of a pike, which he could take on and off as he wished.

I won't be sorry to meet him, I thought. I have an issue with people who change their shape. That's my game and the god thy Loki is a jealous god. I prefer to keep the shapes to myself. I had many already, but a pike was not among them. What was this murky little devil doing with one? I fancied it for myself.

I skipped out the door into the spring sunshine. Yes, reader, it was spring – it was always spring in those early days. The sun, the bright leaves, the young flowers nodding in the grass and at woodland margins. It was good to be alive.

. . . and did Loki live up to his reputation? Did it cross his mind for a moment, or maybe more than a moment, to simply leave things as they were and carry on his merry way. Would he leave Odin and Hoenir to lie and die in the hands of a vengeful and powerful Volur?

Actually, no. Well – perhaps for the merest moment. I am loyal to my friends, whatever they say. Also, back in Asgard . . . Thor and Tyr remained. If Odin died, they would step into his place as fast as weasels. Not good for me. Not good at all. So no, I did not spend any time at all wondering if I should fulfil my promises. The stories, if you know them, tell how Loki made his way first to the ocean, where Ran, Queen of the Seabed, pulls the drowned in her great net down to serve her in her watery halls. There I begged the use of that fabled net to help catch the elusive dwarf, Andvari.

Not true. Ran has such a net, of course, but it was I who taught her how to make it in the first place. Her husband Aegir had taken the waves for himself, so that, although she was the most talented of the two, she was lost to the kelp and the crabs, and long, lonely years of isolation on the ocean bed. Loneliness was driving her mad until Loki came to the rescue. Yes, it was I who invented the net, which serves man for fish and the goddess of the seas as an employment device. Yes, mortal – I fed you fish and I invented drowning – all things have two sides. What is a net but a skein of knots? I am a knot myself, my name is a knot, and all things of knotting trace their lineage back to me.

So no, I didn't need to go to Ran. But nor did I head directly towards Svartálfheimr, land of the murky race. No; I was hungry after my adventure, so I made myself some soup in the Volur's kitchen. Chopped some onions and leeks, simmered the fish bones and head. I am a chef – did you not know that? Yes. And I drew some beer and I sat and I drank and I ate. All the while Hoenir was spluttering and cursing me; but not Odin. He watched me closely, followed my movements. Oh, he knew what was going on all right, but even then, with the prospect of death hanging over him, he was not in a hurry to give me what I waited for. All the time, no doubt, he was trying to come up with a way of avoiding it, but there was no other way. So, in the end, he made the oath I wanted. The oath I had asked him for so many times, and which he had always refused. The oath I had earned, Shit-for-Brains – you must see that by now.

Brotherhood. Yes, Arse-born. And a deep and abiding oath it was, formed in the heart of Ymir himself at the beginning of things. An oath that ignores all other bonds, even those that clasped him to the floor as we spoke.

Well, his life was at stake. He knew – he knew! There was no way round it. My life was at risk from my enemies – you know their names by now, Arse-born – and if the only way I could secure my future was to put his at risk as well . . . well, so be it.

Spittle was exchanged, so was blood. Words were given and taken. Runes were made and cast. The oath was made, deep and powerful, born in the roots of time and space. Thus, Odin and I became brothers, bound with an unbreakable bond, an unspeakable bond, deeper and stronger even than that of blood.

I kissed him then, as was my right as his brother, and, rejoicing, I left the building and made my way directly to Svartálfheimr, land of the murky people, the Dökkálfar, the dark elves, the delvers and miners, the makers. For my brother and his friend, I was happy to do it. And so ends the main point of this story – how Loki secured his rights and safety in the murderous rumour machine that was Asgard. And for a long time, those rights and that safety held. I earned that oath, Arse-born, many times over. But we are on a journey, and I beg your patience before we get to the point where you see how the Allfather, Lord of Creation, maker of oaths, slipped the bonds of the oath he made, like a cheating boy in the classroom. All shall be shown to you. But first, I shall finish the tale I have begun.

Svartálfheimr! No place for a man or a god. What a blasted heath that land is, hard stone and desert, hot lava wells and eruptions, icy outcrops, sulphur pits, mines and industrial waste. They are a manufacturing race; much of your science and industry comes from them, when the early pioneers, Newton, Galileo etc., manage to capture a Dökkálfar or two and torture their secrets out of them. But it's not all manufacture and science; unlike you, they have magic too, a dwarfish magic of their own, runes and spells from the rocky deeps in their dark home, inaccessible to us, even to Odin. In many ways a dangerous place to venture for man, or god. But not, perhaps, for a rat. Much of dwarf's life is spent underground. Surtr's great eye pierces even the dark, muddy clouds above their lands. They cannot bear strong light on their skins, but even without the sun, the Dökkálfar are happier underground, where the kind of secrets they like are hidden. They burrow, they dig, they mine. Many of their passages are infested with rats. The Dökkálfar don't mind. They like them. They eat them, they keep them as pets, they give them names and teach them tricks. So, I made my way to the Tree, then to that branch that leads to Svartálfheimr. I stepped off into the dark rocks of the dwarves' home and hurried on my way down, deep, deep down into the rocks of Svartálfheimr, in the form of a black rat.

. . . Passing through wonderful, intricately carved tunnels, for the dwarves have a sense of beauty all their own . . . past caverns of crystals, some natural, decorated by nature with fabulous forms of mineral exuberance, others made by dwarfish hands, encrusted with diamonds and other gems . . . past the rusting hulks of abandoned machines, vehicles, drills, diggers and various instruments, devices whose use has long been forgotten. Past creations made of half metal, half magic . . . way beyond the human mind, realms you cannot begin to imagine. Although your science has surpassed theirs, you have proven yourselves singularly stupid when it comes to breaking the rules of physics, of making the known unknown and bringing it back to use. Deeper and deeper underground, listening secretly to dwarf talk, creeping out at night into dwarf libraries to read their encyclopaedias and texts . . . deeper and deeper, beyond even the realms where the dwarves lived their day-to-day lives, into the unexplored regions of their dark, hollowed-out world, until at last I arrived in the place where Andvari lived, deeper than the deeps, by an underground lake in a vast cavern, as black and as dark and as lightless as the heart of a dragon.

What a miser old Andvari was! Whilst the others kept their gold in communal vaults and guarded caves, out of reach to the likes of me, he could not bring himself to trust his wealth with anyone, not even his own kind. So he had removed himself as far away as was possible from the other Dökkálfar, below all other habitation, where the rock itself was hot to the touch, and no other living thing ever journeyed.

To him I wormed my way, Arse-born, to perform one of my favourite acts: theft. Among the titles I openly own, Prince of Thieves is among my favourites.

It was warm down there; my rat shape steamed in the darkness. Wet, too; water oozed from the porous stone above and fell, warm as blood, in fat droplets on my scrawny rat back. The dripping was everywhere, echoing in the vast, enclosed cavern in which lay Andvari's Lake, that great, black, deep cauldron of water. Dark, dark, dark. I could sense that water. I could smell it . . . the waft of it, the darkness and heat of it. The hopelessness of it. I was scared, reader. It had taken me three months to go so deep . . . so deep that the Dökkálfar themselves never ventured so far, scared by their own stories of what lay so far down. Only Andvari was here – malicious, tormented by greed, crazy with isolation and the lust for gold. He knew I was there, of course – he could smell me, reader – smell the other life that had arrived at his shores after so long. But though I lifted my rat head into the damp air, I could not smell him. Who can smell a fish in the water and say where it is?

Yes – he knew where I was, and I did not know where he was; or so he thought. He was wrong. I used my brain. Several streams fed into that vast body of deep, black water, running down from above. But only one of them had its source far enough up to carry in its arms the thing that was so scarce down here . . . food. Even Andvari must eat. Only in that one stream would food of any kind come . . . fish from above, perhaps, or pale, eyeless creatures, newts and salamanders and the like, that had learned to live in the dark. Or spiders and beetles washed down from higher corridors where such things lived. Or perhaps the bodies of the drowned . . .

No decent food for a man, or a god, or a dwarf, but good enough for a pike – his one shape, that gave him his chance to hide and keep what he had for himself. Amongst the dwarves it was said that he ventured out and up into the inhabited passageways some nights to steal more. A dwarf may be found with their throat cut, their blood spilling out on the rock. Often it was true. So Andvari got richer and more vicious. None of his kind would begrudge me putting him back a step or two.

I was cold, I was scared, I was hungry. I crept, rat that I was, along the edges of the lake until I came to the place where the stream entered the water. There, I withdrew my net from where I had hidden it amongst my rat's fur. And I changed my shape, Arse-born, and I cast my net over the water. I knew I had but one chance. I did not wish to have to enter the cold water and hunt for the pike that was Andvari. I had my otter's shape now – you know where that came from – but pike can grow large, larger than any otter; and the dwarf was more used to killing in the water than I was. The net was wide, it was light, it was strong, and I knew as soon I began to drag it in that I had my prey. Andvari! You could feel his surprise. How he fought, how he struggled. His life and his gold were at stake, and who knew which was the most precious to him? His strength was enormous, but I was a god with his feet on the rock, whereas he, fish that he was, slipped by his fins through water. I pulled, he pulled; he fought, I fought, each of us fought, but inch by inch I brought my prey to the surface until I was able to reach in, seize him by the gills and haul him up into the warm air of the cave. Then and only then did I strike a light to see my victim.

What a pike was Andvari! So long, so strong, so powerful and broad. Lifting my arm as high in the air as I could, I was still unable to lift his tail off the ground. He lashed out at my feet; but his head was staring up, his fishy eyes stuck sideways on his head and he could not see where my feet danced. Anyway, he was too much wrapped up in my net to flap too hard. I looked up into his fishy, knowing eye and I winked.

'Breathe, Andvari, breathe,' I said. 'Before I decide I've got the wrong fish and start to make lunch.'

I took my time. I carried him away from the water's edge and set him down behind some rocks. I waited. I lit a fire. I pushed him closer and closer to it, and only when the steam rose hot from his flanks did he drop his shape and take his own form . . . a dark-haired, wet, furious, purple-faced dwarf. Somewhat smaller than the pike, I was pleased to see. The Dökkálfar are a powerful race – you can't take any chances with them.

I made my wishes known. 'Your gold, Andvari,' I said. 'All of it.'

'I'll die first,' he spluttered.

'Perhaps.' I blew on the fire and pulled him closer to it. That made his eyes roll; dwarves know all about fire.

Well, it was a long business, and an ugly one too; Andvari truly did love his gold more than life itself, but he did not hate the idea of giving it away to me more than the life I was giving him for an hour or two. At last I learned where the gold was hidden. Underwater of course, deep, deep down at the bottom of the deepest part of the lake. Therefore I tied him up as tight as I could, rolling his clever dwarf fingers into a fist and wrapping him over and over in the net until he could hardly breathe. That water was so deep, even an otter could not reach it; but a salmon might. That was a shape I now owned. So I swam down to take the gold.

There it was, red and yellow and white, all the gold you could ever want. Piece by piece I ferried it up, using a portion of the net to carry it. Slowly the gold on the lake bed shrank and that on the banks rose. Andvari watched and groaned like a dying man . . . which he was, near enough.

In the end I had two great sackfuls – enough, I hoped, to fulfil Otr's ransom. There was one last thing – on Andvari's finger, a gold ring, most beautiful and lovely. I did not leave him with that either, although he begged and wept for it; I could see there was some magic in it, and I was not keen for him to have anything that might taste of revenge later on. When it was off his finger, he stiffened from head to foot, opened his bloody, burnt mouth – he knew the taste of coals by now – and began to chant some foul thing in Svartlish. I know a curse when I hear one, Arse-born, and I was about to dispatch him before it took hold. But I know a little Svartlish myself, enough to tell from a few words that it was not myself he was cursing, but the gold itself. And that . . . that did not trouble me as much. The poor dwarf of course could not imagine that I had stolen the gold for anyone but myself. But wealth has never interested me for its own sake. I knew where the gold was going and a curse on it did not hinder me in any way. On the contrary – I rather liked the idea.

I waited quietly until he had finished his curse. Then I smiled sweetly and held him under the water until he had no option but to turn back into that pike. And then I took a golden dagger from the hoard and slid the blade into his eye, feeling round for the soft bone at the back until I broke through. The pike thrashed and squirmed and died. No; Andvari would not be swimming along the streams of Svartálfheimr into Midgard to take me from beneath, or robbing me of treasures of my own one fine day. Frankly there was little choice – every good thief knows that insurance is best dealt with early on, where possible. Then, rattish again, I dined. As a god I prefer my meat cooked and sauced, but as a beast it was preferable like this. Then, slowly in the darkness, I made the return journey to Yggdrasil and the upper air.

Odin and Hoenir were pleased to see me, you can bet. I had been gone many weeks and they had feared the worst – perhaps they had been remembering the lies spread about me in Asgard. But the gold

I had was no small amount. We took the skin of the slain Otr and filled it with yellow gold and then covered it with red gold. The stories tell how I gave the final ring I had taken from Andvari's finger to Odin, and how it was needed to cover one last whisker that was showing through. The story is a fake of course. The ring was cursed – why would I give a curse to my protector and friend? No; the gold was plentiful, so plentiful that there was even some left over at the end, but I insisted on leaving even that behind, much to Odin's disappointment – he always loved the shiny metal. I left it instead with Hreidmar, who was foolish enough to accept it.

And then, stiffly, the two joined the one and stepped out of the stinking hovel where they had been prisoners for longer than any god had or ever will be kept prisoner – all save one – and out into the bright air.

Odin and Hoenir affected to be cross with me for taking so long, but they could not really be so; the gold was such a quantity. After all, I had saved their lives. It was just fear and tension speaking. I had apologies soon enough.

This is the story of how Odin and I became brothers, Arse-born. It is a story with many branches arising from it. The story of the Volsungs you may know – of the dragon that Fafnir became, changed by the cursed gold; and how he was slain by Sigurd the Volsung, who stole the gold off him; and how Sigurd himself was betrayed by an old woman. All, perhaps, brought about by Andvari's curse. My brother Odin was not happy about all that, as he loved the house of Volsung. But he should have been grateful, Arse-born. I could have let him keep that ring for himself!

My move to secure my life did not sit well with Odin in general, who, I would guess, did not really want to swear brotherhood with a horse fucker. But the oath had been made and he had to stick with it. There were others who were not keen, either. Not long after, passing quietly on my business through Asgard, I was hauled into a dark corner and a cold knife was pressed against my neck.

'Do not think that you have escaped, mare's cunt,' hissed a cold voice – inventing at once a new and wonderfully misogynous nickname for me on the spot. 'You will come to the end you deserve. I will see to it.'

'Only after Odin has had his,' I replied . . . but my words were cut
short as a sharp blow bruised my neck. I fell to my knees and looked
around for my assailant, but they were gone from the scene of the
crime, as all fomenters of war are gone before they are seen, leaving
only their victims to taste the misery they have caused.

I was accused of blackmail and my stock, already low, fell even
further. I promised you, Arse-born, that I would tell you all my sins
and crimes, and you will see that I spoke the truth. Yes, I black-
mailed Odin – small good it did me in the end. Perhaps my misdeed
won me more years in the Nine Worlds than I would otherwise have
had, but ultimately, it did not save me. But how that oath, so deep
and secure, came to be broken, you must read on to find out.

THE FIRST DEATH OF ODIN

Odin, back in the day, was not the god you know now; he has added many qualities to himself over the years. But even then, he was still the boss, the big man, god of royalty, leadership, war giver, battle maker, life giver, seeker of mysteries. Who else would you want as your ally? If I say it myself, getting him to swear brotherhood with me was a masterstroke.

Odin was a god who loved to learn and it was perhaps his biggest mystery that he both loved to learn and was yet, unchanging. I know! – it seems unlikely. But you, Arse-born, come from a tradition in which a god can be one and three at the same time, so let's not complain too loudly. Odin was Odin was Odin, as he was and always will be. Yet somehow, over the eons, he became more than himself.

What was it that drove him on to such lengths? Even he, I suspect, does not understand. Some have said it was simply the search for knowledge that inspired the Allfather to reach so deep into the world, to find the gaps in creation so that he might slip inside or break it open like a nut. Perhaps; but I believe it was the usual old nonsense that pushed him on and on in his crazy search: power. He lusted after power. Knowledge leads to power, does it not? Mystery is another name for a power that has not yet been revealed. Yes, if Odin is the god of anything, he is the god of power. When it came to that, he was ruthless.

In this part of my story, I shall show you how, in his terrible quest to become more, he overwhelmed not only us, but, in the end, the most wonderful thing in creation – himself.

. . . and as a by-product, successfully shafted his sworn brother – me – most royally.

I showed him earlier cavorting around a gigantic turd telling his brother to give it a cunt, and I expect you thought I was dissing the Allfather. Nothing could be further from the truth. Come on! – we were kids, and face it, there was no one there to tell us what we could or couldn't do. The generation before us had pretty well all been murdered off, except his uncle, old Mimir, who had very sensibly crept quietly away down to the roots of the world – hiding, no doubt, from his murderous nephews. Yes – wise was old Mimir, so they all said. But wise does not stand before ruthless, any better than clever, as we've all seen and shall see again before my tale is done.

Let us look at the maturing god and ask ourselves – just how ruthless was Odin? Ruthless enough to slaughter Ymir, the world god, certainly. But that's not all. You will remember the old tale I told earlier of the beginning, and before the beginning, and how the beginning was ended, and of the beings who peopled the first shadows of creation? In the first days there were only two places, not nine as we see today. There was only Muspel, where lived and lives and shall forever live, great Surtr; and Niflheimr, the mist world, the place of no shape or form, where nothing lived or made its home. Between the two existed only the void – Ginnungagap, where nothing was. But as the mist from Niflheimr met the sparks from burning Muspel, the icy water boiled in the air, then sank down into the yawning chasm, where it formed great blocks of ice. From the melting of that ice, then, came the two first great creatures, bigger than worlds, bigger than creation itself, perhaps; Ymir, of whom I have spoken, and Audhumla, the gigantic cow. Ymir fed from the milk of the cow, and the cow licked for nourishment at the ice in Ginnungagap until it melted under her hot tongue.

From that ice, melting with the heat of the breath and the blood of the cow Audhumla, Buri the wonderful, father of all the gods, emerged.

Then there were the two giants, one male, one female, who emerged from the sweat under Ymir's arms, from whom all Jotun are descended. Buri made a union (dare I say it?!) with one of those Jotun, who gave birth to Bor, who married (dare I say it again?!) another Jotun woman, Bestla, who gave birth in turn to Odin, Vili and Ve.

We know the fate of great Ymir of course — but where are the others now, Audhumla and Buri the wonderful, in whose loins all the aspects of all the gods, Aesir and Vanir alike, resided? — those first of all, those wonders of spontaneous creation, they who came into being like Loki himself — not bred, not fucked into life, but springing alive from the void (like me) because the universe wanted them? What happened to them? And what of Odin's father, Bor? Where is his mother, Bestla, interred? Well you may ask. I have, many times, and never any answer came back. In that answer, should you find it, you may learn how ruthless Odin was, and remains.

So ruthless? Yes, yes, a thousand times ruthless! And what else was he besides? There is his reputation for knowledge, of course, and that is not a reputation unearned. Right from the very start he was . . . what's the word? Not clever. I'm the clever one. He was too much himself to be clever. Wise? Well, no, I don't think that's it either. Deep?

Let's call him that: deep.

When we saw him earlier looking at the shits, stroking his beard and murmuring under his breath . . . 'There's a mystery here,' Vili and Ve thought it was hilarious, because what possible mystery could you find in a turd, no matter how big it was? And yet he was right. He always was right about that sort of thing. He had a nose for it. It's hardly his fault that mysteries turn up in the most unexpected places.

Odin had a taste for mysteries, but he was not interested in understanding them. He was never big on understanding. That was not his nature. What he wanted was to *own* it. To make it his. He was like a man who collected a library of beautiful books, made by the best craftsmen, finely wrought leather on the covers, the many pages

wonderfully illuminated within, beautiful calligraphy, with gold leaf
and the finest colours lovingly prepared . . . but who never learned to
read. But don't imagine that the lack of understanding makes him
any less powerful. If you own a bottle of poison, you may not understand how it works but you can still kill someone with it.

Understanding, you see, is a much overrated commodity.

To tell this next part of our tale, we must return, Arse-born, to the
Golden Age, when there was the space and time for the Allfather to
indulge his passion for experiment.

I have spoken of the great world ash, Yggdrasil, that giant tree
with its roots deeper even than the underworld, deeper even than
Niflheimr, that awful place which even the dead dread. Its great
branches envelop and support seven of the Nine Worlds; only
Niflheimr, land of mists, and Muspel, home to Surtr the deathless, lie
outside the realms that Odin created.

Yggdrasil is a myth, of course, in many ways, but true in others.
There *is* such a tree, or at least, there appears to be such a tree. In the
right time, in the right place, you may catch a glimpse of it, towering
above you and soaring below, so vast and wide and tall that the mind
recoils before it.

Now that's what I call a god.

There are even a few places where you can walk up to it and actually touch it, stroke the bark, squash a beetle against it, look up and
see the leaves fluttering far, far above your head – a place where you
can say 'tree', and feel that you speak the truth. One such place of
course is in Asgard, where the gods live and where what is magical
and mysterious feels more at home than it does in your duller, less
colourful realm of Midgard. Back when the world was young, Odin
spent a great deal of time with the Tree, keeping it company. Getting
to know it, if you can have a relationship with a tree. Maybe you can.

An oath he liked to use: the Roots of Yggdrasil. You can see what
it means. At the root of things, at the point of the deepest meaning.
At the beginning, where things began and continue to begin. Where
meaning and creation themselves form and grow.

Yes, Odin was obsessed with the Tree. You may have heard that he
once undertook a journey to find those roots. Which is true. He never

did find them in life, and yet he did get there; and yet he lives. Odin and mystery – you see? It was a risky enterprise, and a painful one. I personally begged him not to go through with it, partly for the lack of success that most of us thought would accompany the mission, but I didn't ignore the fact that were he to succeed, he might come back more powerful than any of us wished him to be. We held a Thing about it. I tried my best to convince him what a bad idea it was, but he did it anyway. He wanted something, he never said what. Perhaps he didn't know himself, but he was certain, he said, that there were secrets at the roots of the Tree that would bring benefit for us all – for us, for you, for all creation. Which swayed the gods behind him, of course.

He had himself nailed to the Tree. There's your cross for you. Astonishing! The agony of it – those great iron nails through his hands and his shoulders and his feet. I remember it – who could forget it? The blood spurting from his torn flesh, dripping off his toes and down his beard. I remember his screams as the nails went in, the sound of the metal sinking through flesh into the wood, the bellows and squeals he gave out when they caught his bones. It was terrible to watch.

You see what price the mysteries cost. You see the conviction and passion man or god must have to reach the places of deepest secrecy. Yet he paid the price willingly.

They came to me to do it, of course, as they always come when there's a dirty job to do. Normally I do it because dirty work has to be done, even in divinity, and the gods are usually not up to it, for reasons of honour, or some other of their ludicrous principles. This time, though, I said no. I saw no good would come of it. I said no; they begged. They made promises. None of them wanted it. Odin himself came to beg me. But no. For once, I stuck to my word.

He wanted Thor to do it – his own son – but Thor would not either, so in the end it went to his brothers Vili and Ve. They agreed, and to start with I don't think there was any relish in them for it, either. Vili lifted him up while Ve held the nail to the flesh, lifted the hammer, paused and struck the first blow. Many of us, I think, believed that Odin had somehow conquered pain and that it would be like cutting a cake or breaking bread, somehow. It was not. At the very first blow he let out a bellow like a bull. It was a hard blow; Vili didn't flinch away, once he'd decided it was his lot. The nail point dove right through the wrist and into the wood in a single strike. The blood gushed at once. Odin screamed. Then the next hand, and I think he fought a little against it, but the boys held firm. Ve paused before he dealt it and looked his brother in the eye. Odin nodded. Bang! In went the nail and Odin screamed again.

And so it went on. Wrists, shoulders, feet, shins. Odin yelled and writhed . . . and then things turned nasty. It began, I think, when Vili began to tell him to ask them to stop.

'Had enough?' he said. You know the tack. Odin shook his head. Ve drove in the next nail hard, two blows, so that the hammer head struck the wound unnecessarily.

'Hold on there . . .' cried Thor, but it was noticeable the way his voice trailed off. The next time Ve asked him . . .

'Beg me,' he sneered. 'Beg me, old man.' – and when Odin did not, he struck him on the side of the face with the hammer. You could hear the bone crack. I thought Thor would pull them off then, but no. He stood there, staring as if he had seen god, which he had. Then the others joined in. Tyr started it with a flint, chipped and sharp, as big as a cat's head. Face it, this was his one chance of getting rid of the master of all. Suddenly stick and stone rained down on the crucified god until he hung by flesh and skin, not bone. And Thor – Thor, favourite son, who you would have thought would protect his father, he still stood back and watched. His rage grew so great his face turned not red, not purple but black. But he said no word, made no move to stop them. What was that rage he felt then, that left him so immobile? That he couldn't join in the frenzy? That Odin had somehow rooted him to the spot? Who knows, he could not say himself. He just stood there, now roaring – yes, actually roaring like a bear in pain. At the end he tore himself from the ground – that's how it appeared to those of us watching – lifted those huge fists and drove them home – not onto the body of his father, whom he would have killed at once if he had, but onto the trunk of the Tree itself.

A note rang out. The Tree vibrated – it actually shook, which was a miracle if you can understand how vast it was – vaster than the worlds that lived amongst its branches, vaster than the universe itself, perhaps.

Everyone fell quiet. When the Tree speaks there can be no further words. Panting with the effort of their attack, they dropped their weapons, they stood back. Odin hung there, broken and ruined, bleeding from a thousand cuts, blackening from a thousand bruises, sagging from so many broken bones, glaring at us from under his eyebrows and blooded hair from those terrible eyes – he still had two back then, when the world was young.

I don't understand it. I didn't then, I don't now. Why did they turn on their leader once he was helpless? I laid not a blow, I swear it, I alone was innocent. I loved the Old Man like a brother. I begged them to stop, but my voice was unheard. Only the voice of the Tree quietened them. They stood still, like ghosts for a while as the leaves whispered above our heads, contemplating what they had done. Then, one by one, they began to slink off, like children caught at sin, like drunkards in the temple. They left him there. And me, too. I slunk off. Even though I had dealt not one blow, the guilt in that clearing was too much to bear. We left him, then, alone, to bear the shame and humiliation, the pain and misery of his wounds, to die as slowly as only a god knows how.

Why? This story is known to men, in one form or other, and that is what they all ask. Why did he sacrifice himself on that tree? And to whom? And for what end?

Once every nine years at Upsala the beasts were slaughtered at the great festival, back in the day. Great bulls, nine of them, only the strongest, in their prime, at their best, the most fertile, whose daughters yield the most milk, whose sons carry the best meat. Then eagles, nine of them too, strong birds whose wings could carry them over oceans if need be, the best of their kind. And the goats, and the cats and the wolves and the horses, each one the very best of their generation that the priests could find among the flocks of kings and lords. The blood flowed like wine and we gods fed and grew fat and happy and rich. Golden days, those festivals. We lived for them.

But not one drop of all that blood ever went to Odin. Not one ounce of flesh or fat was burned for him. His sacrifice took place elsewhere, hidden in the sanctuaries and temples, with only the priests and the kings to witness it. There he is given what is his, and no one without must ever know. But I am a god, so I can tell you what is the due to Odin. No beast will do for him. He must have a man. A man at his peak, of course, strong and vigorous and young. But not just any man. Who can you give to the God of Kings, but a king? Yes. Only the lifeblood of a king will do for Odin. Give him his due. He does not take seven. If you have seven, six of them cannot be the best and only the best may go to Odin, to live by his side and drink from his horn and eat off his plate. That is how it is done. Always has been done, always will be.

You see how it is with him. Only the very best, the highest. So you may well ask, to whom was Odin himself slaughtered? To whom would the best among us, sacrificed on that tree, go? To whom does the God of Kings, the King of Gods go? To whom can he possibly be given?

To himself, of course. Odin goes to Odin, Himself to Himself He is given, His blood to His blood, His flesh to His flesh.

Impossible, you cry? But Odin is the god of the impossible. He collects mysteries as you might collect pebbles on the beach. Yes. Odin sacrificed himself to himself. And who knows, who knew, even he, what might come of that?

Shall I tell you something that I have never told before? It is a secret, I think. Something has kept it from my lips for all this time. There is a shame in it and a mystery in it, perhaps, but I do not know why I have kept it to myself all these years. When the madness was at its height, when the frenzied attack on his person was at its cruellest and most terrible – suddenly I was able to bear it no longer, and I ran to him to help him.

He had told me, he had told us all before that no matter what happened he had to be left to his fate; but I could not bear it. I ran towards him – and he opened an eye, just one; and for an instant he was transformed before me. I saw him not as he was then – a man, partly grey already from too much knowing, being torn to pieces by his own family and friends. I was brought up short, I think, because I had a vision of him suddenly as a creature of impossible age, the ancient of days, white with it; and he had only one eye. He stared at me from that one eye, but not from then; not from the now, I swear it. He glared at me from time to come – from the future. Perhaps in another universe I did save him and he wanted to stop me doing it. I don't know. But suddenly he was there before me, his eyes glittering with power and threat. No! he cried – silently.

I stopped in my run. My feet grew to the ground – that's how it felt. I was rooted to the spot. The frenzied attack went on. Odin achieved his aim.

That word, spoken to me from a future – and not the future we shall have, I understand that now – was a sign of his power. There was no mistaking or ignoring it. When the beating was over we all slunk away, as if nothing had happened, as if we had all gathered for a group shit and were strolling away from our own stink. I myself was among them, but after a day had passed, I went back; I had to. My conscience would not let me rest.

He was still there, of course, nailed to the Tree. The blood had dried on him, his limbs were crooked with broken bones. One of the goddesses had torn his hair and beard out in clumps and his face was swollen out of recognition – a terrible sight. He said no word. I brought him bread and water, but when I held the sponge to his lips he turned his head away.

'Not yet,' he croaked.

'You are mad,' I told him. Then I sat down on the turf at his feet, so that he would not be alone, and we waited together for death to take him.

Nine days it took him to die. On the first day he bled. On the second day his wounds dried up, but his beard was wet with slaver. On the third day he resembled a desiccated corpse. On the fourth day the crows came and pecked out his eyes. On the fifth day, black bile came out of his anus. On the sixth day his breathing became laboured. On the seventh day, he wept. On the eighth day he began to groan rhythmically. On the ninth day, he lifted up his head.

'It is done,' he said.

'Die then,' I said – because no one who had seen his sufferings over those nine days would wish for more.

'I cannot die,' he said.

'You cannot live,' I told him.

'You must finish me off.'

I grew pale then. I alone had struck no blow. Now I felt that he had dealt me a terrible one. I alone of all the gods was not guilty of his torture; now he wanted me to take his life from him.

'I will not do it,' I said.

'You have to, or all this will be in vain.'

His face, his eyeless face, turned to face the ground where an ash shaft spear, tipped with flint, lay on the ground. Frey, I think, had dropped it there.

'Do it, for the love of god,' he grated. I shook my head . . .

I shook my head, but I did it in the end, of course. Why, I'm not sure. Perhaps I could not bear to see him suffer any more. And who was I to stand between the Lord of Creation and his holy goal – even though I had no idea what that goal was?

First I made him renew his oath of brotherhood with me, which he did, although I should have known no use would come of it. The priests that killed the king at Upsala, they never lasted long. The family saw them off. Who does the regicide is supposed to be a secret, but they know it, somehow. They bow to the family afterwards and sometimes, one of the brothers steps forward with a sword right there and then, with the king still bleeding on the ground. You cannot have a king killed, even for Odin, and not take blood vengeance on it.

He swore always to be my brother, even in death. I believed I would never see him again. Then I picked up the ash shaft, stood back and drove it in, hard, under his ribs. The skin of a god is hard, but the heart is harder; Odin's was like a rock. I pushed through the skin and past the bones, into the cavity; then up against his heart. I could feel it pulsing against the tip of my spear. Odin writhed; sweat broke out all over him and he groaned like a tree. I heaved, I pushed, I struggled against his beating heart and fraction by fraction, the flint bit its way inside. My feet scrabbled on the stony ground to keep

footing. I pushed, he pushed, his heart fought me every inch of the
way, I was weeping like a child, but at last it gave way. The spear
slipped within and a great gout of blood shot out – the blood of him
like a river. He lifted his head, shouted at the sky and gave up the
ghost.

I stood back, panting with exertion. I looked around, scared that one
of the others had hidden and seen me, because I was certain they
would come and take revenge, even though they had tormented him
for no reason and I had killed him at his own behest. But there was
no one there. For all the nine days, not one of them had come near.

I turned back and looked at my work. There he hung, Odin, King
of Gods, God of Kings. Every bone in his body was broken, he hung
like a thing on a gibbet, carrion, loveless, hopeless. The wind stirred
his hair and the threads of his beard. Blood, tears and snot fouled his
swollen and bruised face. Soon he would begin to rot. I wondered
what to do with the body. Burn him, I thought . . .

But then it began. It began with the nails; they fell out. Yes, one
after the other the nails fell out. And when the last two fell from his
wrists, then the body of Odin fell too, down, down, down. I rushed
forward to catch him, too late. Through the earth he fell, and with
my god's eyes I followed him down, down through the many worlds,
down to Hel, down through worlds I didn't even know existed, even
to Niflheimr and beyond. And down and down and down until at last
even I could no longer follow him, into regions not even the gods
could know about or see.

I waited a while; surely there was more to come! – but nothing
more did come. The trunk of the Tree still bore the stains of his body
and the holes of the nails. The thin grass that grew among the stones
under my feet was wet with gore. I cleaned up his blood, like a maid.
I waited a day, two days; nothing more happened. A wolf came to lick
the Tree where he had hung and snarled at me when I drove it away.
At last I went to the others and told them I had been to the Tree, and
that he was gone. More I did not say.

So that was it – the end of Odin. Only, of course, it wasn't. A few
weeks later and he was back among us, his wounds now scars upon

him, looking very pleased with himself. Everyone gathered round, patting him on the back, doing their best to look delighted. Tyr's face was like a dog's arse.

Where the Allfather had been, he never said, what he had seen, he never said. Maybe he doesn't know himself, I have no idea. But whatever it was and whatever he did, he brought treasure back with him. Can you guess? Have you heard?

The runes, Arse-born. He brought back the runes. Yes. The deeper magic. Before Odin went to Odin, there were no runes upon or within the worlds. No magic as such – only we gods with our attributes, and the way things were. Since then – well. The laws have been a little more bendy, put it like that. With the runes, anyone can learn.

To start with, the other gods were delighted. Oh, look, sweeties! More power, more secrets, more magic. No longer did you have to stick with your own attributes, you could take on new ones, for a while at least. Well – that didn't last long, I can tell you. As soon as he announced that he was handing the runes out to anyone who cared to learn them – uproar! What? Hand out power like this to the Shit-born? Was he mad? And . . . to the *Jotun*? I swear to god the Thunderer almost shat himself with rage. Or . . . was it fear? I have never quite made up my mind on this matter, whether the most hawkish among us are also the most cowardly, in their deepest hearts. Only those who fear so much feel the need to fight so hard, to conquer and crush. What do you think? Or is it just rage after all? And what is the difference, anyway?

For my part, I thought it was hilarious! I laughed and laughed at the sheer joy of it! First they had fought like demons to stop Odin sacrificing himself. Then they ended up doing it more violently than I think even he planned. Then they were overjoyed at the gifts he brought back – and now look! You could hear the howls of rage all the way to Muspel and back. But there was nothing anyone could do about it. As a result of his unearthly travails, Odin returned among us more powerful than ever. Everyone started frantically swotting up on the runes. Odin didn't have to, they were his, he knew them in his bones. Once again, he had outstripped us all.

What he did while he was there, down so deep, I cannot tell. Odin and I were closer than ever after that adventure, but he never told anyone, even me, even when he was blind drunk, which was most weekends. But we can hazard a guess. The runes must come from somewhere near to the roots of the world tree, where meaning and reality themselves first sprout. Since then, he can re-arrange things, somewhat. So, of course, can anyone who gets to know the runes – I myself am something of an expert in that way. But the runes are Odin's, he is their master and that is how he changes his shape, which was my preserve amongst the gods once upon a time. This is how he has brightness, that was once Hoenir's gift alone, and fertility, and darkness, and how he masters war so well, that was once the preserve of Tyr. Even his own gift of breathing life into the inanimate is enhanced; since then he is able to speak to the dead and ask their secrets. They will tell him whatever he wants to know, at his command. He is able to raise them up and make them walk – for a while. None of it is exactly the original, but still. With the runes he can make the future a tad more certain. Even the past is not unreachable to him. To a degree.

And at what cost? You may well ask. We have seen the physical cost he bore – he carries the scars to this day. But there is a greater cost, a metaphysical one – one still to pay.

'Where did you get them from?' I asked him when he returned.

'From the earth herself,' he replied, and winked at me.

'Doesn't she want them back?' I asked.

'One day, perhaps.'

'She will take them, then,' I said.

Odin went every quiet then and, soon after, he said we were not to speak about it again. Because, I think, he will pay a very heavy price when the time comes, at the end of things, when Surtr comes to call and the gods fall at Ragnarok. Then, his sport returns to the source and he will be required to pay a price that I think no one would want to pay. What that price is, I can only guess.

So Odin became the Great All Knowing, or the Great Know All, as you might say, and became wise and powerful and mighty. It was a remarkable deed. He achieved much. If only he had left it there . . .

THE PRICE OF AN EYE

Listen now to a story carefully hidden from the Seven Worlds for all time. Only I, Loki the unfaithful, father of lies, free-handed spender of words, have the courage to tell you the truth in this matter, of how Odin Allfather lost his hold over the gods of Asgard and all the worlds, by reason of his own over-reaching ambition.

Yes, Arse-born, the ambition of Odin was without end. It was back then, it is now. With runes he had captured wisdom and power from the roots the worlds, but it was still not enough. It rankled that those flipperty-gibbety Ljósálfar, the light elves, had uncovered the secret of eternal youth and not him. It rankled that there were not enough apples to go round. He wanted more, more, always more. But what more was there? He owned the Seven Worlds and all that happened in them. As Lord of All, he owned the present and had the past written to his own taste.

The future, Arse-born. The Lord of the Past and Present wanted to own the future as well. You see how even your mortal ambition, gross though it is, palls beside that of the Lord of Gods. And so, in due course, there was another expedition, one that he made with the breath still in him this time – down to the deeps again to see Mimir, eldest, sole survivor of the days before Odin, that god who dwelled outside of the Seven created Worlds, down at the well at the roots of Yggdrasil. That journey too was successful. And yet it did not turn out as he had planned.

You know about Odin's journey perhaps? How he travelled down to another place – not to the deepest source, not to whatever lies below Niflheimr, where the very rules of the universe are born, not to the place where he found or forged the runes, but to another one equally deep in some ways – to Mímisbrunnr, the welling stream that feeds one of the three roots of Yggdrasil. Mímisbrunnr, where the waters of *knowing* nourish the world ash.

Mimir – what is there to say about Mimir? He was clever, that's for sure – clever enough to be out of the way during the terrible famicide that Odin and his brothers unleashed back when the day was young and Time itself was still getting out of bed and yawning at the world. He was wise, too, which as I think I have pointed out, Odin was not. Wise enough to know not to tamper too deeply with the way things are – wise enough to be content to know rather than act. And as one who was there at the beginning of things . . . as one who made his home by the spring of the fountain of knowledge . . . he was the wisest, the smartest, the most knowing of all of creation. He was there before Odin himself, or any of the worlds as we know them. What Mimir did not know was not simply not worth knowing . . . it couldn't be known in the first place.

Given that Odin had murdered the rest of his generation, you can suppose that Mimir was not happy to see his nephew, and in fact – I can attest to this, as I went along myself, at Odin's request – did his best to keep him away. Mimir, although he knew everything, had no power himself, none that he cared to use anyway. So he used tricks – mazes, false trails, illusions – to keep his murderous relative away from his home by the waters. And although Odin is Odin, he is not necessarily the god of tricks. So he became confused and lost his way, and had to return and find someone who could help him solve those tricks. None other than . . . myself. It takes the god of tricks to understand the tricks of the god of knowing.

So, yes, Arse-born, I was there, too, at Mímisbrunnr, serving my brother. Of the tricks – the mazes, the false pathways, the traps, pitfalls, puzzles and pratfalls – that Mimir laid in our way, and how I, Lord of Clever, found my way past them all, must be told another time. Let us just say that I was there. I was there as we blasted our way through the last wall of rock that cut Mímisbrunnr off from the rest of creation; I was there to see the look on Mimir's face as we walked out. He was there, actually, to greet us.

'You knew we would be here,' said Odin.

'You always were here at this moment,' said Mimir. I could see the frown that plucked at Odin's face at this remark, which told me that he, too, had no idea what that meant.

'And yet you tried to stop me,' he blustered.

Mimir shrugged. 'I always have,' he said.

They stood there and regarded one another for a while – the god of knowing and the god of . . . well. Odin was the god of a lot of things, but at that moment, I would say he was the god of being jealous.

'Show me the well,' he demanded.

Mimir made a little gesture with his hands. 'It is here,' he said.

We both looked around. There was nothing to be seen but the ice cave into which we had broken through.

'It is not here,' said Odin at last.

'It is here,' said Mimir. 'But it is hidden from you.'

I turned to look at Odin. How was he going to deal with that little obstacle.

His hand tightened on his spear shaft.

'Then you must show me it, uncle,' he said.

'I will not,' said Mimir.

'Why not, uncle?'

'Because then you will have no use for me, and you will kill me,' said Mimir with a shrug. You can understand his reluctance.

'There are worse things than death,' said Odin.

Mimir paused and thought. I can guess what he was thinking, as I have thought about it myself many times since; what are the fates that are worse than death? To be roasted alive forever. To be hung by red-hot hooks in boiling pitch. The list, believe me, is endless.

'If you swear me an oath, nephew. I will grant you your wish,' he said at last.

'What is that oath?' asked Odin eagerly.

'That I will draw breath. That I will speak. That I will eat the apples of Idunn, like the other gods do.'

Odin nodded. 'I will swear all that,' he said. 'Here at the roots of Yggdrasil, at the root of knowing, at the stream of knowledge – I swear my oath, Mimir, that you will draw breath, and speak and eat the apples of Idunn, with the other gods.

So Mimir nodded. 'That is the price to me,' he said. And as he said that, the stillness of the ice cave was disturbed by the merest whisper – not the sound of running water, but the sound of water welling up against ice. The whisper, Arse-born, of knowledge itself.

At our feet the water welled. Eagerly, Odin bent down to taste it, but as he did, the water fell away from his lips.

He looked up at Mimir.

'You have paid the price to me, but there is also a price to the well,' he said.

'Yes?'

'An eye, nephew.'

Odin stared at him long and hard. Mimir was known for his sense of irony. Personally I think it was just a last-ditch attempt to put the Allfather off – but perhaps it was true. Certainly Odin must have thought so, since, without a flinch, he took out his knife and carved his right eye out of its socket. There was a small cry of pain, and he clapped a rag over the wound with one hand. With the other, he dropped the dismembered eye into the pool, where the stream welled up from whatever deeps it came from around the hidden roots of Yggdrasil. The water swirled the blood away in a moment. And there it lay, and there it lies to this day, staring out and up from the well of knowledge; the eye of Odin. And if Odin himself sees all, who had only one sip from the well of knowledge, what does that eye see, that lives there?

Then he bent down to his knees to wet his beard – and paused.

'What will I know, uncle?' he begged.

'You will know everything,' said Mimir. 'Everything that is, everything that was, everything that will be.'

Odin, for the first and as far as I know, the only time in his life, paused.

'And what will so much knowing do to me, uncle?'

Mimir shook his head. 'The gift of knowing is mine, not yours,' he said. 'What it will do to you, I cannot say.'

Odin stared at him again, with his bloodied face; then he dipped his head and drank. Mimir and I, we both held our breaths; but when he looked up again, there was disappointment in Odin's face.

'It will come slowly,' said Mimir. 'By the time you reach Asgard, you will know everything there is to know.'

Odin nodded, stood, drew his spear and plunged it directly into the heart of his uncle in one quick, slick movement. Mimir gasped; the worlds trembled. I let out a shriek of fear, because the oath that Odin had made – even he could not break that, surely.

'Help me, quick,' said Odin. 'Before the worlds break.'

And he and I, while the walls of the worlds began to melt, moved fast. Under his instruction, I took my knife and cut the head of Mimir from his body, while Odin prepared herbs, muttered incantations and spells – spells just learned at that moment, perhaps, and played with the runes. In the preparation he made, he bathed the head of Mimir, rubbed oils and herbs into it . . . then he sat back. Above us the Tree itself trembled like a sapling . . .

And the head drew breath. The eyes opened.

'Welcome back, uncle,' said Odin. 'You draw breath. You speak. You will live forever, as the gods do.'

Mimir closed his eyes and a tear escaped and trickled down his bloody face. Such was the fate of him who gave Odin all he wanted.

We packed the head in Odin's pack – I would not go near it – and we headed up back towards Asgard.

So began our journey back up to the worlds; but it did not go well, not well at all, Arse-born. At first Odin went before me with his long stride, but gradually his pace began to lessen, his head began to sink. I caught up with him . . .

'Are you OK, brother? Is the knowledge coming?'

'It's coming . . . it's coming fast . . .' he croaked. He carried on, moaning often, stumbling and holding his head, as if all that knowing was hurting his little brain.

That night we made camp on one of the lesser branches of Yggdrasil, out of the way of curious travellers in between the worlds. We ate in silence – Odin could barely speak for the rush of knowledge into him. In the morning, when I rose to make us our first meal and wash, Odin lay on the ground, curled up like a foetus, his thumb in his mouth, his eyes wide open, staring. His pants were wet.

Well, I did my best to bring him round, but it was no use. Every time I tried to get him to stand he began to weep and cry out. In the end I had to carry him all the way up to Asgard on my back. All the while I was cursing, cursing, cursing because . . . where would I be now, if my chief ally was gone? Who would look out for me, if Odin had lost his wits? Tyr would rise, Thor at his side, and there would be no peace or place for poor Loki then. He wept, I wept – making our way home, he on my back, both of us shedding tears.

I took him at night, in secret – I knew at once this was not to be common knowledge – and I showed his wife, Frigg, what had happened. She told me to be silent, that she would tend him. I went back to my own home, relieved to have shed the problem I admit, and made my way to bed.

And there I left him for a long while; and for a long while there was no news. I expected Frigg to contact me, but no. The Allfather did not appear in public, and so far that had attracted no comment. It was common enough for him to stay hidden away for weeks, months, years, even decades without anyone seeing him. But the rumours circulated, as they always will.

I got word to Frigg; she told me to stay quiet and not to worry, but I did worry, and so in the end I made enough of a pest of myself that she gave in and invited me round to see him, my poor brother. It turned out that she had not needed to ask me what had happened; she had found the head of Mimir in Odin's sack. He had told her all that had transpired and given her advice on how best to deal with the situation. They say that Odin used the head to ask advice, but what use for advice has a man who knows everything? Frigg, though, made good use of the head, then and ever after.

She de-briefed me, swore me to further silence. I had an interview with the head, who told me that for now there was little anyone could do. The Allfather would either go completely mad, or go just a bit mad. Time would tell.

'What does he know, that's made him like this?' I asked. Mimir just smiled grimly and said I could ask him for myself.

I was shown through to him. He sat there, clutching the arms of the chair, his face a mask of terror.

'Brother, what is so terrible that you've been made so grim?' I asked, because he had been a man ready for a laugh up till then.

He stared at me again a while, then suddenly buried his face in his hands and let out a single sob.

'There's not just one, as I thought,' he said. 'There are many – so many! They are infinite . . .' He would say no more.

It took me a while to sort it out. Odin had discovered that day that the future was very different from what we had all thought. Know, Arse-born, that the future is fixed – there is no choice, no free will; that is just the illusion of our blindness. But the future is fixed not to just one path; it is many. To a very great many, in fact. Yes, like the great spaces between the galaxies and stars, so vast as to be beyond mortal or immortal comprehension, so with the futures; they are endless. Every single possible one is real, from which piece of cutlery you pick up first, to who wins the war, to where lightning strikes, to what day kings and peasants shall lie and die. Each second strikes out an unimaginable number of futures, each of which strike out another unimaginable number of futures. Each one exists in its own separate universe. Even infinity might gasp at that; even Surtr the Deathless might quail.

And Odin now knew them all. All of them! Great joke, eh? He thought he was clever enough to encompass the future – but he had no idea just how many futures there were. There they all are, trapped in that little head of his. So he had his wish, the Great Allwise, the God of Mysteries. In the end he knew so much, that he came to know nothing at all.

That look of wonder on his face? It's confusion. The poor fool is utterly unable to work out where, when and above all which world he is in. He knows more than all and less than any. It's tragic in many ways – he was such a smart old dear once upon a time. Now he wanders from day to day like a mote of dust on the breeze. Pathetic. You mortals might learn from him. There is danger in knowing too much.

The day he drank from the well, that day was the end of Odin as we knew him. He had to concentrate so hard to work out which future he was in, which present was unfolding, that he was blinded. His head became bent, day by day. His back curled up until he was staring at the ground like a blind man. The hair of his beard began to grow, curling around his face and head. I swear that within a century or two the hair was growing out of his eyeballs.

Such is the fate of all-knowingness. In becoming so, Odin sealed a number of fates, including my own. Weep for Loki, mortal! And weep for yourself while you're at it. With Odin incapacitated, other, less worthy gods quickly stepped in to take charge, gods who care nothing for the fate of the worlds, and for mankind in particular. Welcome to the Age of Tyr.

But their time too will end, sooner than you think. Surtr the Deathless will leave his station in Muspel and come to wage war on the seven worlds. Muspel will be victorious. There is no weapon or strength or power that can even tinker at the edges of such a force. Already the fires are burning brighter and hotter than ever across middle earth, the ice is melting, the land is choking. The wild places are vanishing under smoke and sun, and the only creatures to thrive are rats and crows, gulls and men. Soon is already too late. There is no escaping the wrath of Surtr, or his flaming sword and his hordes of flame demons. You will all burn.

And what of Loki? I have plans of my own. Deep down here in the cave of my imprisonment, chained as I am to a rock, the forces of war and conflict have me trapped; but the heat of the world above does not reach so far down. It is possible that even great Surtr will not find Loki, were he even to bother looking for something so tiny and insignificant.

And what if I were free? It's not impossible, with the right help. I have allies still. Deep under the earth, deeper even than the dwarves delve, only there can we find respite from the fires of Muspel. I need not be alone. That is all I will say for now, mortal. The gods make a mistake in thinking that I am a creature of vengeance. They want you to believe that when all bonds break and all doors open on the first day of Ragnarok, I will join forces with destruction. That's not so. I am a man of peace. All I ask is simply to be let alone – to be myself, to live on and enjoy the worlds.

While Surtr rages I shall stay here, deep in the flesh of the Ymir; only afterwards, when the fire has died down, only then will I come forward. Those of you who survive will not be without my wisdom, my council, and my tricks. Perhaps even before then . . .

But I am asking too much. Why, after all, should the likes of you help Loki to escape his bonds?

Be yourselves. Mortals! I shall see you in the afterworld.

Now listen and attend closely – I shall tell you the story of my downfall – the truth, not the propaganda, not the Asgard spin. You will see that I am your friend after all.

BOOK FOUR

LOKI IN LOVE

So – times changed. Odin, God of Knowing, knew too much. The Allfather eclipsed himself, became disabled with knowledge and into his place stepped – war.

And what of Loki? Of course, the gibes started again. Horse fucker. Man-lover. Pervert. The Vanir stayed out of sight; the Aesir gathered behind the powerful. War and conflict spread across the land. Genocide was undertaken. Where are the Jotun now? You may well ask. How long is it since they were seen striding across the land, cupping the valleys and mountains in their hands, whispering their love to the rivers and oceans? What of the Dökkálfar and Ljósálfar? Where are they? The elves prefer to dance with the sunbeams than to step the earth these days; the dwarves have abandoned their halls and gone deep, deep into the earth where even the force of the hammer cannot find them. And the rest of us? We must try and live in the world we have rather than the world we wish we had. There remain the pleasures of simply being alive. The sun shines. The earth turns. Spring comes and summer follows. And more.

There is love.

Love, Arse-born. Let us talk about that. Even you, of so lowly a lineage, dream of it and live for it. What treasure is worth more, what life is not enriched by it or lessened without it? The wealthiest among us is poorer than any who have it, and the poorest of us is wealthy beyond measure. Love! I have been in love many times. It is one of the benefits of a long life. I am a passionate person and when the mist of desire falls over me, I will do anything for the object of my attention. Just to be with them . . . to make love with them . . . to believe in them. That is all, surely, any of us can ask?

ANGRBODA

The time came when I grew sick of the gods. To be honest, it had been going on for a long time. That business with the mason. We had to trick him – I'm all for tricks. But murder? No. There used to be a kind of rough justice, a balance, an understanding among the races. The kidnapping of the apples didn't help, of course. I regret my part in it. It got worse again when Thor got his hands on that hammer and that belt – the hammer that never missed its mark and always returned to his hand, the belt that increased his strength three-fold. Odin could have held him back, but never did. The weakness of the father for a favourite son, perhaps? Or did he see something in the future, some gain from letting Thor split open as many heads as he liked? What possible advantage can there be so great, that genocide is excused? Perhaps the truth is, he just liked having a psychopath around. Kings and governments ever since have followed in that tradition, let's face it.

I can't abide a bully, I never could. So when the game stopped being an adventure and it turned into slaughter . . . when feasting became drunkenness and murder became success and poetry became boasting and manners became arse-licking and truth was just another way of telling lies . . . I packed my bag and left. I left my wife Sigyn to her tricks with Tyr. I left Odin staring at his shoes, I left Tyr fomenting distrust, all in the name of protecting Asgard's interests – ring any bells, fellas? – and mighty Thor strong-arming his way around Jǫtunheimr and raping his way around middle earth. Over the Rainbow Bridge I went, farewell to my old mucker Heimdallr – we had some good times in the early days, despite what the Asgard agitprop likes to say . . . and I headed out into Jǫtunheimr to make a new life for myself.

'If you go, don't expect to come back,' rumbled the Thunderer. I took no notice. I was gone, I was out of there. Maybe I was gone forever, maybe not. In my experience, there's always a way.

The Aesir knew I was sickened by the way they ruled the worlds. Frey and Freya and others of the Vanir thought I was bored and heading out for an adventure. Well, perhaps, perhaps. Immortality lasts a long time, believe me. But it wasn't just that. Yes, I was sick of Asgard; yes, I was bored. But the fact is, Arse-born, I had fallen in love.

I have spoken of the goddess Freya. It may well be that no woman, mortal or immortal, could ever match her for her sheer sexual energy. There has been her, many, many times, and a hundred, a thousand, tens of thousands of other loves, male, female, Jotun, god, mortal and otherwise. But I would give them all up for a single embrace with Angrboda. My lovely Angrboda, who held the future in her eyes and destiny in her womb. Angrboda, whose gifts made even Odin jealous. How she lived and how she died has never before been told. Like me, she has been the subject of the vilest defamation. I am here to put the record straight.

When we first saw her she was a mad child, running about in Odin's cave scattering and staring. But in the times in between she changed – from child to woman, from woman to goddess. Mortal, she had Become. Her attributes were foresight and hope. Yes, *hope*. Pray to her, mortal. Angrboda is the light at the end of the tunnel, the break in the clouds, the turn in your run of bad luck, the child of a barren woman, the day of peace after the slaughter. She is the springtime, the turn of the tide, the thaw, the moment of forgiveness. No wonder the gods had her killed. But her day will come, as it always must.

*   *   *

Angrboda left Asgard long before I did. Hope sees far ahead. I remember the day she left, her pack on her back, her dogs at her heels, the gods and goddesses gathered around to see her off.

Everybody begged her to stay.

'Only slaughter can come of slaughter,' she told us. At the time we didn't understand what she meant; this was before the days of the hammer. Now I know. The fact is, the killing of Ymir at the dawn of the worlds may have made the world, but it made it an evil world. With that act, Odin and his brothers invented death and they have lived off it ever since. Angrboda understood all that time ago, and so she ignored our pleas and turned to leave.

'Angrboda,' called Odin. She didn't do him the honour of turning to face him, but she paused in her step to hear what he had to say – as if she didn't already know. 'When you leave us, you betray us,' said the Old Man – inventing in that moment the 'if you're not for us you're against us' trope. She didn't answer, but shook her head and walked on, leaving us staring after her, wondering what she meant and what Odin meant.

But before she disappeared she turned briefly, to look straight at . . . me. Into my eyes. Confused – weak perhaps, because I didn't want to be associated with a traitor – I looked away. At the time I had no idea. I know now that there was only one traitor on the walls that day, and that was Odin himself. Let me admit it, I am a shallow person in many ways – shallow compared to the likes of Odin and Angrboda at least – but it wasn't long before I too began to see it for myself. Once the mason was murdered for doing an honest day's work, once Thor had begun his spree of murder while Odin sat back and watched . . . at that moment, it became obvious to all people of good will and intent.

You must judge for yourselves.

I did not know then, or for many centuries after, that Angrboda would become the love of my life.

It was not so many short centuries later that I trod the same path myself. My feet paused in their tracks, just as Angrboda's had, as I wondered – hoped perhaps – that the Lord of Creation would drop back into this world long enough to bring down the same curse on me as he had on her. I paused, but he said nothing – just stood there, eyes down, lost in the countless worlds. I lifted a hand in farewell and made my way over the Rainbow Bridge to begin my life again away from the gods and goddesses of Asgard with the woman I loved most in all my life; and believe me, I have loved very many.

You know, you must have known, you always knew, that it was never as simple as they liked to make out.

Angrboda, Angrboda! My love. A goddess among goddesses. She was small – petite, you would almost say, like a pretty young fox. She couldn't change her shape but she could disguise it – yes, she knew seidr, the witchcraft. In fact, she *was* seidr, the goddess of the witches, a fact that Odin always hated and feared. Curly hair, so dark brown, a deep, deep brown that was almost black in some lights. Mossy green eyes. Her face looked quite hard at times, but when she smiled, she was like a child. Thor called her hatchet-nosed, which was unfair. I thought of her as my beautiful young witch.

She was so many things. Almost a Jotun, almost a goddess, almost a Norn, who weave the fates. In the end, though, she was one thing above all: a prophet, a seer. Not like the Norns who scrabbled to make the present move forward; not like Odin who knew so much he knew nothing at all. She was of this world, not the many, and she could read the signs as clear as day. She knew what was coming for us, here, now and tomorrow. All the other seers and prophetesses spoke in tongues and confused words, metaphors, elegiac couplets, rhymes, curses, ranting images of things to come that might mean everything or nothing. Not Angrboda. When she prophesied, she told you simply and clearly what was to come.

Maybe that's why Odin hated her. He told me plainly to stay away from her when I first became interested. I thought he wanted her for himself – what a pair they would have made! But the Old Man was jealous, that's all it was. Of course I was curious. I was made to be curious. Wouldn't you be, too? I visited her in her home on the coast, where the river meets the sea, at first because I was passing, then because we became friends. One night as the sun was going down over the bay where she made her home, we became lovers. It was not long after, after a day full of laughter and sex, as we walked along the beach one afternoon, that I first realised that I, Loki, for the first time properly in my already long life, had fallen in love.

I was surprised; I had thought I was immune. I told her. 'I love you.'

She smiled. 'I know,' she said.

'Of course you do!' We laughed, Arse-born, although I have no idea to this day what was funny about that. At that moment I knew I could not happily live without her. I began making preparations to leave Asgard at once.

The gift of prophesy was her blessing and her curse. You know how it is. They read the leaves in your cup, or the ways the entrails of a slaughtered animal are arranged, or how the sticks fall, or how the clouds blow. But with Angrboda it was not just like that. With her everything was a sign. It was like living with a gospel, a testament. I won't lie; it was hard to bear. She did her best to avoid things I didn't want to know, but sometimes she went into a trance and then, terrible things could issue from her mouth. Then I would have to cover my ears, because – yes, I was curious, but who wants to be tainted with too much knowledge? I've seen what that can do to a man. When I went to her, I thought I would be like Odin and learn everything that will be. But I soon learned that life is best when it takes you by surprise.

Angrboda could read the future from everything that happened to her. The wind in the apple trees one morning foretold how many goats we would lose that winter when the wolf pack broke into our yard; the way I left my knife on the table told her how hard the frost would be that week. If I spat or coughed or farted, she could prophesy from it. It was amusing at first, and she delighted in showing me what would happen to the brindled calf in the field from the shape of its hoof, or the kind of harvest we'd get from the way the grass fell under the scythe when they mowed the orchard. But it became exhausting soon enough. Everything that happened meant something else. More than once I lost my temper at it and snapped at her to keep her secrets to herself.

But then the tears would well up in her eyes, because she was a sensitive thing, my Angrboda. That doesn't make sense, does it? Why would someone who sees the fates of everyone she meets written in their little actions . . . someone who sees life and death like an open book all around them . . . why should they go soft at a cross word? But that's how she was. She could calmly see from the mole on her cheek that your grandmother was going to fall in the field and die under the hooves of the heifers, and then weep in the afternoon because a child had fallen sick.

Prophesy often came to her during sex, or before it, in the morning when we lay in bed waiting for the day to begin.

'What did I say?' she would ask.

'I didn't hear. I was hiding under the bedclothes.'

'Thank god for that,' she'd say. And she would get out of bed and go to fix her hair in the mirror, and I would lie there with my hands behind my head and watch her heavy breasts lift as she raised her arms, watch the dimples in her arse as she moved around the room, her neat brown scut, that triangle where the light showed at the top of her thighs. And I would ask her if she would like me to prophesy who was going to fuck her next, or what was her heart's desire, or who it was who loved her more than anyone else in this world or the next. And the answer, friends, was always the same . . .

'You! You, my Loki, my red-haired lover, my beautiful man, my trickster, my love, my only one!'

THE CHILDREN OF LOKI

The one thing Angrboda could not see was her own fate and, therefore, the fates of those near to her. That was dark to her – so she said. But I wondered then, and I've wondered since, if that is merely something she chose to say. I know this much – what a relief it was to me when I believed she could not foresee how things would turn out between us.

We made our home where we had the best of all worlds, where the river comes down from the mountains through a soft green valley, taking the sun all the day long, before winding down to meet the sea. There we built a little wooden house facing south to catch the sun's rays. We planted fruit and grew vegetables and flowers, kept pigs and sheep and goats, a cow or two for milk, and a fat lazy bull, called Odin, who stood in the meadow watching his cows graze, occasionally hefting his hulk across their backs. We did well. Angrboda was no goddess of the fertile fields, but she always knew where the crops would do best and what crops they must be. She always knew which cows bore the best calves, which sheep would sicken and die and which ones would thrive, which seeds would grow the finest beans, which part of the river held the best fish. We had serfs to do our work, and so our days were spent walking, making love, being in love.

Yes, clever and beautiful was my Angrboda. Even though we had been cast out, the gods visited from time to time, often to take advice from her – always in secret of course. Even Odin, who hated taking advice and distrusted anyone wiser than he was, could not keep away. Each time he came he sat before me in his wheelchair – he no longer walked far – and peered up through the hair of his face with that one baleful eye.

'What?' I asked. 'What?'

But he never answered. I took his distrust to be simple jealousy – the man who knew everything was jealous of the woman who knew the value of it. All the worlds were at his fingertips – but which finger, which world? Angrboda's gift could never be his.

That could have been my life – I do believe it. I could have stayed there forever, loved and loving, if the gods had only let us be. Such a good life we had! Just us two tucked away on our own, far from the wretched machinations and snobbery of Asgard. Privilege breeds contempt. I have always been a man of the common people. I have been your helpmate, although you have forgotten it and chosen instead to believe the Asgard lies. I gave you the plough; they pretended they did it themselves. I gave you fire; they changed my name and punished me anyway. I taught you how to work metal – they put an imposter in my place. It's always been the same. The gods you worship would have kept you shivering in the darkness, have no doubt about it. You are a gullible people who always preferred the lies of Asgard to the lessons of your own history. Divide and rule has always been the way of the powerful – you must know that! They despise you but I have loved mortal women and mortal men all my days. I believe we must find love where we can.

I know how it is. Even now as you read this, you are thinking, 'Ah! He has been accused of lying. He admits it himself. Of course. No smoke without fire . . .' It is the nature of lies that they debase the truth. Don't trouble yourselves. I understand. There are those who know the truth, and how to judge. It's a shame you and your kind are unable to be among them, that's all.

HEL

So time passed in our idyll, our hideaway in the soft south of Sweden, by a lake, with the sea not far off, with our farm and our cows and our serfs, all of us happy like one big family, when it came to pass, as they like to say in the books, that Angrboda became with child. It was bound to happen. I was sad in some ways to be losing my sweetheart; but she was turning into a mother and I loved her for that too. I fed her milk and honey and fresh vegetables and fermented cabbages and salmon and beef and fruits and all good things, and she thrived. Odin's ravens, Memory and Thought, flew overhead and reported no doubt to the one-eyed wonder and his regents about our harmless shenanigans. The salmon and trout did their annual run up the rivers. Lamprey season came and went, the berries gathered on the bushes, and soon enough, the time came for Angrboda to give birth.

Imagine the birthing room. There are clean white linen sheets and towels, there is hot water, a fat, comely midwife and a couple of women to assist. I, a mere man, am kept at the back out of the way — I don't think they really thought it right that I should see that part of her body that I desired and loved so much turn suddenly into a fat old hog squirting out a babe, but I loved Angrboda in all her forms, all her moods, all her ways.

Everything is clean and neat for the messy business of birth.

The labour begins. Of this she had no prophesy, I'm certain of that, because I remember the look of surprise on her face a little later on. Surprise – but determination too. And love. One thing you could never say about Angrboda, was that she was without love. If you were with her, you had to love her back; it's the way she was. It could only ever be those who were distant from her who could plot against her.

Her waters have burst. Under her glowing skin, Angrboda heaves and pulses. Inside, her cervix is widening just as it ought to – just as the midwife, who occasionally sticks her fingers up my beloved for a feel, announces that all is going well, that everything is just as it should be.

Angrboda grips the head of the bed, puts back her head and grunts and heaves. The midwife and her assistants bend their heads to look closely between her legs. The baby crowns! Rejoice! – the child is on its way. But not too early, please; let's not count our chickens or our babies.

Then the head. Well! What a fine, pink, plump head that baby has! A pretty child. There are faint whiffs of something unpleasant about the birthing chamber at this point, but nothing that alarmed me. It ponged in there for various reasons. Let's face it; shit happens.

Looking back it may be that the midwife paused, that she hesitated just a wee bit too long before she took hold of the head and helped to guide the baby out of the birthing canal. Maybe. Looking back, I think so. But at the time, all I saw was that fine pink baby head with its neat, wet lick of black hair. Then – whoosh! The child shot out. Angrboda collapsed back on the bed. The midwife stared at the child in her hands; then with a shuddering cry let it drop down to the bed and stepped away.

What is this? What could it be? I bent to look. And lo! That fat pink baby, so full of health, was only half fat, half pink, half health. Doubting my eyes, I took a rag and wiped away the grey film of the womb from her little body, but there was really no doubting it. One half of her was pretty and pink and sweet and young; the other half, divided by a wavering line down her face, was shrivelled and blueish grey. Then I noticed that the birthing chamber was filled with a stink that most emphatically did not belong there. The death-stink. Rot. The taint of dead flesh.

See the baby's limbs! Fat and pink on one side – withered and stinking on the other. See her belly – pulsing with life on one side, taut and bloated with the gases of decomposition on the other. Our daughter was, quite literally, half dead.

The midwife let out a quacking cry and backed off. Angrboda sat up to take her baby.

'Don't touch it, ma'am!' yelped the midwife, as she and her feck- less assistants backed towards the door. But Angrboda was all mother, then and always. She leaned forward, took up her baby and cradled it in her hand. And there it was: one half, a fine healthy child; the other, pale death itself.

'This is our daughter,' my lover announced. She looked up at me and nodded; I nodded back. What else could I do? She was right; this was our daughter.

'Leave us,' she told the women, and they left quickly enough, believe me. Suddenly, after all the bustle, the three of us were on our own. The new girl did not cry. She lay in her mother's arms and waved her stick arms in the air and let out a small, weak bleat.

'Give me a blanket,' Angrboda told me. I did so – my hands were trembling. She wrapped the child up and held her to her breast, murmuring and rocking.

'What does it mean?' I croaked.

She regarded me calmly. 'She is a prophesy of death,' she announced.

'Whose?' I asked – begging inwardly that it wasn't that of her father.

'Baldr,' she said.

'Who?' I asked – because at that point, there was no one of that name alive.

'Not born yet,' she said. And she leaned back with a sigh. The baby began to cry, and she rubbed her swollen nipple against its mouth. The baby gaped and roamed around with her lips, blue and pink, to fasten on to it.

'Baldr. A son of Odin,' said Angrboda. She rested her head back on the head of the bed. 'A son of Odin,' she repeated. She glanced at me sharply; but what she knew, or realised in that moment, I don't know.

'It might be best to keep her inside for now,' she said to the ceiling. Then – 'I want to rest now.'

Dismissed. I left her, exiled with the midwife. I heard her weep a little later on.

So was born our first child, Hel. We loved her as well as any parents could, despite the smell.

Hel was an easy child to rear and an easy one to hide. She did not like the sun, which burned her skin. She favoured the stars and the moon. Even as a toddler we would wake and find her bed empty. Searching outside, we'd find her lying on her back on the grass with the dew wet on her face, clutching a posy of flowers to her chest, quite happy. She had her attributes, so we knew at once she was a goddess. She did not need to breathe, for example – she could lie underwater perfectly still for hours. She was friends with crows, ravens and worms. Yes – if you sat her on the grass and left her for an hour or two, they would come to her – the worm, the sexton beetle, the coffin fly. They would feed on her dead half as well, and yet never consume her.

She was happy just sitting or lying still for hours on end.

But she had her living side as well. She was a gardener – she would sow the seed, watch the little shoots grow, tend them, feed them, love them. Watch them die, dry them, hang them in her bedroom, or sometimes play-bury them, with grave goods and a prayer. Most often, though, the prayer was not to Odin or the others; it was to herself. It was the same with her pets. She would cherish and love them. She would never harm them; but she loved them just as much when they were dead and never once shed a tear for a sick or dying creature.

People fear her, but she never harmed a soul – only loved them better after death.

So Hel grew and played, rarely going out at day, which suited us. Only from time to time on autumn days, when the leaves were dying and falling from the trees, or in winter when the frost had bitten deep and the trees were black against the grey sky on a snow-heavy ground – she wanted to go out then. But Memory and Thought would too often be on high on such days so we kept her in. She wailed and made a fuss at first, but Hel was easily distracted. A good girl. Her one fault was that she liked to hang on to her little playmates, the mice and rats and voles and frogs and so on, long past the time when we wanted them in the house. For that reason I built her an underground home of her own, and she spent most of her days there, happy not to go out, to play with her friends, both the living and the dead.

HADRIGHADA

When Hel was three years old, Angrboda fell pregnant again. This time, we knew we had no idea what to expect, but even so, what emerged from her womb was far more terrifying and terrible than sweet little Hel.

Let me invite you again to the birth, if you can bear it. This time there is no chamber. Angrboda desired to give birth outside – under cover, for we were still trying to keep our family details from Odin. She wanted to be near water, so I had our people build us a jetty going down to the water's edge and beyond to the water itself, so that when she wished, Angrbodr could move down to the lake and immerse herself.

Her labour was not a long one; it was the actual birth that took forever. The birth pangs, the breaking of the waters, all were smooth and as it should be. The crowning of the baby's head, that too went according to plan. We rejoiced – we loved Hel but a normal child would make things easier, that's for sure. So when the head, the squashy head of the newborn – they are never pretty are they? – when that crowned between her legs, I did a little dance – I hadn't known how worried I'd been – and Angrboda smiled.

'Is it normal? Is it normal?' she begged, and I assured her that it was.

I spoke too soon.

And the body came. And it came. And it came . . . and it came and it came and it came. At the first glance I thought that our child had a very long torso for a newborn. But on it went, on and on and on, inching forward with every convulsion of the mother's body. And no torso was this – it was still neck. A metre of neck! Surely that was enough. I hoped that was the end of it, but it was just gathering itself. Then the child began to give birth to itself (that's the way it seemed), slithering, almost oozing at first but then moving faster, still faster, until it was actually shooting out of her. For a moment I had a nightmare that this was no child, but some gigantic endless turd she was shitting out, a terrible scaly turd that was coming before the baby. But of course it was not. Out it came, rushing now, metre after metre of it, as wide as a man's forearm, then as thick as a man's thigh, enormous, scaly, ghastly.

The midwife backed off screaming with her helpers. The bowls were overturned, the hot water splashing onto the floor. The bloody length of what was obviously a serpent was still shooting out of my darling, coiling itself on the bed until there was no room, and the coils toppled down with a crash onto the floor. The creature reared up into the air, three metres or more, and that face, that squashy baby's face turning around high above us, opened its mouth and wailed.

Angrboda stared up at it, then down to see what was emerging from between her legs, still coming out of her, with a face of fascination, horror and yes, love; still, still, still love. Always love.

It was a mythic moment my friends.

Still it kept coming.

'Where's it all coming from?' I begged, because there was too much snake there for it ever to have been all inside her, she who was, as I say, a slight woman, not big, not fat, with slender bones and muscles. Still it came – perhaps from another dimension, I thought, or one of the other worlds that had somehow linked itself to this one. And then I was beset with another terrible notion – that somehow this gigantic serpent had crept in during the night and invaded my beloved via her female part and devoured our child, whose head was simply the last thing to be

swallowed – for no snake before ever had a human head that I knew of.
I seized hold of a pair of scissors, tools the midwife used for severing the
cord, and I prepared to defend my lover, to attack. But . . .

'This is our son,' cried Angrboda. In my madness at that moment,
I looked around for that son, thinking there was some other, a real
boy, for surely this serpent, this snake, this worm, could be nothing
of me and her. But it was the snake she meant – although how she
knew it was a boy, Odin only knows.

On it went. On and on, the birth. It lasted – how long? An hour?
Ten hours – a day? I have no idea. How long was our child? Again, I
have no idea. The lower reaches of him began to coil into the lake, so
I never saw him whole; but the head stayed with us, that baby mouth
wide open, both hissing and wailing at us in a grief of its own.

At last the birth ended; the tail flicked twice in the air and slith-
ered into the sea. I was trembling from head to foot, blood-spattered,
afraid, lost in my wits.

Angrboda closed her legs and sat up.

'Give him to me,' she commanded.

Who can disobey a mother's first command? I reached out for the
head, but it spat and hissed at me, and I had to cover my eyes to avoid
the venom. Angrboda had pity on me. She reached out one long arm
and gently, gently stroked the creature's side.

'Sweet one,' she crooned. 'My lovely, lovely boy. Come to your
mother.' The snake turned and went to her then, making muffled
little panting noises and little wails.

'Come, come,' murmured Angrboda, cradling the serpent to her
bosom. 'You're safe now, safe with mother and father. Hush, hush!
Sleep, little one . . . sleep.'

I admit I let out a snort at the term, little one, for our son was as
big as a train of elephants. Hadrighada nosed his way to her breast
and began to suckle. Oh dreadful day! Angrboda did not flinch,
although there was venom on those fangs. He must have folded them
safely away, because she came to no harm. She wrapped the bedsheets
around him so that only his baby's head showed, and for an instant he
looked like any normal child, his mother's blood still smeared on his
forehead. Angrboda looked down at him, every inch of her the loving
mother. Then she turned those big, mossy eyes on me.

'Something from your side of the family here, I think,' she said.

That was my Angrboda! She never lost her ability to love or to laugh. We both tossed back our heads and laughed. The serpent rolled his eyes back to look at us. She made me stroke the child so that he knew who his father was. And we sat there a while, mother, father, baby, as if all the world was just as it should be.

'And so what does this one mean?' I whispered after a while.

Then she hung her head. Then she wept. Then her voice trembled with fear. Because ./. .

'The death of Thor,' she told me. And that made my blood run cold, because all the world knows how powerful the god of thunder is; and all the world knows how much his father loves him. And all the world knows that together or apart, either of them would do anything to prevent that death.

'He'll kill the Thunderer?' I asked.

Angrboda shrugged. 'Prophecy is only part cause,' she said. 'Because of him Thor will die. Nothing can be done to change that.'

She made a soft chucking noise between her lips and the serpent slid closer, entwining her in his coils.

'We'd better keep this one inside as well,' she said. 'I'm not sure that Asgard will take too well to our son.'

Only later, after a full hour of feeding, as she sat on the lakeside with our son's head on her lap, the rest of his enormous body coiled under the waters of the lake, did she tell me how so very much serpent had come from so small a womb.

'He comes from the future,' she said. 'He is fleeing his own death.'

And so it is. Our son, who encircles the world, lying in the ocean trenches with his tail in his mouth, encircles time as well. Born fleeing his future death to his own birth, he lives until his death . . . from which he flees back to his birth. It seems right somehow, don't you think?

And we named our child Hadrighada, beloved. It was the gods who called him Jormungandr – great monster.

FENRIR AND FENRA

Yes, each pregnancy stranger than the last. And the final one, the third, was the strangest of all.

It began with a kick. I suppose a great deal of life begins in that way, when the baby first puts its foot into its mother's side. She lets out a slight yelp and perhaps a croon of surprise, depending on where the baby has landed the soft blow. The kick and the croon came early in Angrboda's third pregnancy. And then another, then another. Another and another and another. Soon she was getting kicked from all sides at once. There was a scrum going on in there.

'Twins?' I said hopefully. 'Triplets, perhaps?'

'It feels more like seven or eight,' she replied. She looked up at me with her tired hooded eyes. 'Loki, I think I might be going to whelp.'

The pregnancy went on, with more kicks, more blows. How many were there in there? What were they up to? As the months went by, her belly heaved and crunched, tossed and turned. Sometimes a deep, reverberating growl would rise up from her bowels. I'm not talking indigestion here, although god knows, there was enough of that. I don't think she slept for six months – just little snatches of sleep as the little ones rested in between bouts of – what? Wrestling? Playing catch with the afterbirth? We had no idea.

As the pregnancy advanced, she grew. And grew! My god, she swelled up like a whale. I began to fear that she might split open before her time and spill whatever was in there onto the rushes. By this time we were convinced there were seven or eight young ones in there, but of what kind, of what ilk – of what species – we had no way of knowing.

But gradually, as she entered her eighth month, things began to calm down. She stopped swelling – praise the fates! The kicks subsided. Where there seemed to have been a dozen or more at a time, now there were only two or three at most. And she began to shrink. Yes, in her eighth month, she shrank. What did that mean? The belly began to sleep. It vibrated sometimes, and Angrboda was convinced it was snoring. She would smile beatifically and place my hand on her belly.

'See? The little ones are snoring,' she'd say. How sweet! How delectable. How delicious.

So let us for the third time now venture back into the birthing chamber, where the midwife – a new one this time, no sane nurse would bring themselves back after the birth of Hadrighada – prepares the room. The waters broke – a run of water as clear as a stream. I took it as a good omen, bless me for a fool. Then the contractions. Angrboda screamed and howled and heaved – but in this she was not alone; so did her belly. In fact, it did more than scream. It growled. It roared. It whined and cried. It howled . . . long, liquid howls like nothing you ever heard. It went on for hours, the most awful noise and certainly no noise any child ever made. When finally our third child was pushed out, it was no surprise to any of us. First a nose, as black and as wet as a seal's head, and not much smaller either. Then the snout, the long snout, snarling even as it emerged from the maw of her sex. The lips curled and twisted and underneath, the teeth, sharp as knives already, long as knives too, some of them. When Fenrir emerged from the womb, he didn't so much as flop down, squeezed out like icing from a bag – he leapt from the womb, tearing his mother's flesh as he did it. He didn't lie down, not he – he was off to the end of the bed, where he sat and licked the blood off himself with every sign of pleasure. He bit the midwife, who ran off out of the room, followed closely by her assistants. Then I think he might have turned on me, but Angrboda called to him and he calmed down. Then he cleaned his mother up from the birth. Then he devoured his first meal; his own afterbirth.

As Fenrir curled up and fell asleep by his mother's side, the contractions started again. Another pup was born – a slower, more conventional birth this time. A wolf pup, like Fenrir, a bitch this time, who we named Fenra, after her maternal grandmother. A small, plump creature, with no teeth and eyes not yet open, just like any other pup, apparently, if born to the wrong species.

There were many mysteries surrounding the births. Why had so many feet – or hands or paws – pummelled her from the inside so early on? Why had she swelled so wide and then stopped growing and begun to shrink? We wondered about that, but the clue came out with the afterbirth; a jawbone, a small wee thing. And later, examining Fenrir's first shit, I found teeth – some of human children, some of wolf cubs. The answer was clear: the little fiend had devoured his brothers and sisters whilst still in the womb. Such a ferocious little wolf! Only Fenra survived. Why? I have no idea. To this day, I have no idea.

'She is his opposite,' was all Angrboda said. And that was enough. Apparently.

Fenrir spurned the breast of his mother and turned at once to meat – fresh meat, with the blood still warm in it, by preference. Angrboda fed his one remaining sibling, Fenra, at the breast, but her milk was in such copious quantities, enough to feed seven or eight, I suppose, that she had to draw much of it off. She served it in huge bowls to Fenrir himself, and I took some, too – why not, I loved every part of her. But the milk gave me vivid dreams, dreams of things to come that I didn't want, so I gave it up. It made me understand a little, perhaps, of why Hel and Hadrighada had such strange eyes. They too had fed off Angrboda. Therefore, they must know something of things to come.

'So what does this one mean? Whose death does he foretell?' I asked her, when things had calmed down somewhat.

Angrboda turned a face to me as pale as ash.

'Odin's death,' she said. And oh, how I felt my heart sink then. 'We have to leave, Loki,' she said. 'We have to hide. If Tyr and Thor or the Allfather discover our children, they will kill them.'

And she never said a truer word, except perhaps, there should have been no 'if' in that sentence. It was purely a question of when.

THE IRONWOOD

If you raise your gaze skyward on a sunny day, you may see high above you a tiny dot. If that black dot descends far enough, it may become a pair of black wings, spread like a cloak under the day. If so, that will be Huginn or Muninn, Thought or Memory, Odin's ravens, flying overhead, seeking out the doings of the world to report back to their master in Valhalla. You may hear their call, that odd, grunting call that I may liken to that of a pig; when pigs shall fly.

You may; but then again most likely not, Shite-in-Flight, because what possible interest could you have for the Allfather, the Allknowing, or his regents, Thor and Tyr, who now rule in his name over the Seven Worlds? You have no secrets he hasn't heard a million times already. You have no future — not one of any length anyway. Eat, drink and be merry, for tomorrow you die — maybe even this very afternoon. But for me, for Angrboda, for all of Asgard, the ravens are frequent companions — far more than they used to be, back in the days when Odin was himself. They report back to Tyr nowadays, and Tyr likes to keep an obsessive eye on his friends and relatives as well as his enemies. How appropriate that it is the raven, flesh gobbler, battle feaster, corpse lover, the longest lived of all birds, that they have chosen as his eyes to wander the worlds.

Our son was an augury of Odin's death. Angrboda was right. We had to hide. But where could we hide? Where could anyone hide from the far-seeing eyes of Huginn and Muminn?

I had no idea, although of course Angrboda did: the Ironwood, that mythical Ur-forest, where I was born long ago – so long ago that it seemed like a dream to me even then. That dense spread of mountains and ancient trees that no human, or god or Jotun had trod since I had left and my family had passed on. Ironwood belonged to the wolves these days. Not your wolves, Arse-born, such small, soft, furry beasts. Jotun wolves, dire-wolves, huge beasts, savage monsters who fought continually among themselves and killed and dismembered everything that breathed.

'So they say,' said Angrboda evenly, when I pointed this out. 'Maybe it is the density of the trees that makes it so hard for the ravens to see under their branches. Maybe it is the fact that the wolves have hated the ravens since the beginning of time. Maybe Odin likes to spread rumours about the one place where his flying eyes do not go. Whatever, my pretty red-headed boy, it is to the Ironwood we must go, since it is the one place that will be safe for us.

'Will it work?' I asked her. 'Will our children live? Prophesy for me, Angrboda.'

'They will all live,' she said without hesitation.

'And me?' I asked. I did not think, despite his pleas of brotherhood, that the Old Man would be happy with me fathering creatures that prophesied the fall of his line.

'You will live, Loki,' she said.

I sighed; that was good to know. I knew better than to ask about her. When she turned her eye inward to herself, she always saw a blank – so she told me, anyway. I have reason to doubt that, now, as I say. Maybe it was her choice to keep her fate to herself. If so, that was something I chose to respect.

Outwardly we kept our day-to-day life going as usual; we made our preparations in secret. Seed was sown, the harvest taken in. Feast days came and went, and our mortal serfs lived and died. Above us in the skies the ravens circled. We adopted three children from our serfs, two boys and a girl, to show a family.

Then, at the spring equinox, Odin came to visit. You can believe we were worried then. The Old Man sat hunched in his chair, his face crescents of hair, his head down, muttering into his plate. Tyr sat by him, grim-faced Tyr, who kept watch over him like a hawk, occasionally bending to whisper something in the direction of his ear. He hated having to bring the Old Man to us, because he knew Angrboda foresaw and understood everything he did; all his plans and secrets were naked before her. But occasionally Odin, who was lost most of the time in worlds where even Angrboda could not go, would land for a few minutes, maybe even as long as an hour, in this one. Then his head would come up and he would smile and talk, knowing us and who we were and what we did. How Tyr hated that! If the Old Man gave an order then, he dare not disobey.

One such moment came. The head came up and the eye glittered fiercely at me. Odin put down his meat and peered across at me.

'You're going home, then,' he said.

I leaned back. He knew! . . . but how much? I flinched, but Angrboda answered smoothly.

'Yes, Allfather, to the Ironwood.'

Tyr was sitting there, rigid with the weight of all our secrets hanging in the air.

'Nothing but wolves there now,' he said, hoping, no doubt, to hear more before Odin eclipsed into some other universe. 'Your family died long ago, didn't they, Loki?'

'I still have family there,' I told him. 'Among the wolves.' It was a lie – just to scare him and throw him off the scent.

Tyr grimaced with the desire to know. Odin looked across at him and laughed at him – throwing back his head like it was the old days, when he knew me all day, and not just from moment to moment.

'Ah, Tyr, what *are* they up to?' he laughed. Then he leaned suddenly forward and gripped my shoulder like a hawk in his bony hand.

'It's good to know how it will end,' he told me, smiling. He patted my shoulder.

Poor Tyr was shitting himself. 'How will what end?' he growled. But no one was taking any notice of him.

'None of it will be changed,' said Angrboda. 'Even our trying to change it cannot be changed,' she added. A cloud, a cloud perhaps a universe or two wide, passed across the Old Man; he bent his face down to his plate again and began a low growling noise, lost again in a place no one could ever follow him.

'What will end?' demanded Tyr, half rising in his seat. It was a kind of threat.

'What use are all your strategies when none of it changes even one second?' demanded Angrboda. She rose, her face red, tears in her eyes, and left. Tyr strode after her and outside they had an argument – much shouting and banging of doors. But of course she never told him what he wanted to know.

I stayed inside with my old friend, for old time's sake. I was hoping for another few moments of his time here on earth with me. I cut his meat for him on his plate and pushed the food into his mouth, lifted the cup to his lips. Allknowing, Allfather, Allpowerful, but he often forgot to eat and drink. I won a few smiles that night, and some frowns. He clasped my shoulder once again, looked into my eyes and shook his head sadly. But I didn't ask him what that meant, and I didn't ask Angrboda either the next day. Knowing did neither of them any good that I could see, and if everything that will happen is going to happen regardless of what we do, all we have left is to surprise ourselves. Don't you think?

Later, I sought out Tyr. He was not in his room. No surprise there. No one ever saw him sleep, not that I knew of. He was outside Odin's room, spear in hand . . . as if there was any reason there to guard anything. As if he would be any use anyway.

'No passage,' he grunted.

'I've come to see you, not him,' I said.

He grunted, turned away – eyes front like a soldier, rather than the general he was.

'What more do you want, Tyr?' I asked him. 'I'm out of Asgard. Let us be.'

Tyr didn't move his head – barely moved his lips.

'I follow orders,' he said.

'You lie,' I told him. 'Do you think I don't know lies? I invented them.'

He stood, stock still in the half-light. I left him to it, but I had gone no more than a couple of steps when he spoke again.

'He has many worlds to deal with,' he said quietly. I paused in case there was more, but there was no more, so I left him to it.

It was Odin he was talking about — as if the poor drooling fool had any kind of plan for this little world among the billions he had inside him. At the time, I believed Tyr could have put an end to the dangers that gathered round us with a word, but since then I doubt what I thought I knew. Perhaps it was Odin after all . . . perhaps the Lord of All has plans we cannot see. Perhaps he has, after all, found a way to change the iron will of creation. If so, those plans are beyond my ken, and yours, Arse-born. And what we cannot understand, we cannot talk of.

So Odin knew where we were going — but how much more did he know? Our three adopted serf children had helped serve at the table, we showed them to the gods as our own, while our true family remained hidden. Of course, there was no fooling the Allfather . . . but what he knew, how much he knew, when he knew it and if he knew whether it was true here or somewhere else . . . that was another matter.

We continued with our plans, hiding our children, preparing for the move. Keeping Hel out of sight was an easy matter, as I say — she moved at night and lived happily underground. Hadrighada was not so hard, either — he lived beneath the sea much of the time, only emerging at night to join us. Fenra was good — she ran off during the day to play in the woods, or spent time sitting at her mother's feet — learning, Angrboda said, although I never knew what exactly that learning was. But Fenrir was another matter. If you left the door open a crack he was off, off like the wind. A creature like that was never made for the indoors. There was nothing we could do to keep him hidden at our pleasant home in the Swedish valleys. We had to hope that Tyr would mistake him for a common wolf, despite his enormous size.

A year passed. Fenrir was born in the depths of winter, so we had to wait a full year until the nights were long and dark. Then, on the night of no moon, we set off to make the strange journey into and across Jǫtunheimr to the Ironwood, where the dire-wolves ruled and made their home.

There are many stories I could tell you about the long journey of Loki and Angrboda and their children, step by step through the long dark of those winter nights, hidden, in fear, two gods, refugees in their own creation. We had many encounters, many adventures, all of them in disguise.

Those tales, like so many more, are for another time. Our main issue, to be honest, was of course Fenrir. Hadrighada needed the sea – no, not the sea – the ocean. We left him in there, in the deeps, to grow and flourish, feasting on the whales that came up north to feed, growing vast and unthinkable out of sight where he could come to no harm. Hel was no problem – she never was, so long as she had a pet to keep her company, living or dead, she didn't mind which. Fenra was easy too. She spent most of her time at Angrboda's side – still learning. When I became irritated and finally asked *what* she was learning, Angrboda shrugged lightly.

'What is to come, and where to be when it arrives,' she said.

Understand, Arse-born – there is an art to this being in the right place at the right time. Fenra, it seems, was some kind of princess of navigation, of migration, of journeys, of messages. If you see her, you will know something is afoot. She was her mother's child in so many ways, and it annoyed me, the amount of time she spent with her, even coming with us to the bed. She was no ordinary wolf. Although she had no words, she had the eyes of a knowing beast.

But Fenrir, her brother – he, as always, was another matter. He hunted of course – that's nature, although his appetite was prodigious, and he was growing so fast I sometimes wondered if he was going to erupt from his own skin. The main matter was with the killing, though. Fenrir loved the killing – the feeling of a life ending between his jaws, the hot spurt of the death-blood pumping. And I was not fond of killing and nor was Angrboda. What can I say? We did our best. Angrboda taught him not to kill except for food, and he stuck to it often. His sister, Fenra, helped, I think. With her, it was only food that died, a few mistakes notwithstanding.

Yes, Fenrir was a true Aesir in this sense – they all admired killing, including Odin, who perhaps loved violent death more than any
of them. It's a shame they never learned to embrace him as one of
their own. For my part, I never saw the glamour or the glory – only
the universe cut short of another wonder. The fact is, Arse-born, I was
before my time. In your age I would make a better god, more suitable
for purpose. Like you, I prefer to solve my problems with life intact.
We are alike, don't you think? Jaw-jaw is better than war-war, as one
of your leaders once said. We prefer to talk, to negotiate, to arrive at
a mutual conclusion. Of course, en route we may play games, we may
trick, we may even deceive – knowing full well that our interlocutor
will be doing the same. But in the end a deal is a deal and we know
how to stick to them. Yes, I made a wonderful negotiator in my time,
I would make a better one in yours. The Aesir thought of it as coward-
ice, of course. But I like to think that the men and women of the
modern age would know better.

Suffice to say we made it intact to the Ironwood. Then we had to
establish ourselves there – which could be no easy matter. The wolves
of the Ironwood had a fearsome reputation and it was well earned.
The first thing they tried to do, as soon as we approached the first
trees, was to kill us, just as they had killed all previous intruders who
came near their kingdom. A pack of them came charging out at us at
dawn, their favoured time for an ambush.

The wolves of Ironwood elect their leader through battle, and
they obey that leader without question or quarter. Their current
leader, Vanagandr, had ruled over the Ironwood from time before
mind. He was at their head as they came ploughing through the
snow, leaping over the fallen trees.

What can I say? – our arrival marked the end of that rule. I
remember it well. It was early spring, dawn, as we approached the
black trees. The wolves of Ironwood approached at terrible speed, too
fast even for the eye to follow across the white white snow, when a
dark shadow leapt from behind us. A moment later, Vanagandr lay in
the dirt on his back, the foot of Fenrir on his chest.

'Fenrir!' barked Angrboda – for she had seen the slaver in his jaws
and knew how keen he was to taste the life's blood of his rival. But

the wolves, for all their mercilessness, hold fast and true to their own laws. Defeat was enough for them; death would be held against us. And Fenrir, give him his due, held back till the old leader had begged for life. Then he lifted up his paw and stood still as a rock, while his lesser brethren gathered around him to sniff and learn the smell of their new regime.

Fenrir, though he was always painted as a savage who knew no quarter and gave none, granted life at the moment he took his place as Lord of the Wolves of Ironwood.

A good start – a great start, you may say. And yet it was a wasted journey. All that way, all that time – to no avail. We had placed Fenrir exactly where he ought to be, at the head of the Jotun wolves. Fenra, his gentle sister, ruled with him. If he was the teeth, she was the brains. As is the way with wolves, it was the she-wolf who led them in the hunt, organised their tactics, delegated the work. With these two ruling the roost, the wolves of Ironwood thrived like never before.

Hadrighada had his place in the deep oceans; only Hel now needed her place in the world, then we could rest. And we had our plans for her, with the help of the wolves. The fact is, no creature with life in its veins was happy around our daughter, nor was she happy with us. But there was a place for her – a kingdom, in fact. One that lay deep under the roots of Yggdrasil, deep down, where the shadows of the once-living sank after death and made their home. At that time they lived in a democracy of the dead; we vowed, with the help of her brother Fenrir and the wolves he now ruled, to take her down and give her a throne beneath the earth, away from the draughts and dangers of life, where she could be happy at last and rule, as Hadrighada ruled under the oceans, as Fenrir ruled in the Ironwood. Hel needed her place as Queen of Death.

But before we got there, we had news that stopped us in our tracks. Word of Odin. Apparently, under the guidance of Tyr, god of war, he had begun to amass an army. His soldiers were the fallen dead.

You may wonder at his choice of warriors. Odin always had a fascination with death, it only grew with time. After he had excavated the beginnings of things for the runes and learned how to make them speak, he began to spend a lot of time down with the dead boys, fascinated by that journey from which so few ever find a return ticket. He stopped soon enough, discovering that the dead have few secrets of interest and that their existence is duller, if anything, than that of the living. But now he had found a new use for them; an army of the slain, an invincible army of warriors who had died in battle, men and women who could not ever be killed, being dead already.

As soon as we heard about it, Angrboda sighed, sat down and laid her hands into her lap. She spent a moment in thought, and all of us there paused a moment, waiting to hear what was being revealed to her – the wolves of Ironwood, defeated Vanagandr, even Fenrir, who feared nothing and no one, poor fool – all fell quiet for his mother's spell. At last she lifted her head and spoke.

'He knows about our children. So you must go to Asgard, Loki, and negotiate with him for our lives. We have done our best. Now we must throw ourselves on his mercy.'

Uproar! Uproar on all sides. Give up without a fight? Fenrir could not bear the idea. Never, he roared. Never. I was up in arms about it – why should we, we had an army of our own? – although in my heart I knew the answer. I had brought the answer out of the mountains myself: the hammer of Thor. The wolves of Ironwood howled like the wind in a quarry. Never had one of them made a single deal. They fought and won, and one day maybe they would lose. That was all they knew.

But Angrboda was immovable. None of our roaring moved her an inch. I must go and she must stay with Fenrir and Fenra and Hel and the wolves of Ironwood, and wait for my return with whatever deal I could manage.

THE JUDGEMENT OF ODIN

My journey to Asgard was quicker than the long slog across land and sea that I made with my family. For solidarity I had to stay with them on the ground, of course, but on my own I flew on my falcon wings, fast, fast, fast. Even so, it took me a week, flying through air and the void between the worlds. When I landed in the courtyard of my old house, they were expecting me. Sigyn was there, pleased to see me. Apparently. She had been sent, perhaps, by Tyr. An omen I tried to ignore. She had our sons, Narfi and Vali with her — trying, I think, to show me the difference between the children she gave me and those I had with Angrboda — as if love for your own was about a pretty face!

But listen; I loved my kin. I always loved my kin. You do not understand me if you do not know how much I love my kin. But do not doubt in any way at all that I loved Hel, Hadrighada and Fenrir and Fenra as much as Narfi and Vali — maybe more, because, like me, they suffered for who they were. My sons with Sigyn were pretty children, blue eyes, blonde hair, all the things the gods thought beauty should be. They have suffered too, of course, through their association with me. But my children with Angrboda have always been special. They were – they are. They always will be.

The gods are cruel. I never was. I ask only that you remember that.

I went to eat and bathe and greet my family – a quiet time. Narfi and Vali were well grown, strong young men now. They had not developed attributes – alas for them. But they were strong, healthy and happy enough to be living among the gods. We spent a pleasant afternoon, and in the evening they left us to take part in the games, they said. Sporty boys – not like their father. Then Sigyn took me to her bed where we played those games that people love to play, the first time I had been with another for a century or more. I made it clear to her that I was not a man of Asgard any more. No tears were shed on either side. She asked me questions about my life with Angrboda; I kept my council. I knew well enough where my answers would go.

Then, as twilight fell, a noise arose from the plain before our home. A roar, a distant clash. I knew that sound, I had heard it before too many times. Battle!

I jumped out of bed. Who had managed to break past the great wall? Who had brought such an army? Who would dare!

Sigyn remained in bed, her hands folded on her lap. 'Don't worry, there's no enemy,' she said.

'But it sounds . . .' I didn't finish. It sounded so real. I could hear screams amid the hubbub.

'It's just games,' she said. 'They're practising. We can go and see, if you like.'

I wasn't sure that I did like, but I was curious. What sort of games sounded like this? There was real agony there! But listening closely, yes . . . there was also cheering and applause. So we went along . . . and, Arse-born! What a sight I saw that day! May you never see such a sight in your short lives.

On a great plain a million men, women and children fought like demons to the death. The ground was red with gore, the rivers and streams flowed with it. Dead and dying lay scattered on the ground, the dying clutching their innards into their bellies, clutching at their severed limbs, their lifeblood gushing and oozing from their gaping wounds. The air was thick with the stink of blood, the clash of sword on shield, the groans and pleas and screams of the dead and dying. Above the melee the Valkyries, who in mortal battle collect the souls of the slain for Odin, swooped and played as usual, but this time there were no spirits or souls for them to catch, for the dead have already given up their souls. As far as the eye could see, that awful game unfolded.

'But what are the sides? Who can win?' I asked, clutching my shawl to my face to cloak the stink of it.

'There are no winners, no losers,' said Sigyn. 'They will fight to the last one standing. Overnight they will reform, every one of them, and spend the day feasting in Odin's halls. Tomorrow, the battle will begin again.'

I stared at the fighting. From horizon to horizon, the immortal armies fought. The horror!

'How often, then?' I said. 'How long for?'

Sigyn turned her face away from the wind. 'Every night, till the world ends,' she said.

In the centre of that vast field was a kind of circular stadium, and there they were, the Aesir and Vanir, spectators at a sport that had no end, no winners, only losers. At the top of it all, sat the Lord and Chief of the Worlds, Odin himself, waited on by Tyr and his sons — the architects, no doubt, of this endless slaughter. Below him, in concentric rings, the gods and goddesses drank and ate and watched. From time to time one of them would step out into the fighting to show their skills — several thousand years of practice tend to make a better swordsman than any mortal ever could be. There stepped Hoenir with his bright sword, cutting them down like corn and leaving them legless on the ground, begging for their end. There stepped Frigg, Mother Goddess, plucking off their heads like fruit. And look — mighty Thor casts his hammer among them, and a swathe of dead ten miles out and ten miles back, smudged red with blood, opens up among the mortals struggling before him.

So this was Odin's army of the dead. Arse-born, I felt sick — I could not join them, although Sigyn advised that it was politic to do so. My stomach couldn't bear it. My sons were there too, and I made it my business to go to them and suggest they leave, if they had anything of their father about them. Vali wouldn't hear of it – he was having too much fun; the bloodlust was in him. But Narfi, always the gentler of the two, came away with me.

'I know somewhere you may find it more to your taste,' he said. He led me away from that awful place to Freya's sacred meadow, Fólkvangr. What a contrast I saw there! Trestles had been set up. There were games – true games. Running, playing, singing. Skalds sang, there was food and drink, there was love. And in the middle of it, the Lady Freya, who your priests call slut and whore, sat with her brother.

'Loki! Welcome!' They got up and embraced me and my boy. We were given something to eat and drink. Know, Arse-born, that the Lady Freya receives a full half of all the warriors who die on the battlefield – a full half. I urge you, mortal – when your end comes, pray that you die a straw death and sink down to the underworld, where at least you will be safe from pain. But if your turn comes at the end of a weapon of any kind, do what you can to convince the Valkyrie to carry you to Freya and not Odin, unless you want an eternity of fear and pain, and death after death after death. May your death be singular, long and comfortable.

The time was that those who died violent deaths had a similar fate, feasting forever in Odin's halls. So why had things gone so terribly wrong?

'Is it Tyr's idea of fun?' I asked them.

'Tyr has Odin's ear,' agreed Frey. But Freya shook her head.

'Tyr or Odin himself, who knows?' she said. 'It has been going on for decades now. Who knows how or even if it will end?'

'But why?' I asked. 'What purpose can it have?'

But neither of them had any idea. If there was a plan, it was being kept quiet.

I spent some time, a pleasant hour or two, in the company of the Vanir, the gentler and kinder gods. Pity yourselves, mortals, that in that early war so long ago that I told you of at the start of my tale, it was the Aesir and not they who took the upper hand. Your lives, and your afterlives, would have been the better for it.

*   *   *

In the morning I went to put our case to Odin.

I did not fear for my own life. Odin had sworn brotherhood with me and even he, Lord of Creation, could not break an oath like that. Such oaths are deep magic, bound to the roots of creation. I did not fear for Angrboda, either — she was one of us. Even Odin, surely, would not commit deicide. It was the children we were scared for. Each one of them, a portent of divine death. Angrboda had said they would live. What fate, then, had Odin in store for them?

I was prepared to give it my best shot.

It was a formal do. Before then, we always talked as men together, not as lord to chattel. Now I was shown through to a compound with a locked door where Tyr himself stood guard at the entrance, smart and neat, with a red robe over his shoulders that reached almost to the ground and a winged helmet with dyed eagle plumes. 'You vain man,' I thought. I kept that one to myself but couldn't resist . . .

'That helmet'll be handy in a close-up fight,' I muttered as I went past. I know! My mouth — it works all by itself sometimes. Tyr said nothing, just stood there to attention like the grim soldier he was. Inside, the Old Man was alone — another surprise. I thought Thor would be with him, I turned to see Tyr, but he had waited outside — under orders, no doubt, because he was always desperate to whisper in the Old Man's ear.

So I stood before my old friend, my brother, alone. How he had changed since the old days when we and the world were young! Curled up, his one eye shining like a wet stone in its socket. He had begun to bald, his hair was turning from grey to white despite the apples, of which no doubt he had his share and more. Yes, eternal youth was pitted against all-knowingness, and all-knowingness was winning the race; every new world added a white hair to his beard, a new wrinkle to his skin. Hair grew all over his body now, curling up his tunic front, out of his cuffs, around his ankles. He already looked more like some kind of seed-head than a man. But he was there that day — sitting on his rough wooden throne with his ravens by his head, a great wolf at his feet, his face twisted round to regard me. Out of all the possible worlds inside that shattered brain of his, it seemed that he had somehow contrived to be there with me that day, at that moment. Bless me, I thought it boded well!

I put our case. We were a family. Not a simple one, but a family for all that. We were in love – not something that could be said for many of the gods and goddesses in Asgard at that time. Our children were conceived in love. He nodded. I told him they were raised in love to be loving, and he smiled in his beard. I told him about each one of them in detail, how none of them had any argument with the gods; how they may be augurs but they were not the *causes* of fate.

He smiled. He turned his head and nodded to someone nearby but when I looked, there was no one there. I faltered. There he was in the room with me; and yet he was not there. Now he was watching to one side of me. I raised my hand and he focussed on me again, squinting.

'Why not embrace them?' I pressed on. 'Why not make them a part of our clan? I pointed out how another one of my children, the horse Sleipnir, had come into the fold. Why not the others too? Gods could have monsters to work for them. He had ravens, he had eagles and wolves – we all knew he loved his beasts. Why not a great serpent in the depths? Why not a wolf stronger than all other wolves? Why not a Queen of the Dead?

Why not? I knew I could guarantee their loyalty.

Odin opened his mouth, like a burr splitting, showing his thin black lips. 'Your children shall be spared,' he said, in a voice like the dried leaves underfoot. His voice seemed to come from another place, far, far away, as if some trick of time and space alone was letting me hear him. In my stupid heart I rejoiced at his words. 'And so will you,' he added. And suddenly my heart sank like a stone.

'And Angrboda?' I said – she for whom I had the least fear.

Odin smiled, that grim, curious little smile he has when he greets death.

'Your children shall be spared,' he repeated. And I knew then – I knew.

'She's one of us,' I said.

'It will be quick,' he said. And his head dropped down. The interview was over.

'Quick? What use is quick?' I hissed. I seized him by the arm, but somehow my hand slipped off him, as if he was – somehow – not there, even as he stood in front of me, even as I felt his breath on my face.

'But we're brothers,' I said. It wasn't possible. Even he – even he! – could not dispose of the oaths we made as lightly as this.

He lifted his head again – and there was that little smile – a mocking kind of smile.

'In your world, Loki,' he whispered. 'Where you are, I swore. But I am . . . elsewhere. Elsewhere . . .'

Then I understood. Only in this world did his oath hold true.

'You tricked me. You tricked me. You tricked us all,' I gasped.

Odin looked back at me and smiled. From somewhere there was a chuckle, or the ghost of a chuckle, in the dimensions within and between the atoms . . . in the vast gaps between the stars and galaxies . . . within my thoughts, in my veins, in my blood.

I turned and ran. He could do anything, now. He was capable of it, too. On the way I passed Tyr, standing to attention at the door. He did not meet my eye, as if he were just a mere attendant.

'You did this,' I hissed. 'You're behind it all.'

He stood still as a statue, so I seized him by his arm. He turned to look then, first at my hand, then at me.

'The Allfather picks his advice from a hundred million Tyrs,' he said. I stared at him dumbly for a moment. I had heard not Tyrs, but tears. Surely I heard correctly!

'Tell him to spare her, brother,' I begged. I paused, then got down on a knee. 'Do you want me to beg? Then I'll beg. He'll listen to you. Please, brother. She's one of us,' I croaked.

Tyr shook his head. 'She is the mother of death and you are the father of lies. What good did you think could ever come of the two of you?' His cold face, his mouth a hard line under his nose.

I stood up and was about to leave – but then I realised I had said nothing to Odin about the slaughter of the night before. I had promised Frey and Freya I would ask. I made to go back into the hall, but Tyr blocked my way.

'Your audience is over,' he said. Audience indeed! I could have words to say about that. But it was not the time.

'Tyr . . . that fighting. That endless fighting,' I said. 'So much pain. You must stop it . . . night after night . . . There's no need for it, surely.'

Tyr shook his head; there was no emotion visible on his face.

'One day, Surtr will come to claim back his eye. On that day . . .' he began. But I knew — I knew as soon as he said the name Surtr. I cried out.

'Are you mad? You must be mad, Tyr,' I cried. 'You want to fight Surtr! He will wipe us away like snot on the back of his hand. It's pointless! You must know that . . .!'

'In ten thousand years, who knows?' he said.

'In a million years! He is a universal force. We . . . we are all just to be born and die. Even us, Tyr. Even you. Even Odin.'

'The Allfather has given his orders,' grated Tyr. His face closed; the talking was over.

'They will die in agony every day for eternity, then,' I said. But he refused to say more, just stood there to attention like a thing turned to stone. I left him to it and headed back to see to my own.

I went back to my home in a hurry, you can believe that. My own wings were not good enough. Instead I entered Odin's stable, in the home of the Allfather himself, to get my son — wonderful Sleipnir. I would take a son to save my lover. They say that he would allow none but Odin on his back, but he knew his mother well enough and in a second we were flying over the land, through the voids, across dimensions. The journey that had taken me a year on foot, and a week in the air, took me one day on the back of fleet Sleipnir.

I saw the hammer blows in the rock, the raw craters. I saw the felled trees, hectares of them lying flat as if a mountain from the void had crashed down into them. I knew why Thor had not been at his father's side. Ironwood lay bare, every tree down, every rock shattered. The bodies of the wolves were hidden under the fallen timber, but you could smell them by their thousands. Such destruction — for one goddess? It was terrible to see. I did not have to search for long. I came to our house, the place we had made under a great rock, facing the sun with its back rooms in the heart of the mountain and a secret way through deep into the earth. It had been crushed, scorched, destroyed utterly – the rock turned into rubble, the rubble to gravel, the gravel to sand.

And there I found her body – the body of my own true love. Oh, Angrboda, when was there another woman like you? So wise, so all-seeing, so full of news, good things and bad. You never judged, you only saw, but your vision alone was enough to finish you off.

She knew. She knew when she sent me off. Thor would kill me if he caught me, with or without his father's word. He has many reasons held in his heart against me. She saved my life and denied me the right to try to save hers.

Her end had not been a simple one. Raped. It was always the Thunderer's way with women, the rape. I suppose it is a matter of subjugation. Perhaps the violence excites him. Tortured. Odin had promised me she would have a quick death; he had lied. But why? I did not understand at first. I supposed that Thor had overstepped the mark, gone against orders in his passion for murder and destruction. Nothing of the kind had ever been done before to a god or goddess. What was so special about Angrboda?

It was long after at a certain feast in the halls of Aegir, the sea god, that I learned why when I questioned the thunder god.

'Secrets,' he said.

'What secrets?'

'How to avoid our end, when the end comes. What do you think?' he asked, astonished that I had not worked it out.

'Did you sanction this?' I demanded, turning to Odin himself. And the Old Man rocked in his seat. Perhaps he heard me, or a whisper of me, in whatever far-off galaxy he was living just then. Perhaps he felt a pang of guilt for his lies.

Of course he sanctioned it. Angrboda was his superior in her vision of what is to come. Of course he would want to pull secrets from her like teeth before she died.

'But she did not tell, Loki,' said Thor. 'She died bravely. Know this, and be proud.'

I could not disguise my contempt and hatred. I ignored Thor and spoke instead directly to Odin.

'You're a fool,' I told him. 'There is no avoiding the end. Your fate and mine are as fixed as if they already happened, you should know that.'

'There was a chance,' grated Thor to the back of my head. 'If anyone knew, it would be her.'

'So what did you learn, great Thor, when you questioned the Queen of Things to Come? What did she tell, Thor?'

And I swear that his hand quivered on his cup as he buried his nose in his ale. Angrboda must have told him of his own fate, and it was not going to be a pretty one.

'Will you die as bravely as her?' I said, leaning forward and whispering in his huge red face.

He stared at me and trembled. Like all bullies, he lived in fear. You see what I'm up against? These people, these gods. We all live under them.

My grief that day knew no bounds. It was a betrayal of a kind that can never be forgotten, never forgiven. I knew then that the hatred of the gods knew no bounds. I searched among the ruins for many days, looking for clues as to what had happened to my beloved children. None of the dire-wolves of Ironwood had survived to tell the tale, there were no witnesses, no stories to be told, no myths begotten from the murder of a god. Thor made sure of that. Odin would go to any lengths to protect himself, and his reputation as all-wise, but against what? We can only guess what dreadful fate befalls him in some worlds, maybe in this one, too. He deserves the worst that can befall him.

Of Fenrir and Fenra and Hel, there was no sign. Our beloved son Hadrighada lived in the deeps. I could only hope he was still there. I searched long and hard for the others, but with no luck. For all I knew, Odin had lied again when he said they would be spared.

I took her broken remains in my arms and carried her away from that place of destruction back to our old home in Sweden, our true home where we had been happy for a while. I buried her there by the gentle waters, where the sea laps against the shore in a sheltered cove she used to love.

There I built myself a little cottage, a place to stay and to mourn. I had no taste for Asgard, you can believe that. And yes – my heart

4

was full of revenge for a while, I admit it. But what could *I* do? – one little god, full of cleverness and mischief, of course, but what use are cleverness and mischief against those with the real power – the great ones, the powerful and mighty? – those with the weapons, those who write the history books, those who control the stories? To them it is given that they shall do as they will. To us, the little people, you and I – we can only find our ways in and under and between their feet.

BOOK FIVE

THE SUN, THE SUN, THE SUN

The darkness is all around us, and yet still we are not finished! Yes, Arse-born, there are stories yet to tell, and I alone can tell them. The future unfolds, turning a billion promises into one immutable past, but we can only know what is visible to us. The gods possess time itself, past, present and future, but what if we could steal a little bit of it from them? What if we could make our own past, and from it, build our own future?

Does that seem wrong to you? Do not believe that because I love tricks I don't know the truth. The gods will tell you there is a great difference, but I am not so sure. Perhaps you are finding that out for yourself.

Yes, there shall be light before the darkness comes again. Nothing is over until great Surtr comes to show us that existence itself is nothing more than a spark in the night.

But before the light, as ever — the darkness.

THE UNDERWORLD

Let me tell you the stories of the children of Loki. First, that of my beautiful son Hadrighada, renamed by the gods Jormungandr, vast monster.

One day in autumn, it was, when the fish were on the move and I was after them. I stood in the shallows casting my net, when the surface of the water began to tremble, to shake. Little wavelets began to form; foam gathered in the dimples. Soon, the whole cove, land and sea alike, began to shake and quiver.

I thought it was – what? An earthquake? A tsunami? It was neither. As I stood quaking on the shore, a word began to form on the air. It was a word spoken not by any throat or on any lips or tongue. It was a voice that arose out of the water itself as, vibrating against the air, it created sound. A roar that formed itself into a word.

'Father,' said the sea. 'Father.'

'Hadrighada,' I cried.

'Is it safe?' asked the sea. And bless me, I said yes.

Then he came – Hadrighada, rising out of the waters, a tear (I like to think) in the corner of his vast eye, as he turned his gaze from me to the grave of his lost mother.

But as he rose another came – rocketing out of the west at such speed that the air cracked and the wind wept. A chariot; two blazing goats before it. A man as tall as a tree, red beard flowing, arm raised. Yes! – mighty Thor. All this time I had been watched. They had spied on me, waiting, waiting. Now was their moment – so they believed.

'Watch out!' I cried. But my son, his vast head and half a mile of neck coiled already above the water, turned to watch. Thor screeched by him and hurled his hammer . . .

And Hadrighada . . . Hadrighada . . . he caught it. In his teeth.

I remember Thor's face, who was travelling fast, as he turned his head to watch. Mighty Thor, like a fool at the fairground who just lost all his money at a cheap trick. Mighty Thor, wonder of the hammer . . . suddenly cast as nothing.

He turned and I think he was about to flee. But Jormungandr, who was still rising out of the water – there were two or maybe three miles of him coiled about – who can judge such things? – he flipped out his tail and caught the Thunderer's chariot, so that the whole thing tipped arse over tit and splash! – into the drink went the great warrior.

'Little Thor,' hissed the serpent my son, when the bedraggled red head emerged from the water. 'You will leave my family alone hence-forth, will you not?'

Thor, splashing in the shallows, looked up at his hammer which was twitching in my son's jaws – the hammer that nothing before, from a range of mountains to the solid earth itself, had even slowed down, let alone kept from his hand.

He coughed and nodded. 'I give you . . . I give you my word,' he said.

'That doesn't count for a lot,' I said.

Hadrighada nodded and turned to look at me – blaming me, I think, because he had been ambushed.

'Sorry,' I muttered. 'He must have been hiding.'

Thor coughed again. 'Can I have my hammer back, please?' he said.

Hadrighada dropped the hammer, which sailed back into his hand. He held it and twitched. I could see what he was thinking . . . one last throw . . .?

'Best not,' I said.

He nodded, clambered back into his chariot . . . and fled, the great Thor – fled the scene of his most miserable defeat. Leaving behind nothing more than a dirty smell. Because – yes, yes. The mighty Thor had shat his breeks.

So what do you think of that?

Hadrighada and I, we mourned together by the graveside of the most wonderful, but alas not the most powerful of the gods. It was good to have someone else with me to say prayers by the graveside, to share my tears and recall fond memories together. He stayed an hour or so before he left – back to the lonely deeps where he made his home, away from warfare and cruelty, away from the little doings of little things like gods and men – in the vast deeps, where no trouble ever visited him, and he could be left at peace. Such was the nature of my son, Hadrighada – so terrible that despite his endless power, he wanted only to be left alone, lying there, encircling the globe, his tail in his mouth, his end and his beginning as one, from the dawn to the dusk of the Nine Worlds and back again.

And what of Fenrir? – another of my children so powerful the gods were unable to tolerate him. Let me tell you of his betrayal. They lured him to Asgard with flattery and promises, and tested his strength with great chains, chains stronger and thicker than any that had yet been made, composed of the hardest metal that Volund the smith god could make. He wore them in good faith as a test of his strength, and broke them like wool, so instead they tricked him into wearing a cord, an unbreakable cord, of which you may have heard – made of six wonderful things: the promises of Odin, the mercy of Thor, the justice of the gods, the breath of the dead and the love of a murdered child. Who can break such things, that are already so broken? So Fenrir, that free soul, was tied to a rock underground, forever. It breaks my heart. He did not think ill of the gods before then. He would have fought by their side had they only asked. His problem was that he did not fear them either. So now he, unlike the rest of us a true immortal, must wait till the end of all things to be free – when there shall be no time left.

*   *   *

Now let us finish this part of our tale. Join me in a summer's day. The sun is setting but the warmth of the day remains in the rocks and stones, in the earth, on the sand and pebbles of the seashore where I sit. I was hoping Hadrighada might drop by to see his father. I was watching the birds fly in formation low over the waves. I was feeling lonely, unloved. The gods had taken everything from me. I was wondering if perhaps it was time to give up my godhead and become what I had always envied – a mortal man. Seventy years is enough time to fill and I had already lived a thousand times that. What more could life offer? A youth lived so long becomes monotonous. The living think that the dead have a bad time of it, in the land of shadows where nothing ever happens, but there is an honesty to nothing. In this world, which never stops, you soon reach the end of things to do. Then you have to start over again and believe me, that feeling, that there is nothing new left to do, makes the heart sink like no other.

And yet – the heart lies. Life turns, it seems the same, but nothing is ever old and nothing is ever repeated.

I sat by the gentle movement of the sea. Idunn was due to call by with an apple for me, and I doubted I had the strength or conviction to say no. In the end, despite everything I have learned, something always seems better than nothing.

Out in the bay, a head appeared. A seal. It rose in the water before me, facing me directly, then began to swim towards me. It dived, rose again, dived, then began to swim straight forward in a determined way. It caught my eye, because when you see a beast doing something with such intent, it is usually not a beast.

The seal arrived among the wavelets that dappled the shallows, and I rose and walked down to meet it. As I drew close, it raised itself up on its flippers and shook itself as a wolf will when it wishes to shake itself dry. And as it shook, it changed . . . shaking off not just the water of the sea but the shape it wore . . . its flat fur rising up and flapping in the force of the movement . . . its snout growing longer, its eyes narrower, its head broader. Its hind flippers turned to tail . . . but no more suspense. Before me was our fourth child, sister of Fenrir, beloved Fenra.

Well, we rolled in the sand together, we kissed, we played in the shallows and held each other tight. We cried, we wept for the loss of our loved ones and the beautiful life we had made for ourselves. Lovely Fenra, goddess of secrets, traveller, messenger, lone wolf; always full of love. Angrboda and I believed that Fenrir had spared her in the womb because of her nature. Fenra . . . my beautiful cub, now grown to her full bitch-hood. She was, even to my eyes, with my man shape, beautiful. And a shape changer too! That I had not even known. Yes, she was a creature of secrets and hidden places, my Fenra, appearing when needed, then vanishing again; the only one of my children the gods were unable to catch. Perhaps they did not even know of her existence. The songs of the Skalds missed her altogether.

We had so much to talk about! – but Fenra, beloved cub, was the only one of my children not blessed with the power of speech, although she thought deeply enough for ten. Where had she been when the Thunderer came calling? How had she escaped? Did she know the whereabouts of Hel? Where had she been living? She could answer none of my questions, although I had no doubt she knew the answers. And yet she had a message for me. Once we had said our hellos, she lay her foot onto the sand where the tide had left it damp, pressed it firmly, lifted it and raised her head to me and smiled, I swear, because there, plain as day, written in the sand were the words . . .

'Visit me.'

I turned to her foot and examined it. And yes, the message was there, in reverse. Plain as day, written in a hand that I knew. It made my blood run cold. Angrboda! My only true love. Angrboda, the slaughtered, the betrayed, the raped, dead love of my life, had some-how found a way to send me a message from beyond the grave.

She wanted me to come to her.

But how? Only Odin knew the way down to the underworld, where the dead live, and even he quailed before such a journey. I knew one way, of course – the road we all take, sooner or later. And I must admit – I had not expected my love to ask that of me.

But it was not that. Fenra led the way to the little cottage I had made of wood, set back from the sea, and nosed out my shoes and my travelling sack. We had a journey to make together, by a road untrod-den, I believe, by any living thing before me – down to death.

*   *   *

Of that journey, Arse-born, you may know nothing. It is not for you to understand such things. Of course, you will surely find your own way before very long and once there, it will not be for you to come back. The route you must take is the same for us all, god, giant, man or elf. So, you may believe that I followed my daughter in a state of great anxiety. Yet I went willingly enough. It has been said by those wiser than myself that it's not death but the dying we fear – the journey to that dreaded kingdom, rather than the kingdom itself. But for me, on that occasion at least, it was not so dire. Down we travelled, down and down, and across and through dimensions of time, state and being. All those boundaries must be crossed on the road to sweet death. There came a time when I looked down and saw that my daughter was no longer with me. I surmised that, unbeknownst to myself, I had already died. I stood there then and trembled, for who does not fear death? I touched my skin; it felt warm. I put my wrist to my mouth; I felt my breath. My pulse moved, my heart beat. I seemed alive. I paused – but there was no going back. Love had called me, reader, and you must know by now that I am a creature ruled by love, only love. Despite all the lies that have been told about me, it is love I live for.

And so I made my way, seeking love, into the halls of death itself.

Or should I say, herself?

Of course. Death had a queen – none other than my daughter Hel, who it transpires, learned the way there long ago, when she was only three years old. Her games led her there . . . and back. Yes. Both living and dead at once, she alone has the right to go and to return; and she alone has the right to grant passage. She received me in all her glory, her posthumous beauty shining, her halls decked with bones, lit with the spirits of the dead. I knelt before her – the only living thing allowed in her terrible halls.

We feasted my arrival, as an honoured guest of the dead; and by my side sat my beloved Angrboda. What a sweet pleasure that was, for I loved her dead as well as I had alive. We drank, we toasted our daughter queen. And when the feasting was over and we had time alone together in her tomb on the edges of darkness, she told me what had happened.

She knew, of course – she knows so much. She knew Thor would come, she knew she would die. She sent me away on a fool's errand so that I did not have to see it while she stayed and fought the Thunderer, although she knew she could never win. She fought and lost, she endured torture while Hel made her way to death, travelling not by air or land or sea, but by means that you, Arse-born, can never understand. So Hel escaped, and Fenra with her.

Upon her death my wife presented herself to Odin at his halls of Valhalla, because by rights, since she died in battle, she had the right to drink by his side. It was a bravado act – she would never have stayed with the one who ordered her murder. She turned her back on him before he even spoke, and no one could stop her leaving, though they tried. Angrboda was dead and already had been consigned to the rule of the true Queen of Death, of whom Odin is a pale travesty. The Valkyries barred her way, Thor tried to stop her. Yes, Odin himself tried to take her, but she was ruled by a greater power than his. She only showed herself to teach him who was strong and who was weak. Once, he wanted to rule over all the Nine Worlds, but that dream now is dead. Odin, with his overreaching ambition, wanted to be Lord of All; instead, he is only Lord of Some.

Fenra escaped down to the halls of Hel with Angrboda, and she could have stayed. But our daughter wolf, goddess of secrets, is a restless spirit. Instead of a life in the dark, she made her way back up to the world where she travels far and wide, bringing back news of the living worlds to Hel. Odin has his ravens; Hel has her sister-wolf, Fenra.

And Fenrir could have come down, too, but he was his father's son and succumbed to false promises and flattery. They said he would be a general; instead he is a captive until time ends. My dear wife failed to save him through his own pride. But she herself is now free of pain. Our son the serpent dwells where he feels safe, Fenra is free and our daughter Hel is a queen whom even Odin has need to fear.

And that, you would think, is all. Angrboda, dead; Loki, the living dead. Fenrir trapped. Odin foiled and Hel Queen of the True Immortals – the dead themselves.

But of course there is more. There is always more.

I stayed a long time down in the halls of Hel – many lifetimes in your terms. Of Loki's time among the dead, the tricks he played, the games, the broken hearts, the sadness – I will not say joy – is again a story for another time. But death itself, for me at least came to an end. One day Angrboda herself came to tell me that the time had come for me to go back to the land of the living. I was surprised. I must be honest, I was not entirely unhappy about the idea of going back to the surface, to life – to live again! I had petitioned my daughter many times to let me rise to the surface, even if only for a day.

'But why?' I asked Angrboda. 'We're happy here, aren't we?'

'Are we, Loki?' she said; and I admit I could not meet her eye at that moment. I thought I was happy. I even believed I was happy. But I was not happy. The fact was, I was tormented by an old, old companion of mine.

My friends, I was bored. Bored of the dead and their grey skin, bored of their cold embraces, their dark humour. I longed to feel water that had been warmed by the sweet sun on my limbs. I yearned for the taste of food on my lips, the grass under my feet. Yes, I yearned for many, many things. Not my old companions, I promise you. I did not miss the gods or any of the living, with their frantic greed to hang on to what they own, to seize more than they want, to deny others the spoils. The dead have lost everything already, maybe that's why they are such restful company.

No; let the living make their own misery. But I did miss the green woods in spring when the light of Surtr's eye shines through the leaves. I missed the sea with his sparkling waves, the bright green fields, the warm wind on my face. In one word I could sum it up, my friends; the sun. Oh, how I missed the sun. The sun, greatest of creation's glories. Its warmth, the colours it casts. The love of life and the living, my friends, all of it goes back to one thing – the sun.

'That's love for you, Loki,' she told me sadly. I shook my head.

'Do you doubt that I love you? Do you want me to die for you, so that I must stay here forever? I will.' I said that to her, even though it made my heart tremble.

Angrboda smiled grimly, but her sunken cheeks, her deep-set eyes, her grey skin did not smile with her.

'You could have done that long ago,' she told me. 'All you had to do was to stop seeing Idunn.'

I blushed. Of course, I knew she knew, but it was something we both silently agreed not to speak of. I had eaten the apples Idunn had carried down to me. And that's not all I'd tasted.

'Anyhow,' she said briskly, sweeping her sadness away in that manner she had. 'It is foretold.'

'By . . .?'

'By me of course,' she said. 'There is another you will love.'

And – well! You can imagine what my head and my heart were doing. A new love? Really? I was feeling guilty even before I'd met them.

'Who is it?' I said.

'Oh, fuck off, Loki,' she said. Which I suppose I deserved. It was thoughtless to ask her of all people, even though she was the only one who could know. Perhaps there was too much eagerness in my voice. But even then, I was unable to stop myself.

'Do I know them already?' I said.

Such was the nature of our goodbyes – with a quarrel. I can't blame Angrboda, but I find it hard to blame myself, either. If you had lived among the dead for so long, would you have said no to a fair young thing with hot blood and red cheeks? Come on! I decided long ago that guilt was not a useful emotion, and so it was that I headed up to resume life among the living with a spring in my step and a shine in my eye. When I burst through the doors of Hel and reached the sunlight, I cannot tell you how my heart sang! It was the first time I had felt the sun on my skin in over a thousand years. The sun, the sun! Odin may have brought the end of days on our heads when he stole Surtr's eye, but once you have missed the sunlight, you understand any number of days without it are worthless.

So it was that after 10 x 10 x 10 years, a pale and woeful creature called Loki emerged from the darkness into the spring sunlight. He lifted his arms and he rejoiced.

The sun.

THE SUN

Arse-born! I can't tell you what it was like to have the sun on my skin again. Colour! Blue sky. Green grass. Brown earth – yes, even brown was lovely. And the light. And taste and smell. And warmth and joy and . . .

Life! I loved it so much, I wondered if that's what Angrboda was talking about when she said there would be a new love for me in the world of the living. I was intoxicated, I was drunk, I was inspired, I was beyond myself. I loved the world so, so much, it would have been a sin – except, how can anything a god ever do be a sin?

I emerged on the edge of the bay where I had last been in Midgard. The sun was rising. Small white clouds fluffed up the heavens and dappled the water. A village had sprung up on the bay where we had once been happy. Fishing boats were moored by a neat wooden jetty, cows and goats grazed on the hill. There were crops in the fields. I made my way to the humble dwellings to accept tribute. And Loki found it good. It was good, all so good. Good to be back among men and women. Good to taste their simple food, to accept their simple hospitality, to sleep among and with the living. I could have stayed there forever, but something called

me. I did not know what it was then. But something called me to
Asgard, and I went.

I took the long way round – on foot, past fields and through woods,
over mountains and hills. I lingered in the green of our creation. I
thought to myself (how many makers have thought the same thing?)
– what genius I had in my youth, when these things flowed out of me
without understanding of how and why. We learn, we grow wise, we
forget the free simplicity of those days when we did it well just
because it looked good and felt right.

I passed through many villages and homesteads on my way,
stayed at a fair number of them. I saw many temples. Not many to
Loki – I was never a simple deity and people love their divinities
to tell an easy tale. Odin was there – but not so many as I would
have expected. Thor on the other hand was everywhere. Thor Thor
Thor Thor Thor. Well, I thought, a simple god for a simple people.
Tyr was there, too – there was a lot of Tyr. War is forever with us.
No one wants it but it comes anyway, and when it does, no one
wants to own it, but everyone wants to win it. Tyr never goes short
of sacrifice.

And – there was a new boy. Baldr. I'd heard the name before. You
may remember how Angrboda said that Hel was a portent for his
death, even before he was born. So here he was. A son of Odin and
Frigg, it seems. A god-prince. At his temples – and there were very
many temples – the people knelt in the early morning and prayed
with a smile on their lips. Baldr the beautiful, they called him. Baldr
the good. Baldr, who shone like the sun, Baldr the clean, Baldr who
banished ugliness with his presence. Baldr who forgave, Baldr who
loved. Baldr the brave . . .

. . . Sounds unbearable, I thought. But I know the propaganda
machine of Asgard – none better. Enough to reserve judgement till I
had seen him for myself. But one thing warmed me to this young,
unknown god – the first of us to achieve such fame amongst the Arse-
born for many, many years. Above his temples, in his temples, among
his temples, one image occurred more than any other. Glorious and
bright and beautiful: the sun.

*   *   *

They met me at the Rainbow Bridge – Heimdallr had obviously told them I was on my way. It was not a triumphant homecoming. There were no balloons or trumpets for Loki. They didn't let me go directly to my house, where my wife Sigyn and my children waited for me. Instead I was taken straight for an audience with the Old Man himself in his great hall of Valhalla. It had been extended somewhat – as far as the eye could see, in fact. The palace itself was a metropolis. There he sat on a great throne, very grand. A wolf at his feet, an eagle on the back of his chair. Both monsters; that must have been the last dire-wolf on earth, captured no doubt, from the Ironwood for the glory of Asgard. My old brother had become far, far too important for any ordinary-sized eagle or wolf. Looking at him, it was hard to recall the days when we had cavorted in the youth of the world about two giant turds, and created mankind from shit. He was a young man then, full of vim. Now he was Odin Allfather, Allseeing, Allknowing. The big All.

Yes, well, they were all very big and I was very small, that was the impression I got. Oaths were exchanged, mainly on my part. I think they were trying to quell my spirit. Frigg sat there by the Old Man's left side, Thor at his right. Thor, not Frigg on the right, you notice. Once Odin and Frigg had been a team. Now he had Thor – Thor the strong, Thor the hammer; Thor the thick. Tyr was there too, standing guard over the three of them. Standing guard! He didn't fool me. I knew who was the boss there. Poor Frigg; she looked surrounded. And the new boy. Baldr was there too. And yes, he was beautiful. Yes, he was. He looked over at me, and I looked back at him, and we did not so much as nod.

All the others, the gods and goddesses, were all there too, standing round while Tyr welcomed me in Odin's name. None of it felt very welcoming. It was in the nature of . . . we're having you back, but you better be thankful and behave yourself this time. Even though everything I had ever done was done to help the gods of Asgard.

The rules were read out. Odin's choice of voice? The new boy, Baldr.

'Rules?' I said. 'Since when did we have rules?' Judging by the buttock-clenching silence that followed, I should have kept my mouth shut.

I suppose it was only to be expected. Let's be honest, the gods and goddesses were never a particularly open-minded bunch of people. In the beginning, when the world was young, they had taken things as they came, but as time went by, they became more and more themselves. They hardened like an artery. Once they had taken the Jotun, the Dökkálfar and Ljósálfar and the men and women as they were, but like all those who fight for dominance and win they had taken it upon themselves to look down on the other. They had come to see their own habits as normal and good and the habits of others as deviant and bad. They had learned to value offence as more important than tolerance, and manners more than wisdom. As the people, so their gods.

I won't give you the commandments of the gods. Why bother? They don't stick to them, why should you? There was a lot about theft; apparently what you owned once, you owned forever, which was news to me. There was a time when things used to get used then dropped and picked up by someone else who needed them. Somewhere along the line, someone had invented *property*. The gods had become rich. There was a lot about sex, too. No same-sex sex, which had become even more of a no-no, it seems. Why such fun – why any fun – should be evil is, was and always shall be beyond me. No one actually said no sex with horses, but it was implied. Quite a lot was implied, hidden quietly away behind one particular word they had fixed on: *deviance*. No one actually said what deviance was, but I could tell what it meant by who they were all looking at.

Me. I was deviant. Somehow or other, no one actually said exactly why or how . . . I was all wrong.

I glanced at Freya. She twitched slightly but refused to meet my eye. The list went on. At the end of it, Baldr put away the parchment the Great Rules had been written down on – it was a long roll – and everyone looked at me to see how I would reply.

Various things passed through my mind. I wondered if I should relay the story of Freya and Brisingamen and the three Dökkálfar. I wondered if should recount the story of the time mighty Thor had such a damn good time man-loving with me. But I kept my council, for now. I shrugged and smiled and said, 'Of course! Of course.'

I had other things on my mind.

*   *   *

After the 'welcoming' was over, the drinks and canapés came round. Yes, friends, how times had changed. Frey and Freya came up to say hello. I did then, in private with my old friends, feel moved to remark that a lot of rules had come along since I was last around.

Frey shrugged. Freya sighed. 'The gods don't get old, but we can't stay young either. What do you expect?'

They were both looking over my shoulder as they spoke and I turned to see what they were looking at. Baldr, across the room, chatting to his mother.

'Good-looking boy,' I remarked.

Freya glanced at me and laughed. 'Forget it,' she said. 'No one touches Golden Boy. Tyr won't have it.'

'Not that he needs guarding,' added Frey. 'I doubt if he even touches himself.'

'Really?' I turned again to look at him. So young – so beautiful. The goddesses were twittering around him like a bunch of excited finches. 'He'll have to marry, I suppose.'

'Not interested,' said Frey. 'He's the god of beauty and innocence. He doesn't care for any of that, it seems.'

'He's too good-looking to be sexless,' I said.

'He seems to be. He's going to leave a lot of upset and very frustrated people in his wake,' said Freya. She licked her lips in a kind of grimace.

Frey's eyes slid to the left and then back; Freya's followed his. I glanced over. Heimdallr the watchman was watching us. He can read your lips from half a mile away.

'He's not interested,' said Frey again. A little later, they left.

I said hello to the others, pressed a little flesh, exchanged a few chaste kisses. Later, still sober, I went home with my wife and children where we celebrated quietly among ourselves. Heimdallr had given me an invitation to drink with the other gods, and although I had no appetite for drinks, I knew I ought to go. I left early, on my own. Strolled through the twilight and sweet night air towards a certain brightness that glowed softly among the birch trees that grew behind my house. I followed the light – I always follow the light – and wandered on for a mile or two until at last I came across Baldr in the woods waiting for me. We embraced.

And then we fucked. We fucked like bulls, we fucked like bears. We fucked like men, as only men can fuck. We fucked and fucked and fucked among the trees. Then we lay down and whispered of love, of the deep, deep love that had sprung up unbidden between us, with no apparent cause, for no apparent reason, without any knowing or planning or forethought. A magical, wonderful love of a kind the world has not seen before or since. What did it mean? Where had it come from? As soon as we cast eyes on each other in Valhalla we knew we were made to be one. And in the woods we were one.

It was a miracle. And we knew this: that our love had to be kept quiet. Long before we wished it, we went our separate ways – I to drink with the gods, Baldr back to his beautiful lonely palace. Truly, he was the god of beauty. But the most beautiful thing about him, Arse-born, was the thing he could never be except with me: a man who loved another man. The penalty for which, in those new days of rules, was death.

Yes, Arse-born. Just as Angrboda had foretold, I was in love again. Once again, it was a love fraught with danger.

BALDR

Beautiful, beautiful Baldr! When I worshipped the sun on my re-emergence into the world of light, it was his reflection that I saw in the bright disc of Surtr's eye. Surtr sees all. Some say he sees it twice – once through his severed eye above the bone roof of the sky, once from his place in Muspel, where he waits and watches. It is the duty of us all to live lives that are worth his while to watch, for you can be sure that on the day that we cease to amuse him, he will leave Muspel and come our way. Then everything you know will be destroyed in fire, a fire of a kind none of us know or can even dream of.

I like to believe that as a man and a god I have fulfilled my part in the destiny of this world we live in. What about you? Live, love! Kill if you have to. Give Surtr something to wonder at, because it is only wonder that stands between us and destruction.

Yes, I have acted out my part, but Baldr did not need to live a life worth watching. He required no drama, no action, no deeds to make him interesting. His beauty alone was enough to keep Surtr bound to his place forever. What a tragedy, then, that he was sent so soon down to the underworld, the one place in the Nine Worlds where the eye of

Surtr cannot reach. I worry, dear friends. I worry that Surtr will come sooner than he need, just so that he may look again on the face of lovely Baldr.

No one and no thing, in life or beyond it, ever approached Baldr in loveliness. All things adored and worshipped him; all things wanted to be near him. Even the wind fell quiet in his presence so as to allow the full weight of his beauty to settle within the heart and mind of the beholder. Beautiful, beautiful Baldr. And his gift was given freely, for we can all gaze upon beauty. A cat may look at a king; even the louse in your pants could gaze on Baldr and feel the better for it. And Baldr, accepting his due, enjoyed being looked at. His place was the centre of attention. It is in the nature of beauty to give itself away to all, and yet never grow the less.

And reader! – he was *mine*. Unbelievable? I know; but true. The god of clever and the god of beauty. What could possibly go wrong?

People ask me from time to time, what was Baldr the god of? Was it beauty? Certainly. The sun? Maybe. Love? Yes, of course – but there was only one worshipper at that altar; myself. Perhaps he was the god of adoration. I do not know. I only know I loved him. And he . . . I don't know why or how! – he loved me back. For a long time, I believed that he loved me because I was the first one to recognise him. The very first moment I saw him in Valhalla, I knew him. I felt that I had always known him – who he was, what he was, why he was.

He had a secret and I knew what that secret was. Or so I thought. How wrong I was.

Yes, reader, though I did not know it yet, my vision fell short. And yet that day in Asgard I did truly recognise Baldr, just as he recognised himself in me. What astonished me was the other gods didn't see it. They didn't use to be like that – but then, back in the day, they didn't mind that sort of thing. They *did* that sort of thing! And now here they were wandering about as if such things were unheard of, unspeakable, unrecognisable.

There were exceptions, in secret. Frey and Freya as you might expect.

'Not surprised, now I know,' said Frey. 'And yet . . .'

'I know,' I said proudly. 'Only with me.'

Frey and Freya pouted. They were both having to get used to
being denied under the new regime, but they found Baldr's faithfulness – to me of all people! – hard to understand. A god, saying yes to
me and no to *them*? Unthinkable! Monogamy in itself was a new
rule . . . and not one the gods of sex liked very much.

'Odin is so full of knowing, he knows nothing,' complained Freya.
'Tyr sits at his left hand and whispers war to him, Thor sits on his
right and whispers more war to him and that is all he knows. The
gods have become narrow.'

'We're the same, we haven't changed. But now we have to be
ourselves under cover,' said Frey. 'The Vanir remember. We don't
forget what pleasure is.'

He raised a cup of wine and we drank.

That night – I remember it well – we had good times, hidden
away in a huntsman's hut in the woods – myself, Freya and Frey.
Those two, who had always been the closest and happiest of lovers,
had to meet in secret now since sex between brother and sister –
twins, in their case – was now forbidden. The powerful love their
rules so much! This you may do, that you may not do. So it was in
Asgard. I had come back to a heaven ruled by an oaf, a psychopath
and a senile. If I had ever imagined that Thor would rule the roost,
I'd have stayed with my dead wife and daughter, believe me. But
there was too much to love now in the world of light for me to ever
wish to leave it.

Yes, Arse-born, it was good that night to feel Freya and Frey's lips
upon mine, their tongues against my skin. I enjoyed it. But I did not
tell Baldr of my fun. He had already begun to talk fidelity to me, as
the young sometimes do before they realise the length of time. When
you can live more or less forever, you learn very quickly that variety
really is the spice of life. He would see soon enough. So I thought.

Around that time as well I went to visit Frey and Freya's father,
blameless Njordr, in his beachside home in the soft south, not so far
from where Angrboda and I used to live in the old days. Njordr, poor
lonely man – his Jotun wife Skadi couldn't bear the sandy coasts and
had gone to live in her mountain home, and he could not bear to live
in her mountain home but had to have the sandy coves on the coast,
so they saw very little of each other. He played sometimes with the

daughters of Aegir, elvish types who lived as waves on the sea most of the time. But he was alone mainly, and found it hard to bear. For a while he had even come to live in Asgard with the others.

'But the politics,' he said. He shook his head. 'You've been there, Loki.' And he cast me that even, long look he has, as if he could see inside your head. Perhaps he could.

'If you mean is Asgard ruled over by murder-head and knuckles, then yes, you're right,' I replied. 'Two dogs taking it in turns to piss in Odin's ear.'

Njordr looked panicked. 'Hush, hush,' he croaked.

I looked up. There were no ravens in the sky.

'They say he uses ants, these days,' hissed Njordr. 'And bees. They get everywhere,' he said, peering anxiously at a beach fly that was trying to land on his sweaty old shins.

I laughed – but quietly, as I had no wish to humiliate the poor man. Flies and beetles were eavesdropping on us now! Why on earth would Tyr want to keep records of every little exchange?

'I don't know,' said Njordr. 'Why do you think he does?'

So we dropped our talk of politics for the sake of his nerves. We spent a pleasant day instead. We fished, we drank, we ate shellfish, and in the evening we frolicked together, Njordr and I. Aegir's daughters came to visit me and we played with them, too. But not amongst the waves, as we used to once, or on the beach, but at the back of an old sea cave, where the water had wormed its way several hundred metres into the rock. Only there did Njordr and the daughters of the sea feel safe enough to drop the pretence and play the games we all love to play.

Such fun was dangerous of course, but emotionally these encounters meant no more to me than they ever had. I assumed that the others were up to the same things as well; those who make the rules are usually the first to break them. I kept my games quiet from Baldr, not out of deceit, you understand. When you have a new lover, a new young lover who is still learning the ways of love, it's bad manners to talk about your other encounters. Don't you think? I supposed he had dalliances of his own, and if not, he soon would. Neither of us mentioned them only out of delicacy, nothing more. So I thought.

So I thought. You see the dangers of being out of the world for so long? When you come back, things have changed. I thought Baldr was one of us, the way we used to be. In fact, he was something altogether new.

I remember the moment when I first began to realise that he was not the person that I thought he was. I was lying on the bed in his home. Baldr was at his dressing table . . . yes, he had that, a table where he sat to dress his hair and check his appearance in the way the beautiful people do. Don't call it vanity. If you were as beautiful as he was, you'd find it hard to keep your eyes off yourself as well. I was watching him myself. I had two views – the back of his head and his face in the mirror. I was thinking how lucky I was. Baldr was teasing a lock of hair here and there. And then he said . . .

'You would never betray me, would you, Loki?'

I was surprised. I have never betrayed anyone in my life. Not on purpose, anyway. He was peering in the mirror, and as I watched, he rubbed a little brush over his eyebrow, leaving it darker. Then, he dipped another finger into something on his dressing table and rubbed it on his lips.

Make-up. It wasn't unusual at that time for people of all sexes to wear make-up. This was strange though, because it was the kind of make-up women usually used. It was also odd that he was doing that whilst asking me such a strange question. I wasn't sure what he even meant.

'I never would, I never shall,' I said. 'Why would you even ask?'

'I think I'd die if you were to be unfaithful to me,' he said. As he spoke he was applying the shadow to his other eyebrow and then he turned to look at me. 'What do you think?' he asked.

I studied him carefully for a moment. Betrayal and infidelity? Since when were they the same thing? In Asgard of all places . . .

'Dark brows don't suit you as well as the usual blonde,' I said. 'You know, Baldr, yours is a beauty that cannot be improved.'

He sighed. 'I get fed up looking the same way all the time,' he said. 'Maybe I should dye my hair dark as well, what do you think?' he added, turning back to the mirror.

It was a complicated moment. Betrayal. Infidelity. Make-up. I admit I had no idea what to make of it. Did it mean that I had actually betrayed my love without even knowing it when I had been about my frolics with the Vanir? Or was this simply Baldr's way of asking me to sleep only with him?

I didn't understand. I didn't question him further at that point. I needed a little time to consider what all this meant. In the meantime, I kept my meetings elsewhere to myself.

Let us jump forward in time, Arse-born. It is a lovely day in Asgard's summertime. Surtr's eye is shining low in the sky in the late after-noon, and the soft heat from the earth that you get at the end of a long, hot day is rising around me.

I lay on the edge of a meadow, by a pool. I had daisies and orchids in bloom around me. Birds sang. What can I say? Summer in Asgard! Don't come to Asgard looking for ugly things, you might think – although if I had chosen to walk half a mile further I might have seen beyond the meadows and the woods and the low hedgerows, to where a coil of razor wire threaded its way across a blasted heath.

Thor's place. We never went anywhere near that border if we could avoid it. Baldr, who could not abide anything that was ugly or dirty, really should never have had a place next door to the Thunderer. His house was spotless. You could have licked the floors and come up with a clean tongue. And Baldr's place drove Thor mad. It was a security risk. Any number of elves and tiny Jotun could be crawling through that long grass and bushes, ready to loot, rape and pillage. Something was going to have to change.

Lying low in the fields as I was, I could not see the barbed wire, the mined land, the blasted rocks. All there was for me was the grass, the soft water, the damselflies, the fish rising . . .

But reader, I was not happy. Why so, Loki? I hear you ask. Your normally bright heart is not normally sunk so low. What ails thee, sweet prince?

One simple reason that I'm sure you will understand; my lover had just celebrated his wedding.

Yes. *Wedding.* It was the custom now. Although Baldr had never been attracted to a woman, he had now married one for the very little reason that he was supposed to. As one who never did what he was supposed to, I was not particularly respectful of that decision, but I did understand it. What can I say? I had married myself. Sigyn and I had been in love once upon a time, and there had been no need for weddings; now, Thor and Tyr insisted on it and neither Odin nor Frigg saw fit to disagree. The Allfather and his wife wanted grand-children, I expect. You might have noticed how rare children were at this time among us gods. The apples kept us young, but our seed aged. We gods fucked as much as ever but very little came of it any more. Baldr, who had true youth at this time, was expected to play his part.

So it came as no surprise and yet . . . and yet! I was upset, Arse-born. I was surprised that I was upset. I didn't feel that I had any right to be upset, to be honest. But I was.

I can't explain it myself. It was Baldr who had first brought up the idea of monogamy; infidelity was betrayal, he said. You heard it your-self. I'd only gone along with it to please him and now, here he was spending the afternoon after his wedding with his wife. And as a result, for perhaps the first time in my life, I was *jealous*.

It makes no sense to me either – not then, and not now. Somehow, I had changed. Perhaps I was getting old. Perhaps I'd just got used to the idea of sleeping with only one person. Somehow the idea that sex and love were the same thing had taken root in me. I remember when it was first announced that he and Nanna were going to be wed, I smiled at him and asked him how about faithfulness now.

'Oh, come on, Loki,' he scoffed. 'You know I have no choice. It won't change anything.'

'Oh, I don't mind,' I replied. 'I just want to know if this means we can sleep around, like we used to.'

I was teasing, but sweet Baldr looked at me and, bless him, his eyes filled with tears. 'I know you sleep with Sigyn,' he said. 'And I hate it. And now I have to sleep with Nanna. And I hate that. We do these things because we must. Not,' he added firmly, raising a finger . . . '*not* because we choose to.'

I smiled a kind smile. I loved him for being jealous – a feeling at that time I looked down on as childish. Good, wise Loki, looking on his young lover's sufferings with a forgiving eye . . .

'It's a good disguise for us,' Baldr added. And that was true, because if it ever came out that we were lovers . . . You cannot begin to imagine how homophobic things had become since the military had taken hold. Exile, even death, would be the least of our worries.

So Baldr had been wed that morning. We had arranged – no, let me be honest – *I* had insisted – that we meet up after he had done his 'duty'. His term, not mine.

The other gods carried on with their drinking and feasting after the wedding. Ale, mead and meat were still as popular as ever among the oafish classes, but I had no appetite for it. I went to the lake early, to swim, to clear my head, to relax, to try and forget that the one I loved was banging away with another. That pool by whose banks I rested, that beautiful pool, was one of our favourite spots. It was hidden behind flowering elders and rowan trees, there were primroses and violets and sweet woodruff growing by. It was very pretty. So pretty, that although I was never a very pretty sort of person, even I could appreciate it.

Or at least I was trying to. The thought of Baldr with a woman kept getting in the way. He had to fuck her, of course. I understood that – the whole marriage was just about babies. But why was it taking so long? He had been worried that he might not be able to perform properly, so perhaps, I thought, he was putting it off . . . showing Nanna round his palace, introducing her to his servants, showing her all his pretty things, just to avoid the baby-making. Perhaps I was being indulgent going down to the pool to engage in a little romantic angst. Perhaps I would have been better drinking with the boys that day. I don't know. All I can tell you is that I told my love where I would be, and when I would be there, and I went to the pool early and I swam and I rested and I lay in the sun and I waited for my love, and my love never came. The hours ticked by. I flicked stones into the water. I tickled the trout in the nearby streams. I drank the flask of mead I'd brought with me.

I got impatient. I ran up and down. I complained to the trees. An hour passed, then another. Any idea that this was just some kind of mistake was wearing very thin. More time passed by. To be fair to Baldr, he had warned me that he might not be able to get away. If he was to do this as a disguise, and god knows we needed a disguise, then he had better do it properly. Sneaking off on your own wedding day is not a good look for a young husband.

Yes! I know! All very sensible. And yet . . . and yet I was enraged. I was perplexed. I was upset, confused. I did not understand what was happening to me. Jealous? Loki? Of course not! The mere idea. I was way beyond such foolish emotions. If I was suspicious, it must surely be simply that there was something to be suspicious of . . .

And so, as the afternoon slid into the evening, and Baldr was sliding yet again at that very moment into Nanna (in my mind at least) I began to conceive of the very reasonable idea of sneaking into the palace and spying on the honeymooning couple, to see what was going on.

Such is the nature of jealousy.

At first I dismissed the idea as unworthy of me. But then – what harm would it do? I'm a shape changer – I am THE shape changer! I would certainly never be caught. They would never know. Just to check up that Baldr was truly delayed, you understand, and not (as he insisted he never could or would) actually enjoying the company of his wife too much to be bothered to come and see his real love – me!

This is a very familiar kind of scenario for regular readers of romantic fiction, I expect, of which this is not an example. The forlorn lover hides himself behind the curtains or peers in through a window – something like that? You won't be getting any of that here. I am a god. I turned myself into a falcon.

I flew to Baldr's home, Breidablik. I flew fast – I was in a rage by this time – and I was out of breath by the time I arrived and perched myself on an apple tree, panting hard. I cast my hawk's eye up and down the building. The shutters were all drawn. I suppose that might be expected on a honeymoon – but *all* of them? Every window in the house was darkened, from basement to the upper stories, as if there was an act of mourning going on in there rather than acts of love. Repeated acts of love, if what my broken heart was telling me was true.

I flitted to the window in the form of a wren, a bird that everyone sees and no one notices. I did it too soon I expect – holding a shape is not easy even for the god of transformation. You have to concentrate to hold it true. It's like a muscle – you can wear it out.

I tried to peer in, but the shutters were very close. In the past Baldr had justified this on the grounds that he would not let the others see what went on within; but now, of course, I was wondering if he did not want *me* to see what was going on within. I flitted from one window to the next until at last I found them, in a room at the back of the house. A room where we usually slept.

I ground my teeth. What right had this . . . this *woman* . . . to invade our special places? The shutters had been fitted tightly, and even as a little bird, it was hard to see in. But these were the long-ago days when glass was in short supply, so there were gaps.

I changed again . . . into a fly this time, a shape often looked down on but one I have found useful more than once. I flew in through a tiny crack into the room where the new husband and his equally new wife were having their fun and . . .

It all seemed fine at first. Nanna was dressing up for him. She had on a very fine dress, make-up, hair beautifully done. I would say she had never looked so beautiful. I was impressed. She was a good-looking woman but this time, she really shone – really gorgeous, actually. It was difficult to take the eyes off her. Baldr, on the other hand, was dressed as if for war, with his leggings and shield and with the short sword that he used at games by his side. He looked somewhat diminished for some reason. But it was normal enough fun . . . husband and wife in their finery. I was relieved that the finery hadn't come off, but on the other hand disappointed that he was putting off coming to see me for the sake of posing in front of the mirror.

Then I realised.

Nanna wasn't Nanna; he was Baldr. And Baldr wasn't Baldr – she was Nanna.

They were cross-dressed. Well! Reader, I was so surprised and . . . I don't know! I can barely remember what I felt just then, to be honest. I'd just changed from man to hawk to wren to fly, which was stupid. My sense of who and what I was had slipped and I lost my concentration. I was sitting upside down on the ceiling watching the two of them at their antics at that moment. I fell. I panicked. I turned back into myself . . .

Bang! On my back. In the middle of the floor.

They screamed, both of them at the same moment, and jumped like cats. Me, I had every drop of breath knocked out of me by the fall and all I could do was crawl around on the floor trying to breathe.

Baldr clutched at his heart and glared at me.

'You bastard,' he cried. 'You utter bastard, Loki. Spying on us!'

'No, no,' I croaked pathetically.

Nanna was staring at me as if she'd just seen a ghost. She clutched at her head and spun round in circles. I guess she was thinking what to do next. Baldr was glaring at me with his pretty face twisted into a rictus of surprise and outrage. To her credit, Nanna recovered first.

'We were just playing . . .' she began, when she was interrupted by Baldr's brain suddenly kicking into life.

'I was supposed to meet you!' he said, remembering.

'Three hours late,' I gasped, still trying to pull myself upright.

'No problem,' said Nanna – suddenly all bright, as if my presence there was nothing unusual or wrong. 'We were just playing about. Come in, Loki – oh, silly me, you already are of course! – come and have some mead. Or ale. We have meats and other dishes too . . .'

She was rattling on. And on and on. She was more nervous than I was, despite the fact that it was me who had broken just about every convention of decency and privacy you can imagine. Baldr meanwhile was staring at me, the rictus gone. On his face now was a different look. It was more or less . . . thoughtful.

'We were just dressing up . . . Playing games . . . honeymoon . . .' gabbled Nanna.

'Yes! I understand. No problem.'

'We're so sorry!' she said.

'No! I'm sorry,' I said, desperately trying to work out what was going on. She was apologising? What had she got to be sorry about?

'Baldr,' she said. 'We have our first guest. Shall we get changed into our proper clothes and . . .'

'No,' said Baldr suddenly, snapping out of his trance. 'No, Nanna. Not this time. Not for Loki. Not for him.'

We both turned to him and stared.

'You know I love him,' he said to Nanna.

'No no no no no no,' I babbled. What was he playing at? Admitting to man-love? He knew better than this.

'Oh, no no no no,' burbled Nanna. 'I mean – Yes! I mean, he's such a good friend to you, I know all about that . . . so happy to have you here, Loki . . .' she gurgled. And then . . . 'Don't, Baldr. Don't . . .'

She was begging him, I could see that. But begging him about what? . . . but by then I was beginning to wonder . . .

'If you want to play at dressing up . . .?' I said.

'Yes! Why not?' gasped Nanna, grabbing at straws.

'We're not dressing up,' said Baldr. 'This,' he said, gesturing down at his body in women's clothes . . . 'This I who I am.'

'Let's get changed, shall we?' begged Nanna, coming over to pull at his arm. But he pushed her off.

'No. I want him to know. I want you to know, Loki. I am . . . I have become . . . *a woman.*'

'I don't think you are,' I said lightly, nodding down to his groin, where the most well-proportioned penis in Asgard nestled.

'You don't understand. In *here.*' He banged his heart. 'In here, Loki. I feel it here. Inside,' he said. And he – *she* – dropped to her knees and wept.

I nodded like an idiot. Nanna dropped her head. 'Oh, shit,' she said. I went over to my stricken lover and knelt beside her, patting her back. She flung her arms around me and howled. Nanna flung her hands into the air.

'Of all the people to tell,' she wailed. 'Not him, Baldr. Not *Loki.*'

METAMORPHOSIS

Like I say – give a dog a bad name. Poor Nanna was certain I was going to spill the news all over Asgard. My reputation had dropped so low during my years away, she was certain that her brand new husband was doomed. Baldr, who had seemed quite happy as a he for so long, was now a she. Let me he honest – I was susprised, but I had no trouble with it. I'd been a she on and off my whole life, I hurried to reassure her. I wasn't going to tell a soul. Why would I? Baldr was my lover. If *she* went down, so did I.

Poor Nanna, she'd had a series of disappointments on this, her wedding day. She'd spent the whole afternoon trying to coax Baldr into doing the business, and after a number of failed attempts, her new husband – let us honour him as a her from now on – had broken down in floods of tears and confessed that only men turned her on. Nanna put a brave face on it and had suggested doing the whole dressing-up-as-a-man thing to get her interested, but it hadn't worked. She had got it up sure enough, but as bold Sir Percy approached the golden gates, she lost her nerve at the last minute. Dressing up like that had been a last-ditch attempt. And finally, she had admitted to her what she had so far never told me – that she now considered himself to be a woman.

Nanna was furious. 'What is he, a poof or a pervert?' she hissed.

'All three,' I replied. But it was no joke. If the other gods found out, all the beauty in the world would not be able to save Baldr, or myself. And where would Nanna's hopes of marriage and a family be then?

It is a strange thing to want to control love – there are losers enough in that game without manufacturing more. But kings and politicians have always wanted to own the future almost as much as they want the present – and love is the road to tomorrow. Of course things are somewhat looser these days, but before you pat yourselves on the back let me ask you how you would feel if your child, or partner, perhaps, were to spend a night with a horse? I am a god with many shapes; you are mortal with only one. Perhaps we can agree, when you tread the world in so few seasons and forms, it's best to concentrate on one thing at a time.

You know something of me by this time – enough to know that I am the most broad-minded of fellows. I take a person as they come, man or woman, Jotun or god, bird or beast. (I don't think I've told you about the bird – that must come in another book.) Like me, sexuality has many forms. It may be a toy, a whim, an act of brutality or an expression of love. It may be anything from a pastime to a passion, but the one thing it never is, is fixed from person to person. And yes, the same is true of gender. *I* was able to smoothly move from calling Baldr *him*, to *her*. And I was pleased to see (no one is perfect!) that Nanna was upsetting her every time she opened her mouth by calling her *him*.

It was hard for Nanna. Fortunately, she, like so many of the gods, was not as convinced in the laws of Tyr as she had to appear, but even so, nothing she had ever been through could have prepared her for this. She was desperate – desperate for Baldr, desperate for children. Desperate to have her place as a wife and mother amongst the gods. She knew very well that the new rule in Asgard would never tolerate a man who was a woman. At the point when I fell off the ceiling, she was still half hoping that this was just some weird sex-play. But when Baldr burst into tears and insisted that *she* actually was a woman, Nanna knew that things were as bad as they could get.

I had many times come across men and women, elves and Jotun who felt themselves as belonging to a different gender from the one they appeared to be. I myself once had a very enjoyable affair with a Jotun, born a man, who lived as woman. She ignored all the male activities, prefering embroidery and such womanly tasks of her era over fighting, pillaging and shouting. That didn't go down well with her fellow Jotun, let me tell you, and soon she, high born though she was, was put on to cleaning, cooking, being beaten and other menial tasks normally kept for the low born. I took pity on her and whisked her away to one of my palaces, where we spent our time playing in the surf and making love. While I was away on my travels, she sat at home and wove herself a series of beautiful garments to wear when I returned. Alas, she decided eventually that her femininity had become too gracious to be ignored even by her Jotun brethren, and took a trip back home, where her family promptly emptied the privvy on her head and then threw said head, minus her body, into the local swamp.

Such has always been the traditional fate of those who cleve to a gender other than the one that sits between their legs. As it happened, I had my doubts as to whether Baldr was now *truly* a woman, in his heart or anywhere else. He seemed more confused than transformed to me, but either way, it made no difference to how I felt. I loved my Baldr, as a him or a her, in a dress, in trousers, whatever. Love is love as far as I'm concerned. To the other gods, however, that would not be the case. To them, it would be simply disgusting. Perverted, corrupt, anti-godlike . . . deviant, in a word. And of course we all know whose fault it would be, don't we? Exactly. Another example, if one were needed, of that revolting Loki, source of all deviance in this world and the next, finally losing all forbearance and corrupting the most beautiful of the gods to his own disgusting level.

It would all be my fault, no doubt about it.

Once I'd calmed Nanna down and convinced her that I was going to keep my mouth shut – not an easy task; my mouth is the most famous part of me – I set about comforting Baldr and trying to show her – gently, calmly – that she was over-reacting. She'd had a tough time! She'd had to hide her true self for so long. She'd just got married to a woman! She'd been expected to make babies with her. Our love was a very deep love, and she obviously felt on some level . . .

But no. She pushed me away.

'I'm a woman, Loki, I'm a woman. That's all. Why can't people accept me as I am?'

'How can you be a woman, Baldr? I'm a woman. Look at me. I'm a woman! Not you – me!'

This from Nanna, tearing off her robe. This is woman! But Baldr just shook her head and wept.

'No one understands . . . no one. Not even you, Loki . . .'

These kinds of scenes – calming Nanna down, trying to get Baldr back to some semblance of normality, them winding each other up, went on for some time. There were months of it, in fact. The truly terrifying thing was that Baldr was threatening to go public with it, which would certainly bring a terrible and painful fate crashing down upon us all. Nanna loved her too, poor unfulfilled girl, which, of course, meant that she saw me as her rival. It was a long process, but in the end, through great efforts on my part, we became friends, or at least allies, thank god! It was necessary. Baldr had not wandered from her fixation one little bit.

'I'm a woman, I'm a woman now. Why can't everyone accept that?' she kept wailing. Privately, I still thought that all the hiding and secrecy our love entailed, the dreadful fear of discovery never far beneath the surface, and now having to be a man to a woman, had got to Baldr. She was upset, I reasoned, unsure of who and what she was – not surprising in the oppressive world of Thor and Tyr. But I kept my doubts to myself. On the contrary, I told her that yes, of course! Now that she had poinited it out, I could clearly see it – she was a woman. As a result, we had a glorious week of love and celebration, and I hoped, foolishly, that my acceptance might be the end of the turmoil and settle things down. But no. Happy though she was that I accepted her, she didn't turn to me. Instead, she started locking herself away with Nanna for long 'girly chats'.

Girly chats? I found that hard to believe. There were rows. She was insistant that it really was just chats, but even so, somehow or other, between them, they managed to get Nanna pregnant. I was as jealous as a dog. Nanna of course was over the moon about it, but far from leaving Baldr alone, she was spooning over her more than ever. She harboured hopes that she was getting back to 'normal' – whatever that is! If she could get her pregnant, she could be a man, couldn't she? She had to be! But Nanna's girlish hopes were soon cruelly shattered.

It all came to a head maybe six months or so after the wedding. I was sitting in my own home with my own wife when there was a thunderous banging at the door. It was Nanna, bursting in like a Jotun, floods of tears, wailing, groaning, clawing at her hair. She even tried to fling herself into my arms – a gesture which I quickly repulsed. Things were complicated enough as it was. Instead, the girl stood in front of us, trying not to howl.

'What? What?' I said in a panic. Sigyn threw her embroidery down and glared at me.

'What is this? Loki?' she demanded.

'Nothing, nothing, let me just take her outside, you don't want to be bothered with this . . .'

'There's no one else I can talk to,' sobbed Nanna.

'No, no, not here,' I began. The last thing I wanted was to get Sigyn involved. It had been centuries since she had any loyalty to me, and the only reason I could see that she was at home with me at all was that she might spy on me for Tyr. Once she found out Baldr's and my secret, I could not imagine any other conclusion but that we were both doomed.

'He really is a woman. He really is,' sobbed Nanna.

'Loki? What's been going on?'

'I don't understand what's happening,' Nanna wailed, and she flung herself at Sigyn, since I wasn't having it, and sobbed her little heart out.

It was a difficult situation. Frankly, I was petrified. And things were about to get a lot worse.

'He's growing breasts!' wailed Nanna.

'Baldr?' demanded Sigyn. 'Oh, Loki, what a mess. What a fucking mess!' she hissed. And so it was. A big, fucking mess.

*   *   *

The result was that all three of us went round, Sigyn magnificently sailing in front, Nanna fluttering behind, pathetically grateful for having another woman in on the whole thing, me skulking behind, feeling sulky. Apart from feeling very much reduced in my own love story, things had suddenly got even more dangerous. But as it turned out I was wrong about Sigyn getting involved. She was great. Baldr was delighted at having someone else involved as well and she, Sigyn and Nanna got down to some serious talks. I was there too, but it was obvious I was something of an interloper, so I left – in a huff by then, I admit. I got into a worse huff once their serious voices and tears turned to laughter. By the time I went back in, things were positively merry in there.

When she saw me, Baldr, who was sitting between Nanna and Sigyn, rose to her feet and stretched out her arms. She was wearing a light linen robe, dyed a soft blue, which fell open. Her semi-erect penis – Baldr was always at least semi-erect – rose from her body like a bird taking flight. her blue eyes shone with joy, her blonde hair about her shoulders, her perfect body lightly toned and tanned as always. Beauty, beauty, beauty.

'Baldr is *Becoming*,' announced Sigyn. 'She is turning into herself.'

Well! Once it had been pointed out, it was obvious. I was annoyed – I should have known. But it had been so long since a young god had gone through the change we call the Becoming, it had simply not crossed my mind

I have mentioned the Becoming before, I think. Not all of us gods are born with our attributes. Some are, some aren't. For some, it never happens. Others Become. Thor had a Becoming. He was always a strongbox with a taste for bullying, but as he reached adolescence he turned. His muscles swelled. His beard coiled and grew bright red. The thunder and the lightning took to growling around him and lighting up his way whenever he walked in darkness. So it is – he gained his attributes; he *Became*. Did I mention how my daughter Hel changed when I saw her in the underworld – she had the spirits of dead kings and queens fluttering around her like garments, and the ghostly green light of putrescence shimmering around her head. And Frey, who became lit with a silver light, whose skin seemed to turn to silver when he became a true god in his youth.

So with Baldr. She had changed; she was still changing. It made sense. We had seen this kind of thing before. Not in quite the same way, of course, but still – it was familiar territory.

But with was one big difference. Thor and Frey and the others who had Become, had changed into something that fitted very neatly into the whole macho Aesir ideology. But Baldr? What was she Becoming? A woman? Was it as simple as that? Or was there some-thing more complex – more divine, perhaps – going on? Her penis, I noticed, didn't seem to be shrinking. On the contrary. Was she perhaps turning into a being of more than one gender? There had of course been gods of that kind before, although none of them had been so foolish as to try and make their home in Asgard. I had visited Haemaphrodite in Greece, and Hapi in Egypt before. Interesting folk. No one had worried about them there. But how would Asgard see such a being? As a bloke with tits? A woman with a willie? Something in between?

There had actually been one example here of a god with both genders – Ymir. Look what happened to him.

One thing was certain – if Tyr and Thor ever found out, Baldr – and Loki, too, no doubt – would be in the very worse kind of trouble.

Now that she had begun to change, Baldr started to go fast. She grew taller. Her limbs became straighter, longer. She developed dimples on her face and behind. Her breasts swelled. She became stronger and quicker. The bones in her face became more elegant – high cheek bones and eye arches. Her charisma – she was never low on charisma – went up several gears. Her penis became more beautiful than ever, her lips fuller, redder. Her hair grew, her muscles swelled. A golden light began to shine around her body, gathering and brightening towards her heart and face. Her hips widened. Her skin shone silver and golden in certain lights. Birds, butterflies and other creatures of the wild began to gather around her in adoration. She gave up eating meat and fish. If you stood long in her presence you became beautiful yourself. Between her legs, a perfect vagina formed just behind her testicles – sweet as a little pink flower, musky as perfume. I know; I took her second virginity one night on bearskins in front of a roaring log fire. Later that same evening, she had me – both as a man and as a woman. Of course, I am able to be all things to all people – but never, oddly enough, both at once. That gift was reserved for Ymir once, and now Baldr alone.

Yes – Baldr was *Becoming* – changing from the god he was into what she was always meant to be – a goddess of beauty, of love, of sex; as such, she was both genders at once. None of us knew what it meant yet. How could we? We didn't see the full result of it till later. Her androgynous beauty increased daily. You would think that would make everything all right, because we all love beauty, don't we? Beauty makes everything right.

You wish. If you think that, you don't know the world we made. I can't blame you. I myself don't know the world we made. The fact is, the worlds have become more than we gods ever intended or wished them to be. We have become creatures within them, just like you. I myself have no idea why it is that love and beauty inspire such hatred in certain breasts. I can see that they do. Beyond that, my mind cannot stir.

Of course, Nanna and I did what we could to keep the androgynous nature of the Becoming a secret. Sigyn was willing to help us, for reasons at that stage I could not understand. We strapped her breasts close to her chest, padded her waist and shoulders to hide her blossoming womanliness. She began to smell of musk and roses, and so we had to dowse her daily in manly perfumes, which she hated.

But her beauty we could not disguise – it was simply impossible. And as her beauty increased, so did her divine aspects grow, and trouble began to brew. Whoever stood with Baldr, their own beauty increased, no matter what kind of beauty it was. As a result, everyone wanted to be with her, no one could get enough. Still thinking her a man, the goddesses wanted to spend time with her, to sleep with her, to bear her children. The men wanted to play with her – to walk and run with her, to drink and eat with her. Thor became stronger in her presence; Tyr dreamt more and more ambitious cruelties when he spent a hour by her side. He begged her to join in the planning and execution of the war games that took place every night in the fields of Valhalla – games which revolted Baldr, who was as gentle as the lamb. When she refused, Tyr flew into a rage. Anger erupted all around. How strange, Arse-born, that someone who only ever felt love could inspire such division?

Baldr herself was painfully aware of the tensions around her, which troubled her deeply. Her time became devoured by the demands of others; she became a god even to the gods. I saw her less and less often.

And eventually – it had to come – things got so bad she'd had enough of it and decided to lock herself away. She sent word out that she was retreating from the world for a while, and the gates of her home Breidablik were closed. Only Nanna stayed inside with her. The grounds around the halls were locked. She took no callers, no visitors. She disappeared from our lives, for no one knew how long.

This, you should know, is not an unknown thing among those who eat the apples of youth. Even the mighty Thor had been known to close his gates and stay at home a while. Perhaps it is possible for you to understand, despite the brevity of your time. In this respect, no one was particularly surprised. No one, that is, except myself.

I was surprised, not because she took herself away, but because she took herself away from *me*.

I didn't realise at first that I was excluded. I went in secret, slipped through the trees and hedges to our private door built in the shadows at the back of her palace. But my way was blocked. Thorns and dense shrubs grew there instead of lilies and roses, and when I made my way to the door, that was locked too. I whistled and shouted; there was no answer. I persisted, and in the end I was rewarded by the head of Nanna appearing in a window above.

'He's not seeing anyone, Loki,' she told me. She still hadn't given up the idea of having a husband at this point.

'She's seeing you,' I said, sick with jealousy.

'I live here,' she told me.

'I *love* here,' I replied.

Nanna shook her head. 'What makes you think I'm even seeing him?' she asked me, the dissembling cow.

'You're not leaving the house, either,' I said.

'I'm sorry. Don't think it means he doesn't love you, Loki – he does. But this is his time alone. I'm sorry . . .'

She made to close the window, and I tell you it felt as if she was closing time on my soul.

'Wait,' I begged. 'How long? How long is this going on for?'

She paused and glanced over her shoulder, which drove me mad as it made me think, correctly I believe, that she was there behind her, just a few yards away, keeping carefully out of my sight.

'Baldr!' I bellowed.

Nanna turned to look at me. I fancy her eyes were glittering with triumph.

'As long as it takes,' she said evenly. And she closed the window on me. On my life. On my worth.

On my love.

'Baldr!' I roared. Oh, reader! I roared, I screamed, I begged. Of course I changed shape almost immediately and made a dash for that window in the form of a falcon, but the window was already shut. I dashed myself against it and peered in, but the room was empty. I flew in small circles around the palace, seeking a way in, but all the windows were locked. I changed into a fly. No building, no matter how secure, can keep us flies out – and soon enough I found a way in, but when I tried to enter, I could not. The space itself refused me. Don't ask me how. Maybe Odin had a hand in it, maybe Mimir, maybe Surtr himself; maybe the world demanded it, as it demands that some of us be and some of us be not. Perhaps it was part of the structure of how things were during that time. I only know that I spent all that night flying, crawling, burrowing, drilling, digging, banging, knocking and kicking at and all around Breidablik. At the end of it I lay exhausted, beyond myself, out of my wits and beyond my strength, in a cocoon of silk I had spun at the edge of the door, weeping spider tears, my heart broken because now I would no longer see my love . . . for who knows how long?

Well, reader; time passed. It does, no matter what, have you noticed? Even when your heart has been broken into a thousand million pieces. Reader, I missed her! How I missed her. I grieved as only a god can grieve. We all did, of course. Baldr inspired love in everyone; but only I loved her as a lover loves.

And yet . . . and yet! Everyone wanted her back, but not everyone was happy to want her back. Some of us – Frey and Freya, Njordr, myself and the Vanir, only wanted her among us, for any reason, in any way, in any form. But some among the Aesir were not so straightforward.

I remember Thor and Tyr at this time. How they looked, how they talked. Did they love Baldr? Of course they did! Baldr was the god of love, they had no choice in the matter. But love, my friends, does not need to be kind, or generous or peace-loving. Love does not exclude hate. Love can be cruel. Love can be manipulative. Love, to put it briefly, can be a weapon. They were prepared to break the hearts of any who stood in their way – and if that included their own hearts, so be it.

Remember that to them, Baldr was a still man – she had not let them into the secret, for fear of her life. Of course, it was perfectly possible for them to love another man in that kind of back-slapping, ho ho ho, let's get drunk and go fuck some girls kind of way. But Baldr was not only a goddess of love, she was also a goddess of desire. Imagine then, how *that* made the likes of Thor and Tyr feel. Imagine their discomfort as they stood next to Baldr, feeling stronger, more handsome, cleverer and more cunning than ever, unable to take their eyes of their new best mate . . . and twitching with desire in the secret folds of their gowns every time 'he' smiled in their direction.

Delicious, don't you agree – the lust of homophobes. But in this case, hideously dangerous.

Rumours began. Perhaps, the rumours suggested, there were those who did not love Baldr *properly* . . . perhaps, the hidden voices wondered, perhaps they loved him too much? Not the likes of Tyr and Thor of course – Heaven forbid! – But perhaps there were other gods who perversely thought that love itself might be better than right and wrong . . .

You know the score; you've seen it before a hundred times. At its root were the usual politics; Tyr and Thor were worried Baldr would come back greater than they and usurp their place at Odin's right hand, robbing them of the power they lived for. I kept telling them – Baldr was not interested in ruling over others, but my words had no effect. They saw how much she affected the hearts and minds of those around us and they fretted. And as they fretted, they planned . . .

Every day at the evening feasting, the conversation would turn sooner or later to Baldr. Of course, the other gods had no idea that 'he' was turning into an androgyne deity, but they all knew he was Becoming. How long, everyone wanted to know, would he be gone? In what way would his Becoming become? They knew what he had been – so they thought – but what next? What did it mean? When he re-emerged . . . if he emerged . . . what then? How much more beautiful would he have become? How much more *powerful*?

How much more would he *deviate* from the way of the true gods . . .?

Decades passed. Thor and Tyr consolidated their power and became more themselves. Odin became ever more lost in the multiplying universes inside his head. Frigg, Baldr's mother, retreated and did not concern herself much with the world, missing her beloved youngest son as she did. The terrible games that took place on the plains of Valhalla, where the slaughtered of Midgard re-slaughtered one another each evening, dying and maiming and being maimed for your daily viewing pleasure, continued to grow. Cruelty and power abounded. Tyr plotted and planned for the final battle, while Odin sat on his throne, bearded like a bear, one-eyed, seeing who knows what . . . lost in the futures, or the pasts . . . a castaway in some strange mad place where other lives ruled and lived and died. We could only hope that one day, the Allfather would come back to us and place mystery at the centre of our lives again, instead of war and pain.

Over it all great Surtr watched from his standpoint in the east, unmoving since he first awoke, still watching . . . always watching, always waiting. Who can help but wonder what will finally bring him across to us with that frightful sword and sweep away our lives? Perhaps it was that daily vision of Surtr the insurmountable standing there in distant Muspel, just a few of his giant strides away, that drove Thor and Tyr on to plan battle, to hone their skills and strategy. But no amount of skill and strategy can arm you against Surtr. The day is coming, mortal! Do not doubt it. But don't bother to fear it either. What use is fear against the inevitable? Every day he comes closer.

*   *   *

Baldr spent a hundred years behind locked doors, and every hour of it was an arrow in my heart. My woes were multiplying. Angrboda lost, regained, then lost again, only for me to find a new love who now locked me out of their doors, their bed, their life. Yes, Arseborn, I have spent many years with a broken heart, but I do not seek your sympathy. Many times I sat outside the doors of her house and howled at the moon, for Baldr, for Angrboda. I have lost much; my wounds run deep. I did myself and others a great deal of damage in those years, I admit it. If you want to judge me, there are plenty of stories from the lost years, the loveless years. I was beside myself, beyond myself, outside myself. I lost control – my head along with my heart. I do not ask forgiveness. Only that you know, there is more to Loki than the tales they tell.

I tried in those years to rejoin my Angrboda. Yes, reader, I knocked closely on the doors of death, but I was not allowed in. Death and her mother conspired against me. She who knew the future must have seen that I still had a part to play in the way of things. Deprived of her, I took what pleasures I could. I made my way to Ran, Queen of the Seabed and the deep waters, and to the company of the drowned who reside with her. Ran and I spent many years together, comfort given and taken on both sides. The goddess of the drowned would have preferred to take to the surface where her daughters played, but by Tyr and Thor's decree she was kept low, far from the sun, in the deeps with the fishes and the bones of the dead.

Yes, Ran and I had our time. And I spent many years in the arms of beautiful Freya and her brother Frey, in Freya's hall of Sessrúmnir, where half the slain dead reside. Almost weekly Tyr came banging on her doors demanding that her hordes join in the war games and the daily slaughter in Valhalla. But Freya was a queen who pitied the dead and did not let him in, though he stormed and blustered and threatened. Her half of those slain had a better time of it than those in Odin's halls, who got drunk as pigs each night to dull the horrors of the day gone and the day to come. They traipsed out ashen-faced to the daily slaughter. Death is not an experience any of us should welcome more than once in their life, let alone the horrors of the battlefield. Night after night after night. In Freya's halls they are allowed the peace and calm of their ending years, as they drift in and out of sleep on the long, slow, long slow journey down to Niflheimr, where the shadows fade.

Yes, reader, I craved death and, being denied it, sought out the company of the dead instead. I was as near to happy as heartbreak can be in the good company of Frey and Freya, of Ran and her drowned companions, and with others of the Vanir. You should wish for the sake of your own kind that it had been they who won the ancient war, instead of the warlike Aesir.

Hard times for your hero. But all things come to an end – for man and mankind, for gods and all their kin. Even the heartbreak of poor Loki came to an end. Enough of sadness and regret! Let me instead tell you about the day Baldr reappeared in her true godly form. If I had the gift of images, I would draw her image in the air. But the air would collapse beneath her picture. I do not think there was ever a space so full of beauty as Baldr made the air that day. Weep, you who have been denied the right to see her.

It was a day of feasting. Oh, I know, I know. It's always a day of feasting in Asgard, don't ask me which one. So, so many – and in those days, Loki was at them all. I ate the meat and the mushrooms, and I drank the mead, and the ale and the juice of the poppy, trying to forget my losses. The gods of the north liked their fun then as now. You might think it was the mushroom giving me visions that night, but I promise you, if you speak to anyone else who was there they will attest to the truth of my words – as if words can do justice to the vision that was Baldr that night.

When the hall door opened, it was not Baldr who entered at first. A tall warrior stood there, in fine linen leggings and coat. Tall and stern, but a silver light seemed to glow about them. We all turned to look, slowly at first because they stood so still, but more and then more and more of us gradually noticed his illumination. Some say Odin was watching the door even before it opened, but of that I cannot speak.

After many long moments, someone spoke . . .

'Nanna?'

Yes; it was her – or was she now a *him*? Acknowledged, he stepped aside; a golden light flooded through the door behind him. And *she* was there. In stepped Baldr, into our feasting hall and the full splendour of her magnificent godhead.

What can I say? How pale words are, what weak things, almost squalid. Vision itself might pale before Baldr that day. Around her head her golden hair was a halo. Above it, a helmet of some blue stuff, turquoise, perhaps, or lapis lazuli, but shining like beaten metal. And yet it seemed soft. Does that seem strange? Overdressed, perhaps? But that day Baldr out-conceived the idea of fashion; she could wear what she liked. Everything turned to beauty on her person. Her body was framed by the trim of a shimmering robe; folds of gossamer hung about her breasts and hips in the soft pinks and blues of the pale sky at dawn. Her skin shone gold. Her eyes, so wide, were blue, such a blue! – not the cold icy blue of the meltwater, but the warm, rich blue of the deepest, warmest skies. Her full lips – perfect. Her nose – perfect; her hands, perfect, her arms and legs, with their long muscles and evident power – all perfect. In that moment, as she stood before us in her glory, she redefined beauty and desire in one perfect form.

Nanna and she stood there together, Nanna to one side, allowing Baldr to shine forth in all her transformed glory.

At last, she began to move forward – to move towards me! A deep silence had descended on the normally raucous crowd. I sat, so drunk, drooling, untidy, smelly, ugly, old. That's how I felt. But she came towards *me*, with Nanna in attendance. As she drew close she held a hand out towards me.

'We are ready for you now,' she said.

I rose, I put my hand in hers. I became beautiful. She and Nanna led me out of the hall. I can barely remember the journey back to Breidablik. Looking back, perhaps I did hear, somewhere at the back of my mind, the explosion of noise that erupted in the drinking hall a little after we left – but perhaps not. My mind and body were so filled with beauty. All else fell behind us. We seemed to glide over the ground like mist, like thought – like love itself. Inside Breidablik, Baldr's halls were transformed, too. Nothing like it had ever been seen or known before. Hangings, tapestries, silks, carpets, paintings. Artworks from all over the world.

And . . .

Well, we had our time, that's all I will say. I have not taken you into any of my bedchambers before, and I won't start now. We had our time. Baldr and I and Nanna too. It was understood that the new divinity was not to be monopolised – and yet I felt no jealousy. Perfect beauty inspires perfect love; my love was transformed just as Baldr was. Just a few hours we had, not long. Hours of beauty, grace, love, passion. Then the front of the house crumbled and fell to pieces in a rain of crushed stone and rage. The hammer came crashing in, with the dead troopers close behind. Baldr was taken, I was taken. Nanna they let alone. They dragged us off to Asgard for the judgement of Odin.

I have snatches of memory. The Old Man sitting there, his beard coiling all over his face so that even his one good eye was all but hidden. His helmet slouched over his face. His mouth open, drooling. Frigg sitting by his side was still tall and fair – but the mother, a mere woman, was not allowed to speak in these days of the patriarchy. It was a farce. Tyr bent his head to the Old Man's mouth as if he could make sense of the mumblings that came out of it and pronounced the death sentence for us both. Pervert gods, we were named. That was the phrase. No one had ever sentenced a god to death before. I was held by force of arms. Baldr they took and forced up against a wall. Thor took his place. A terrible silence fell over the hall as the killer god took his aim – not that he needed to; the hammer never missed its mark. Brutality against beauty. We all know how that ends. Baldr stood, peaceful as beauty must be, and awaited her fate. Then Thor hurled the weapon of terror to extinguish the most beautiful being, or thing, or place, that had ever been.

And it missed. The hammer that never missed, missed.

Instead, it circled around the beloved one's head, swept across the hall and flew straight back to the Thunderer's hand. Mighty Thor stared at it as if he had been tricked. He blinked slowly, like a cow. Then he roared and hurled it again, with a such a force that you would have thought Surtr himself could not swerve it one inch from its path.

Baldr stood there, tall, proud and lovely. She never even blinked as the hammer tore towards her with a terrible scream, at such speed that it boiled the air behind it. And it missed again! It missed and came trailing sheepishly back to its owner's hand.

Uproar! Again! And again! Thor threw and threw. The hammer refused him. Then he rushed up to Baldr and seized her by the neck, or tried to; but now his own hands betrayed him and instead of throttling and tearing as was their habit, they danced in front of him like gnats on the night air. Thor bellowed and roared. He threw spears and swung swords and rocks. A bench, a table – a wall of the long hall. But nothing would touch the god of beauty.

Others tried, weeping as they did as they were commanded. Again, failure. One after the other they came forward. But Baldr, it seemed, was unharmable.

'Enough!' A single voice rang out, with queenly power and passion. The mother – Frigg herself, who had been silent the whole time.

Silence fell on the hall.

'All things, the living, the dead and the unliving, love my daughter, Baldr,' said Frigg, 'and all things, the living, the dead and the unliving have sworn not to harm her. Your violence is wasted here.'

Tyr and Thor looked at each other.

'You dare to undo the commands of the Allfather,' Tyr hissed.

'Odin commanded nothing. He hasn't commanded a fly for centuries, as you well know. It's all you and your sidekick pretending.'

The way she said it, *pretending*. The accused gods flinched like children.

'Now stop wasting our time. We have work to do.'

Frigg swept past the guards, who had lost their will to obey. The bonds fell from Baldr's arms, and she followed her mother out of the hall. I tried to catch Frigg's eye as she went past, but she kept her head turned away from me, from which I knew that much as she wanted to save her daughter's life, she was no fan of Loki. But by the time she had left the door, a fly had followed her out into the air; I was free. Unwelcome as I was in Frigg's halls, I made my way away from Asgard and my sentence of death, across the worlds and the arms of Yggdrasil to Jǫtunheimr, where I had friends who would see me safe until the heat had died down.

BOOK SIX

THE FATE OF LOKI

So now you know something of the Aesir and poor Loki. Of course, as they say, I am a liar. I lie to trick, to amuse, to play. I lie to protect myself and those I love. I am complicated, I am flawed. I love too much and I think too little. But they lie too, the other gods, and they lie for other reasons. They lie for themselves. They lie as governments lie – for the power of life, death and wealth. They lie to cling on to power, a regime that outrages decency and love, that damages the health and wealth of all. They care about only themselves. You and I are small things that occasionally get in the way and must be flicked aside. And if we will not be flicked, we must be crushed.

You can see this, I hope. But perhaps not. The Aesir propaganda machine works well. Behind the mask, the killing goes on. They have destroyed my family and my love twice and blamed me for it both times. It is their way, and your governments here in Midgard have learned well from them. So you may ask yourselves why it was, when, some mere years later, messages were sent to me to my hideaway in Jǫtunheimr telling me that I had been pardoned, that I accepted an invitation to return.

THE RULE OF BEAUTY

I did not trust them, of course, the messages. But trust was not the point. I missed Baldr, that's what it was and that's all it was. I had hoped that she might come to join me in my exile, but she did not. Apparently a goddess's place was in heaven. It was our fate to be parted, to live in sorrow. Sorrow is a part of beauty, she said, and that I should learn to embrace it.

To make beauty out of sorrow! Why would you? Everything that Baldr touched turned to beauty – even pain and sorrow, it seems. It was almost as if life itself was irrelevant to her.

So when the invitation came, I did not pause to think whether the promises of safety were true or not. I was allowed back into my beloved's company, that was enough. So I went. Maybe I would die – probably I would die. What did I care? I am a god made to lie and to love. That is all.

I went home.

Know, Arse-born, as I flew back on my falcon's wings, I looked down on the world and the world had changed. The fields blossomed. The people smiled. Honey flowed, crops grew, peace reigned, families prospered. The good ruled the land. Queens were exalted as much as kings. Hatred — where was it? Poverty — where had it gone? War? What war? When the crops grow and are harvested unhindered, when the greedy are held in check, the people prosper.

It was a new Golden Age.

I could not know how or why this bounty had come upon the world, but I did not pause to taste the pleasures of a peaceful Midgard. With a flick of my tail and wings I sped on faster than ever to my destination — to Asgard. To love!

Asgard too had changed — how it had changed! Doves of peace had replaced the hawks of war. The gods shone with health and contentment. Love was in their eyes. No longer did the slain fight and die and suffer each day in Odin's fields. Instead they walked out among trees and meadows, lay by streams, played games, hunted, loved; their life in Valhalla was better than it had ever been on earth. And in the great hall at the nightly feasting, flowers crowded the tables; butterflies played around the heads of the feasters. In the rafters, bird song fell like soft rain onto their ears.

And at the table-head, in between Odin and Frigg, the goddess who had brought all this about sat in glory and beauty. Baldr! Now I understood why she had refused to join me in exile. All things flow from heaven, as thoughts flow from the head to the body. While she resided here — not just immortal but unharmable — she could spread beauty and love throughout the Nine Worlds.

And now she had brought me to her to share in her glory.

I sat by her right hand as we feasted on delicacies that were as pretty to look upon as they were on the tongue. After, came the games — no longer the slaughter, no longer the pain and the fear and the dread. Baldr herself became the target for all, standing in her brightness to the head of the hall, as the others came to throw at their weapons at her — stones, rocks, swords, arrows. Everyone laughed with joy as each one missed its mark and fell harmlessly to the floor. That was the world I returned to, Arse-born. There is something to rejoice and wonder at! War itself had lost its edge.

I am not sure who it was who gave me the spear. One of the goddesses — Lofn, I think, the marriage broker. I remember it was a gift that I received with joy, for I believed in that moment that Baldr and I would be together forever.

I did not throw it at once. Indeed, for a while I thought I might not throw it at all. After all, why would I cast anything at the one I loved? But the joy of the game was infectious. One after the other the gods and their attendants threw their weapons, one after the other they crashed to the floor. At last Baldr herself caught my eye, saw the spear and beckoned to me —

'Come, Loki! You too.'

How can we resist the command of a lover, when it is given with joy and love? So I stepped forward and I threw, with all the strength of my glad heart.

And somehow, Arse-born, I was not surprised when it failed to miss its mark. When it pierced her holy flesh, when it murdered peace and love and hope. In that moment it as was if I always knew. 'Here it is,' my heart told me, even though for the past few hours I had been telling myself that everything was well.

Baldr fell, the blood welled up at her throat where the blade stuck. The gods all cried out — even Tyr, who planned the whole thing, let out a terrible groan of pain. The blood flowed — beautiful blood, unsurprisingly. A great pool of it spread around us all. And misery returned to the heart of Loki, and to the world.

Yes, even Tyr groaned, but as I turned to look at him, I saw the triumph in his eyes, and I knew then I had been pardoned only to be used. I had murdered love — I and no other. The gods would listen to no excuses. All would blame me. It was all over for love, all over for peace, for man, giant and elf, and all over for me, too.

Baldr fell and so ended the brief honeymoon with love for the Nine Worlds. I knew she was dead before she hit the ground, from the groan she let out, a groan that I knew carried with it her dying breath. That groan was echoed throughout the hall. Every god, every goddess . . . the birds in the roof, the butterflies and the flowers at the tables, even the timbers of the hall, the thatch in the roof, all groaned with her.

And me? — I fled — I fled as fast as I could. What now was there to live for?

*   *   *

So did the gods kill beauty and love, peace and prosperity, diversity, tolerance, kindness and hope with a single spear. What would the world be like today if Baldr had lived? – if Odin had spent more time and interest in this world, instead of exploring the impossible others? – if Loki had only taken that spear and broken it over his knee. When we think of Baldr now we think of death, of her pale beauty in the darkness of loss. How different it could have been!

Of course there were efforts to bring her back. Frigg sent her messengers down to the dark realm and Hel could have released her had she wished; it is within her power. But she did not wish. Why I do not know – I have not been allowed back into her realm, much though I have longed to be there. No doubt she has her reasons. For a while I thought that she, advised perhaps by her mother, denied Baldr leave to return to the sunlit realms simply to spite me for my infidelity. But in my heart I always knew better. I am just a pivot for the great events of this world, which happen above and beyond my plans and desires. I can only hope, and you can only hope with me, mortal, that Baldr's place in the underworld and my exile from all that I have loved, serve a greater purpose, a good purpose, one beyond our understanding. Why else am I here, and he and Angrboda are there?

Perhaps it is the case that peace does truly lie with death, not life, just as the tombstones say. Long for it, then, say I! Long for it, Arseborn! If beauty and truth lie with peace in the grave, who in their right mind would not want to lie there with them?

IMPRISONMENT

My story is nearly at an end – although *perhaps* there will be more chapters ahead for poor Loki. That is up to you, Arse-born, and we shall speak of that shortly. But first, let us answer the obvious question: what had happened, that despite the oaths from all things in all the worlds that Frigg had begged, one of all creation had broken its word?

It was not like that. There are many, many things in this world. Perhaps it was inevitable that one of them should be missed. Tyr had discovered one small thing – the mistletoe that grows neither on the ground nor in the air. Frigg thought it too young. It's the custom among us that the young may not swear an oath. The spear that Tyr ordered to be put into my hand was tipped with mistletoe wood. So ended Baldr, the hope of the world, broken on the usual rocks of violence, in-fighting and greed. Those who love war require conflict and death. They have made sure of a plentiful supply.

Again I went knocking on the doors of my daughter Hel and again I was turned away. I accept my fate, Arse-born – I must, as must we all. But it is hard, it is so hard, to have everything taken from you and yet to be forced to endure this life, this endless life.

I tried once and once only, to get back among the Aesir and the Vanir, to take my place as a god in heaven. Where else was there for me? In Jǫtunheimr there was only death. Thor was set on wiping out that race. When did the people of these days see the Jotun striding out across the mountains, or hauling the winds in a bag, or wading across the seas? The worlds are the poorer from all sides. The Ljósálfar have long ago entirely taken to the upper air, the Dökkálfar retreated deeper and deeper underground. I dwelt in Midgard an age or two, hoping to find love one more time, but the heart of Loki had been broken twice and could no longer be put back together again. At last, in despair, I went to see my fellow gods at the autumn feasting that took place every year in the halls of Aegir, who rules the ocean waves, the tempest and the sunrise over the water. I did not think they would let me in, and they certainly would not have if it wasn't for Odin. The Old Man's face had disappeared under his beard, which coiled so thickly out of his cheeks and forehead as well as from his chin and lips and even his empty eye socket, that he was hidden in fur. He sat bent over at his seat – still at the head of the table, for all that was worth. When I made my entrance, amid all the calls for me to be gone or die, his voice emerged above the din – a cracked thing, as much a creak as a voice. Everyone turned to look, for he had not uttered a word for a century or more.

'Let him drink with us,' he said.

They all turned. Thor coughed and looked over to Tyr, who shrugged. Slowly everyone took their seats, unsure what to make of the Allfather's sudden but all-too-brief return to the here and now. I sat, and one of the goddesses came to fill my cup, as guest of honour, invited by Odin, who had deigned to speak for me after so many years of silence.

Why? I do not know why, nor do I expect to. Perhaps, wrapped in the grip of some ancient mystery, I have a place in the Nine Worlds and destinies still to fulfil, after all. Time alone will tell.

I sat. I drank. I spoke. I did my best to convince them to let me return to take my place in Asgard. Across from me sat Sigyn and I saw her shake her head at me when she caught my eye, so I knew how small my chances were. But we can try, mortal, can we not – god and man, mortal and immortal? We can only try.

Of course the word had been put out that the spear had been planned by me, made by me as well as thrown by me. I wanted to end the life of beautiful Baldr because it is in the nature of evil to destroy what is beautiful and good. I was jealous of the freedom with which she handed out her love. According to these lies, it was my shape-changing powers that had enabled her to grow breasts and a female part. Baldr, beautiful in all other things, had been ruined, made morally repugnant because of me. Such a filthy thing as Loki, such an evil thing, could not be countenanced. I had turned what was beautiful into a perversion – that was the word.

Of course, you have to ask yourselves how many of those gathered around Aegir's table believed this nonsense – how many knew that it was all a set-up by Tyr (Thor was too stupid to make such a plan). The answer, I would suggest, is . . . all of them. Asgard was ruled by fear these days. The planning of Tyr, the strength of Thor – who can go against such power? You have to hand it to the god of war – it was a clever stroke. He got rid of the new power behind the throne, established his own morality at the head of things and cleared his enemies away.

Well, I had my chance to try – not to turn the tide! – I knew I was too small to attempt any such thing – but to convince them perhaps to be a little less judgemental against poor Loki. But I took a wrong turn for once. My instincts, once so sure, let me down. Perhaps I had become bitter – perhaps I no longer had the heart for it. Instead of just begging, or tricking, or making them laugh, I decided on a different course. I reminded them of their own pasts, their own follies, their own sins, if you will. It was the theory of, let he who has not sinned cast the first stone. It was unwise – I see that looking back. Of course, it was doomed to failure.

I reminded Odin how he had once liked to bend me over a barrel and have his way. I reminded Thor of the time he had made love to me, when, disguised as Sif, I had played a trick on him; how, at the end of it, he had exclaimed that mine was the best love-making he had ever had.

I reminded Tyr how he used to like boys. I told how Freya once slept with three Dökkálfar for the sake of a trinket, and of how Frey had been lovers with his sister for half an eternity, and how they often

MELVIN BURGESS

invited other gods into their bed, and how often those other gods said yes. Oh, believe me – I had tales on them all. But as I talked I could see it was not going well. Frowns deepened, the few smiles that had been there for me disappeared.

I persisted! I had decided, against all sense, that for once I would allow the *truth* to speak loud and clear, without varnish or gloss. Foolish Loki! To trust the truth – what halfwit does such a thing? I was stupid to ever imagine I had a chance. It was not the killing of Baldr that sentenced me – they all knew what had really happened that day. As for my so-called perversions – it's true that the likes of Thor and Tyr hated all that; but it was not that that spelled my doom either.

It was *power*. I had been on the wrong side, the losing side – Baldr's side. Baldr had taken power from Thor and Tyr, so she had to die. That was it, plain and simple. Baldr was so loved they could not be seen to do it themselves, so I had been tricked into the murder. They all knew this – every god there. Yet each one of them sat and kept their silence. No one spoke up for me. Even Frigg, great Frigg, mother of so many, knew which side her bread was buttered these days. She had lost the battle to save her child and did not care to join another one to save me.

The simmering frowns soon burst out in anger. They thought I had come to be quiet and godlike. But no! As usual I had come only to insult them with my lies and inventions. Wasn't it enough for me to have killed the best of the gods without coming back to the feast to tell stories that everyone there knew were untrue?

Heaven help me – I was surprised. Even I, the father of lies as they have called me, and not without justice, I admit – even I was surprised at how barefaced and opportunistic their untruths were.

'Everyone knows the truth,' I insisted. 'Every one of you knows it.'

But it was no use. I was sent away again for the last time. They would not kill me there, in Aegir's house, under Odin's eye. But they would come for me sooner rather than later. They told me as much and I knew that on this matter at least, they would keep their word.

I might have guessed it! – it was talking that finished me off. If I had pleaded forgiveness as if I were the guilty party, shown my willingness to get along with the great ones, admitted every lie they uttered, maybe then they would have let me back. But liar though I am, I know the truth. At bottom – I know you may find this hard to believe, Arse-born – liars like me *need* the truth. We understand it and love it, for without it, how would our tricks work? For the likes of Thor and Tyr, on the other hand, truth is just another weapon – one that can be used against them. For that reason they wish to disarm truth. They discredit it, they make it worthless. They do it by making it indistinguishable from lies. What use is truth, when no one believes in anything any more?

I went back to my fortress in Jǫtunheimr, but the Jotun would not let me into their kingdom; I had become too dangerous. I could have gone to Midgard, which is a great realm, but I did not want our wars to take place on earth, where they would have caused so much death and destruction. Instead, I went to a hill not far from my own home in Asgard, where I built a hut with four doors so that I could see them coming and flee in any direction; and I prepared myself for my fate. It was a pretty spot for me to end my days. There were birch and aspen trees, trout in the stream that rushed past and a waterfall where I bathed each morning. I collected berries and fungi and hunted in my own lands. And I wondered and worried about when they would come, and how they would do what they came to do.

I tell you now, Arse-born, I did not fear death! Why should I? Death for me had far more to offer than life. Angrboda and Baldr, the loves of my life, dwelt there. As far as I was concerned, death meant reuniting with those I loved. I tell you, as I drank the chilled waters of the stream, and fished for trout, I was looking forward to the day when I would meet my lovers again for the last time – forever. But how? How would they send me there? I was not expecting a quick dispatch. And that – yes, that I feared.

I did not have to wait long. Soon enough they came tripping up the hill. Thor led the way with the hammer over his shoulder. Tyr brought up the rear. Odin was there too, carried on a couch.

I looked at the hammer – the hammer that I had won for the Thunderer, let's not forget that. Soon, I thought, my brains would be spattered over the walls, my blood would join Baldr's, flowing onto the ground. At last I could go to my final home, my place in the underworld. But . . . let me admit it now; I am not a soldier. I had hoped to wait for them with dignity and courage, but, reader, the truth is, since we are talking truth now, that I lost my nerve at the last minute.

I panicked. I ran outside and looked around for escape. By my side, the stream ran fast and sweet so I took to that, to the cool, quick water. I took the form of a salmon and hid under the waterfall, where the white water roared and ran deep.

Well, they knew. Of course they knew. They dragged with a net for me, and caught me with my own invention. So poor Loki had to meet his fate running and hiding through lack of courage, rather than standing square and looking his enemies in the eye.

I expected my sentence to be carried out painfully, but certainly. They have creative ways of sending a man to his end. But it was worse than that. I had miscalculated for the last time, Arse-born; it was not death they had in store for me.

I was tied, hands behind my back – too tight of course – trussed up like a chicken and made to walk ahead of them down to a cave that sank deep, deep into the earth. Down and down we went, down so deep we could feel the heat, where Surtr's fires burn at the planet's heart. There my family awaited me; my sons, Narfi and Vali, bound and ready. Vali they turned into a wolf – it was always in his nature. But the wolf that had been my son was never so cruel in human form. He flung himself at Narfi – yes, his own brother; and the gods knew who I favoured – and tore him to pieces. My gentle Narfi, who never wished anyone any harm. And with his ice-cold entrails, mortal, they bound me to the rocks. You see? What kind of monsters do such things? How do such creatures come to be gods? They wanted my torture to be not only eternal, not only physical, but my heart too must live in torment. To what end, Arse-born? To what end do they do such things? Explain it to me. I myself cannot imagine why.

And there I was left, bound with my son's guts, deep under the earth to the hot rock, smouldering, burning, kept there to remain in perpetual torment until great Surtr comes to end all suffering.

And even that was not the end of my anguish. They tied a serpent above me so that the venom would drip on my face. And . . . agony!

Mortal, you cannot imagine! That was no normal snake. Who made it and how I do not know, but I can only think it was an invention of the Dökkálfar. No normal venom could cause such pain.

You may have heard from the stories how Sigyn, my beloved wife, stayed behind to catch the venom in a bowl? Not true. She hated me, if anything more than the others, since she blamed me for our sons' deaths – as if I would ever have done that! It was her doing as much as mine. Tyr no doubt noticed how she had failed to betray Baldr to him. He learned, as I did before him, that Victory is fickle, as fickle as lust. This was her punishment as much as mine. And further, that now she had to return to Tyr's side forever – for who could challenge him now? But this she did understand, because return she did, many years later, to build a shelter over me to keep the venom off. Each day the venom falls – drip drip drip. Each day I watch it trickle down and away; and after a hundred years or so, the drip drip drip eats through the stone she has placed over me – and then it hits me . . .

And my suffering is truly beyond imagining.

Sooner or later Sigyn comes back to replace the stone – more often later than sooner. No doubt she has other tasks to attend to.

There is another visitor, from time to time; Idunn. Yes, she comes with her apples. She waits, of course, until I am old – until I can feel death waiting outside in the corridor for me. Then, when I am sure that the final visitor is about to call, there is a light footfall and there she is, with her basket, smiling, pink-faced, young and lovely.

And each time I turn my face away. Truly, Arse-born, I want to die. I would love to die. But they do not allow it. Each time she forces a slice in my mouth and crushes my jaws so that a little of the juice trickles down my throat. She is patient, she waits as long as she needs to, for each slice to go down. Then, when I am young again, full of juice and vigour – she goes.

So my torment goes on forever, agony without end. Pity poor Loki, mortal, whose only sin was seeing before his time, and living life to the full.

And I beg her as she leaves – 'Why make me live? Idunn! Why make me live?'

But she never answers.

Only once, just once, was there another visitor. Not in the flesh . . . and perhaps not at all. In a dream, he came to me . . . at least I think it was a dream. Perhaps now he is beyond any physical shape, I do not know. But once I fancied Odin was here in my cave with me, and I asked him the question that I ask of Idunn – why? Why make me live? What have I done that is so bad? Surely, of all beings in all the worlds, he knows the truth?

There was no answer except that within my own thoughts . . . a dry whisper in the wavelengths of my mind . . .

I saw an image, reader.

Long, long ago, when Odin and I were first friends, we set off into the world, which back then, you will recall, was not so fixed as it was now. Odin's powers were so much weaker. Great as he was even then, he was not able to make the spells stick. As a result, the mountains and soil and sea of the worlds kept returning to their original form – the stinking corpse of great Ymir.

It was I who fixed the spells for him, and each time I did, he turned and smiled and tapped his skull.

'It's in here, Loki – all fixed forever in here . . .'

Now that whispering voice came to me . . .

'Not my mind, but yours, Loki. In *your* mind the world is fixed. Therefore, old friend, of course, you can never be permitted to die . . .'

'Tricked,' I hissed. 'You tricked me! You tricked me, all this time . . .'

I saw the shape that was Odin fade into the darkness. I was alone again. He never returned. Just that once he came, to tell me that without my life, the world will return to its source – the stinking remains, the endless decay that is Ymir. Not Odin; it is Loki who stands guard over creation – between you, Arse-born – and the pit of filth.

I suffer each day . . . for you.

So, mortal – there you have it. Loki was not sunk by his lies, as they often claim, but by the truth. Here I am tied, time immemorial past, and here I stay, till great Surtr comes to end my torment. Unhappy Loki! Unloved, alone, abandoned, friendless. In Hel I could be happy, but from Hel itself I am exiled. Did anyone ever suffer so from love as I? Now you know too, why the world you live in suffers such torment from day to day and year to year. So much pain! War, hunger, poverty – all done in the name of the gods, all done so that Thor and Tyr, the least worthy amongst us, can hang on to power. The great god of the mysteries, all-knowing Odin, is blinded by his own knowing; Angrboda the goddess of hope and Baldr the god of beauty live in the underworld. One blessing you have from that though, for when you die, unlike poor Loki, your life will be the better for sharing death with them.

But mortal! It does not have to be like this! You have grown, mortal. You have become so much more than the gods ever intended. You do not understand the mysteries, but with the gifts you have acquired for yourselves you have gone far. You know science. You understand how things work, how they move, how they are powered. Even the gods do not measure up to that knowledge. One day they will wake up to the threat you pose them, and then there will be war, a war between the immortals of Asgard and the mortals of Midgard. That will be a war to end all wars – believe me, mortal, only Surtr can bring destruction on a scale greater than that.

That day you may truly fear. But – why wait?

Mortal – let us talk business. Poor Loki still has a trick or two up his sleeve to play, torn and bloodied though he may be.

Know then, that my daughter Fenra survives. Yes – she lives. The gods have sought her for all these aeons, but still she eludes them. And hidden, she travels. She carries messages between me and my wife, my lover, my sons and my daughter – down to the underworld where Hel rules. And further afield. She has made contact with the Jotun, those few who still survive, hidden in the deep fjords, beneath the mountains, in the oceans. She has spoken with the last Ljósálfar, hiding in the sunbeams and the leaves of summer, and with the Dökkálfar, deep in the mines where they still invent and create and build.

The bonds that bind me are beyond my wits, but perhaps they are not beyond yours. Mortal! – free me! Find me and free me! I do not expect to lead you, but I can show you the way to Asgard. Together we can make a better world. They say that at the end of all things, the gates of the underworld will open and then Baldr the beautiful will walk out again. I can tell you now, that story is true. So let us not wait for fate. We can do this together. Ragnarok may be the twilight of the gods, but it does not need to be the twilight of mankind. We can make a world of beauty and love, rather than one of pain and war. I offer you my services – my guidance, my cunning and tricks, my knowledge of the gods and the Nine Worlds.

The rule of Asgard must end! Alone we are weak; together we are mighty. All the beings of all the worlds are tired of war, of the rule of might, of the hammer of Thor, the blindness of Odin, the machinations of Tyr. The might of the old world combined with the science of the new – what could stop us? We can defeat Asgard and bring new life to the world, even to its furthest corners.

We have plotted for hope in the darkness. Help us bring that hope to the light. I was sunk by truth in Asgard. Now I offer truth in Midgard, to fulfil my last desire – that I may finally be a part of something truly great: an enterprise that will benefit all except those who would oppress us. To bring beauty and truth, love and hope back to a hopeless world! Surely, Arse-born – surely it's worth a try?

The End.

ACKNOWLEDGEMENTS

First and foremost, special thanks to Martin Riley for his encouragement of Loki in all his moods and guises, for playing games and for allowing the Trickster to walk on earth, in school, at home, whenever he could.

My very first introduction to the Norse Pantheon was through a book my dad brought home from when he worked at OUP – *Tales of the Norse Gods and Heroes*, by Barbara Leonnie Picard. That's where I first fell in love with Loki, his tricks and deceits. Her telling of the old stories doesn't seem to me to have been bettered so far.

Thanks to Mark Booth at Hodder, who gave Loki his chance and helped him on his way so sympathetically. And who also showed the book to Brian Catling, who did a number of versions of the big liar, one of which hangs on my wall. Thanks for the pictures, Brian.

And thanks too, to to Messrs Johnson and Trump, for the fine example they set – a great help in the writing of it.

And to the Mrs, without whom, none of any of this.